CHILLS

Mary SanGiovanni

LYRICAL UNDERGROUND
Kensington Publishing Corp.
www.kensingtonbooks.com

LYRICAL UNDERGROUND BOOKS are published by

Kensington Publishing Corp.
119 West 40th Street
New York, NY 10018

First Electronic Edition: September 2016
eISBN-13: 978-1-60183-748-6
eISBN-10: 1-60183-748-8

First Print Edition: September 2016
ISBN-13: 978-1-60183-749-3
ISBN-10: 1-60183-749-6

Printed in the United States of America

This book is dedicated to Brian Keene, who braved the winter for me.

ACKNOWLEDGMENTS

The author would like to thank Adam, Michael, Suzanne, and Christy SanGiovanni; Michele and Mike Serra; "Seedling," Brian Keene; Paul Goblirsch; Peter Senftleben; and the five brave "victims" in this book, who were kind enough to lend her their names, for their support, encouragement, and patience.

Chapter One

Jack Glazier had worked Colby Township Homicide for going on nine long New England winters, but he had never seen blood freeze quite like that.

It certainly had been cold the last few nights; it was the kind of weather that cast phantom outlines of frost over everything. That hoary white made grass, tree branches, cars, even houses look fragile, like they might crack and shatter beneath the lightest touch. An icy wind that stabbed beneath the clothes and skin had been grating across the town of Colby for days now, and the place was raw.

Jack hated the cold. He hated it even more when his profession brought him out on brittle early mornings like this one, where the feeble sunlight did little even to suggest the idea of heat.

He had caught a murder case—a middle-aged John Doe found hanging upside down from the lowest branch of a massive oak tree at the northeastern edge of Edison Park. The body had been strung up off the ground by the right leg with some type of as-yet-unidentified rope. A crude hexagon had been dug roughly in the torn-up grass beneath the body. Scattered in those narrow trenches, he'd been told, the responding officers had found what they believed to be the contents of the man's pockets, which had been bagged as a potential starting point for identification.

Jack glanced up at the silver dome of sky with its gathering clouds of darker gray and listened for a moment to the low wail of the wind slicing at the men gathered near the body. They worked silently, their minimal conversation encased in tiny breath-puffs of white. The air carried a faint smell of freezer-burned meat that agitated Jack in a way the smell of dead bodies never really did. It made him think of lost things, things forgotten way in the back of dark, cold places and left to rot slowly. There was no closure and no dignity in it.

Of course, he supposed that closure and whatever little dignity he could scrape together for the victims of murder was part of *his* job.

It took an effort to focus on the body again, to duck under the strung-up lines of police tape and move toward it. He found that the closer he got to a decade of dealing with dead, clouded eyes, gelid, mutilated flesh, and distraught loved ones, the more energy it took to give himself over to getting cases started. He wanted them solved— that drive had propelled him to the rank of detective lieutenant and it made him good at what he did—but it was the *starting* of the investigations he had lost the taste for. It was getting harder and harder to stare the next few months of brooding and nightmares in the face.

As for the body itself, the throat looked like it had been cut—bitten, really—and there were lacerations on the naked torso, shoulders, bare arms, and face. Jack, who did his best to suppress his morbidly imaginative streak in these situations yet frequently failed, could imagine the John Doe dangling in the glacial night air, wracked with shivers as his blood poured from his wounds, cooling the fire of life in his body until there was no movement, no feeling. He was an end scene, frozen before the roll of the credits, his screen time cut suddenly short.

All of the John Doe's blood had formed, drop by drop, fringes of crimson icicles from the lowest-hanging parts of his body, as if every part, every tissue of the man had struggled to escape that branch and its pain and death. The overall effect stripped the humanity from the corpse, leaving it a gross caricature of what it once had been.

A uniformed officer whose name slipped Jack's mind—Morano or Moreno, something like that—nodded at him as he made his way up to the crime scene. Crouched beneath the body a foot or so from the outline of overturned grass clumps, Colby's thin, bald, and bespectacled coroner, Terrence Cordwell, was packing up his kit.

"They're calling for about eight to ten inches of snow, starting around midnight. Can you believe that? Probably keep up most of tomorrow," Cordwell was saying to Dave Brenner, his assistant, who had switched from the digital camera to the film. Dave was documenting the churned-dirt hexagon and the body with another series of close-up photos. Both men nodded to Jack as he joined them.

Brenner stepped carefully into the hexagon's center and took a close-up photo of the body's neck wound, a gaping tear like a second frown across his neck, then stepped outside the core of the crime scene, around to the back of the torso. He whistled, holding up his pocket ruler beneath the body's shoulder blades, and took another couple of photos. "Hey, Glazier. Where's Morris?"

Jack crouched and peered closer at the neck wound. It looked deep and uneven, like several serrated sharp objects had torn and gouged at the neck at once. It reminded him again of a bite. "Nephew's baptism. He's the godfather, I think."

"Poor kid. Hey, shit weather, huh? Too cold for May."

"Cold, yeah. Not unheard of, though, I guess."

"No," Brenner offered grudgingly over his shoulder, and Jack heard the whir and snap of the camera taking another picture. "Up north, maybe. But still awful late in the season for more snow around here. It's a sign that the planet is fucked, if you ask me. Global warming and shit."

Jack didn't answer. He wasn't particularly fond of Brenner; the guy always seemed to have one more thing to say than Jack had the patience to hear.

Instead, Jack rose and turned to Cordwell. "So what's the deal with this guy?"

The coroner peeled off his rubber gloves. "No ID, no wallet—but he's got teeth and fingertips, so if he's in the system, we should be able to find him. Dead eight, maybe nine hours. With the cold, it's hard to say for sure until we get him back to the cave. What I can tell you is that he froze to death before he had a chance to bleed out, although the hypothermia was likely accelerated by the blood loss. These lacerations and that neck wound were meant, I'm guessing, to speed up the process. They're animal, most of them. Not certain what kind yet, but we bagged and tagged what I'm pretty sure is a tooth."

"Animal bites? So what, someone fed him to something and then strung up what was left?"

Cordwell shrugged. "More likely, it happened the other way around. Someone strung this guy up and left him to . . . whatever did that to him."

Jack frowned, moving slowly as he examined the body. One of the hands was missing. When he pointed it out, Cordwell shook his head; they hadn't found it. The leg from which the John Doe was strung up was virtually untouched. Jack imagined a man would know that it would have to be kept intact to support the weight of the body, but how the animal or animals managed to avoid it, Jack could only guess. Likely, it was simply too high for them to reach. The other leg was mangled, but not nearly as badly as the head, arms, and torso. Those wounds alternated between slashes Jack figured for a knife and more of those ragged tears, right down to the bone in a lot of places. Jack shook his head at the brutality of it and moved around to the back of the body.

Then he saw the brand. In the entire space between the shoulder blades, ugly, angry pink swells of skin formed a large kind of symbol Jack didn't recognize, featuring asymmetric swirls crossed with an irregular lattice of lines. It looked deliberate; in fact, it surprised Jack that the design was as clearly and intricately formed as it was.

"Hey, Brennan, you get a picture of this?"

"The burn marks? Yeah. Creepy shit. Occult?"

"Maybe. Looks pretty new."

"You know," Brenner said with a careful, measured tone, "if this is some kinda devil-worshiping thing, they'll probably want to bring Ryan in on this."

Jack frowned, glancing at the younger man. "Don't think we'll need Ryan, necessarily."

Brenner shrugged. "Maybe not. Maybe the brand doesn't mean anything at all, other than deluded satanist fantasies of some nut job thinking he's some grand high wizard or something. But you know, if it's not—"

Jack turned the full attention of his gaze on Brenner and the rest of the sentence dropped off.

It wasn't that Jack didn't like Ryan; they'd worked very closely a few years back busting a child sex ring that had strong connections to a radical Golden Dawn sect working out of Newport. She'd also been called in to work with him on collaring a big-name drug dealer in Boston whose specialty product, in addition to persuasive pulpit revelations delivered in an abandoned Russian Orthodox church, was a powder rumored to make devoted users both see and attempt to kill demons. Occult practices, ancient grimoires, devil worship, blood sacrifices, and rites to archaic gods and monsters—that was Ryan's thing, her specialty. She'd worked all over the country as a private consultant to law enforcement evaluating occult involvement and assessing risk, and was known to be efficient and discreet. She also was apparently able, through resourcefulness or mystery connections, to skirt a lot of red tape and paperwork regarding freedom of religious pursuit that usually hung up other investigations. Jack thought she was brilliant, aloof, and intense, but the kind of woman one was dismayed to be inexorably drawn to.

Ryan was good at what she did, although to say she was popular with the people she worked for or with might be pushing it. How she'd come into her line of work or developed a reputation for being one of the country's leading experts in it was something she guarded closely. Jack suspected it contributed to what made her eyes dark and her smile fleeting, and any true attempt at getting close to her impossible. Her experiences formed the ghosts of truly haunted expressions beneath those she offered the world. And Jack thought she was a bottle of vodka and a .38 away from blowing all that she'd seen and learned about the fringes of the world out the back of her head.

Cordwell clapped him on the shoulder, jarring him from his thoughts. "I'll have a prelim report for you in a day or two. Stay warm."

Jack nodded as the men moved away, ducking under the police tape. He saw Cordwell motion to one of the technicians, say something, and then gesture in his direction. Jack assumed the tech had been told the body was ready for transport.

He stood a few moments, his eyes drawing over the details of the body, the contorted features of the face, the wounds already starting to take on that freezer-burn-like quality to match that smell that, when the wind shifted, found its way inside his nose on the back of the cold, dry air. He made his way over to the small blue tent top that had been set up over a folding table, designated as the detectives' safe area. He figured Detective Reece Teagan would already be there, getting a jump start on examining the items Cordwell said had been found in the dirt.

And so he was—Teagan's scuffed sneakers were propped up on the corner of the evidence table as he leaned back in a metal folding chair. He was squinting intently at the contents of a plastic evidence bag with a red label, an unlit Camel cigarette hanging out of his mouth. With his free hand, he absently ran his fingers through his hair, a quirky little habit that sent it up into dirty-blond spikes. When he noticed Jack's approach, he nodded a hello, which sent those spikes drifting back, more or less into place. Jack noticed for the first time that some of those spikes had the occasional strand of gray—not nearly as much as Jack had seen mixed in his own black hair the last year or so, but enough to remind him again just how many cases had come and gone for him with Teagan, Morris, Cordwell, and their winters in Colby.

"Jack. You seen these yet? Right feckin' warped."

Teagan had grown up in Westport and Inistioge in Ireland before going to Oxford and then working as a detective sergeant, and although he'd been almost ten years in the States, his brogue was still strong. It seemed a continuing source of amusement to him that American women swooned and giggled when he spoke to them, calling them "love." His accent and accompanying rakish grin never ceased to earn him confidences, phone numbers, and, when need be, forgiveness from the "birds" he occasionally dated. That he was a pretty good-looking guy beneath the facial scruff, with a lean, strong build to boot, didn't hurt his cause, either.

"How's that?" Jack pulled up a folding chair next to him and leaned in toward the evidence table. Nodding at Teagan's light jacket, he said, "Aren't you cold?"

"Fresh air, mate. Take a look at this stuff." Teagan gestured at the evidence bags. Jack examined the contents of the first few, taking note of some change (thirty-four cents), a key ring with car keys (although the Toyota they belonged to was conspicuously absent), and a receipt for chips and coffee from the nearby convenience store.

"Not sure what I'm supposed to be seeing here. Looks like the stuff on the floor of my car."

"Not those," Teagan said. "These." He slid a few bags over to Jack. The first bag contained what looked to Jack like a chunk of splintered wood about six inches long and three inches wide. He held it up by the bag and turned it over, then saw what Teagan meant. The back side of the wood was flat and smooth, and into it was burned or carved a series of runic marks that formed neat lines across the whole surface. Jack looked at Teagan questioningly, and the other man shrugged.

"Cordwell says this one's a tooth." He handed Jack another bag with a slightly curved bit of ivory substance about five or six inches long. One end held the remains of a rough kind of root while the other tapered to a very sharp point.

"What the hell has teeth like this around here? Is he serious?"

"Damned if I know," Teagan said. He slid another bag toward Jack. "And there's this card, here."

It was the size of a business card, although it was entirely black and there was no writing on it on either side. Jack studied the matte finish on both sides for signs of fingerprints but couldn't even find a smudge.

"Calling card, maybe? Business card?" Jack asked.

"No idea. Though, whoever it belongs to might want to be re-thinking their business plan."

Jack handed it back. "Maybe they can get something off it. Or off that piece of wood there. Cordwell seems pretty sure this was some kind of orchestrated animal attack."

There was a pause. "Cordwell's saying they might call Kathy in on this," Teagan said, his gaze fixed on the piece of wood.

"Yeah, Brennan said the same thing to me," Jack replied. "For her sake, I hope all this black-magic bullshit is coincidental. Last I heard, she could use a break from it."

"Her input couldn't hurt," Teagan said thoughtfully, handling the bag with the wood sliver. "Even if she only identifies this . . . language, or whatever it is."

"You know superficial involvement, at least in cases, isn't how she operates."

Teagan reined in a small smile. "Yeah, I know."

Jack prided himself in thinking he understood the thoughts, feelings, and motivations below the surface—the ones others wore in their eyes and their smiles and nowhere else. He was fairly certain Teagan was in love with Kathy. The way he looked at her, the softness that crept into his voice when he said her name—it wasn't an investigative stretch to see his longing for her, however smooth and subtle he thought he was. Kathy, though, likely had no clue. In spite of their individual eccentricities, or maybe because of them, Teagan and Kathy were probably soul mates, but knowing her as Jack did, he was pretty sure she never allowed herself to entertain the thought. And Teagan . . . he approached his job with the relentless instinct and perseverance of someone resigned to giving up anything like a normal life. To Teagan, there were dead folks and the folks who killed them, the psychology behind how and why, and not much else.

"Well, I'm off. Could eat the ass of a low-flyin' duck," Teagan said suddenly. "We on this thing together, yeah?"

"Yeah, looks like," Jack said, leaning an elbow on the table. "You, me, and Morris. Tomorrow, nine a.m. My office."

Teagan nodded and jogged off to his car. Jack watched him go, then turned his attention back to the chunk of wood in the bag. He took a deep breath, frigid in his nose and throat, and let it out in little white puffs. It was time, he knew, to start the job.

Although the official start of summer was a month away, the forecast of eight to ten inches of snow for Colby, Connecticut, raised few eyebrows, as late in the season as it was. It had been a particularly harsh winter; temperatures often dropped into the negatives and a leaden sky had dumped snow by the foot on a weekly basis for months. When it didn't snow, the rain during the day turned to black ice at night. The children's spring break had been eaten into by the accumulation of snow days. The county had run out of salt for the roads by early March and had been having a tough time acquiring more to clear them.

Still, most people believed this storm would be the last of them for the year, and patiently suffered the weather to exhale its arctic breath one last time over all. The town of Colby warmed up the snowplows and salt/sand trucks in preparation for winter's last hurrah, and the townsfolk swarmed the local supermarkets, the Targets and Walmarts, the Costcos and the gas stations, to stock up on gasoline and supplies.

Most were still blissfully unaware of the body found hanging from a tree in Edison Park, but they felt it, in the vaguest, unarticulated way. They felt the cold trying to wrench their skin from their bones, and they felt something else, too—a kind of forlorn loneliness trying to wrench peace of mind from their souls. Just as they stocked up on food and bottled water, shovels and gloves, they squinted into the night outside their homes before drawing blinds and locking doors, double-checking on the kids in bed and huddling closer to each other than usual. Something other than a late winter was in the air, and it chilled them just as much, if not more, when they thought too long about it.

Though not even the gossips would give voice to it, the people of Colby knew something was coming with the snow.

The first time Kathy Ryan ever fired a gun, she was seventeen. A good-looking farm boy with strong arms, warm hands, and big brown eyes had shown her a .38 from his own gun collection. He'd stood close behind her, his chest pressed against her back, his arms around hers, and those hands guiding her fingers and palms to the right positions. He'd made sure she understood the basic rules—always point the gun down and away from everyone, and never even touch the trigger until she was ready to shoot—and then he'd positioned a plastic jug of water ten feet away in his dad's field. He told her where to aim to hit it. She fired seven times, and hit the jug every single time. She remembered being surprised by how loud the firing of the gun was, so loud it set off a ringing in her ears and an excited pounding in her heart. It was a sound of momentous *thereness*, a sound of something happening, of a definitive change from what had been only seconds before. It was a powerful, scary, sexy sound, and she was hooked.

Seventeen was twenty-two years ago, when there had still been some people, albeit few to name, who knew Kathy Ryan as something other than a homicide detective. Back then, she had been just "that pretty young daughter of that hard-ass Jim Ryan, with the dead mama and the brother no one talks about." It was a mouthful of tag line for Kathy, who had felt back then that a lot had been shoveled her way in those seventeen years, and she was fighting an uphill battle with the world just so she could look at it with simple wonder and amazement.

Jim Ryan's only daughter had bright green eyes, a shining stream of blond hair that the tomboy in her felt compelled to pull up off her soft, narrow shoulders, and a smile of innocent amusement. She'd always been thin, but it had looked right on her then, the kind of tight body boys liked. Back then, her smooth, lightly tanned skin had been unmarred by anything but a light dusting of summer freckles.

No scars, inside or out.

The Kathy Ryan who stared into the mirror hanging on her stark apartment's bedroom wall was still pretty nowadays but in a lean, angry, indifferent sort of way. Those bright eyes had retreated to a safe distance behind dark circles and dark memories; they were eyes that were not afraid to lock gazes but which seldom offered any indication as to what was behind them. Her mouth rarely smiled, and when it did, it was a sardonic twist or an uncomfortable flutter that telegraphed how out of place it really was. And there was the scar.

It tripped down through her left eyebrow and over her eye to land firmly just below the socket, working its thin, jagged, white way across her cheek to her jawbone, where it unceremoniously ended. When she looked in the mirror, she seldom paid much attention to her eyes or her mouth, but she could never quite overlook the scar.

The paradox of her face, she thought, mirrored the juxtaposition of opinions others held about her. It created an unusual reception of mistrust and avoidance up close, and from afar, an almost secret awe. Professionally, she was always requested ahead of a long line of similarly educated peers to handle certain cases, to assist in more troublesome interrogations, and to consult on certain task forces because of her experience and her ability to get the job done. But those requests were made in offices with blinds drawn, over heads and under personal radar, with minimal paperwork and never, ever to her face. Kathy Ryan didn't care much about all that; if police departments wanted her to work a case, no matter how they asked for her, so be it, so long as she was paid.

It was such a case that had gotten her out of bed this morning, the third day into her somewhat forcefully suggested vacation. There was a homicide with ritualistic overtones, Morris had said, and the mayor of Colby himself wanted her in right away, as early as she could make it there. The case involved an as-yet-unidentified middle-aged man found hanging upside down over an invocation circle. He'd been branded with what sounded to Kathy like a powerful sigil, and among his belongings were a totem and a small calling card she recognized well. So she'd swigged from the vodka bottle in the medicine cabinet and then brushed her teeth. Then she showered, slipped into her underwear and a bra, and pulled on a pair of jeans and a sweater.

As she did every morning, she looked at the collage frame on her dresser, gently touching the empty matte squares where the pictures of her and her family had been. She'd removed the ones of her brother and father first, and then that last one of her mom. She never looked at the remaining two of her anymore, only at the empty spaces where her old life used to be, and only for a minute.

Her thoughts returned to the case. Whoever this John Doe had been, he'd pissed off a group of very bad people. That calling card probably meant a Black Stars sect, in which case the snow wasn't going to be the only kind of storm to hit Colby.

She grabbed her purse and keys from the dresser beside the mostly empty picture frame and left the apartment.

Chapter Two

It began to snow again as Kathy reached the tan brick Colby Police Department building where Jack Glazier's office was. She flashed her credentials at the unsmiling, bulky policewoman at the front desk and nodded to the officers she passed on the way through the bullpen to the senior detectives' offices. They nodded back with a mixture of unease and politeness that she had come to expect from them. She got that reaction a lot from people who knew her profession. It was almost as if they thought the remnants of it—otherworldly bad mojo, curses, haunts, and evil—clung to her hair and clothes like smells or smoke, and that those intangible things might somehow poison their space or infect them if they got too close to her. Because of the possible outside chance that their fears were not superstition, she didn't take their reactions personally.

Jack's door was open, and Kathy found him sitting behind his desk. Teagan leaned on a corner of the desk, tossing and catching a glass paperweight, much to Jack's tightly controlled dismay. Teagan smiled at her when she walked in, and she found herself smiling back. Oliver Morris sat in a chair across from Glazier. He offered her a small wave, and she tipped her chin at him in return.

"Hi, Kathy," Jack said. "Get here okay?"

"Sure," Kathy said, sitting in the remaining empty chair next to Morris. "Long early-morning drives are my reason for living. So what've we got here?"

"Well, let's not waste any more time with pleasantries," Jack said with a small smile. He slid the file across the desk to her. She leafed through Jack's and Teagan's notes and read over Cordwell's report, then leaned back in the chair as she studied the crime scene photos. There was a photo of a chunk of wood with runes carved into it. She recognized most of them as an archaic language rarely seen, even in occult circles.

"Can you read that?" Jack asked.

"Yeah," Kathy answered after a moment. "Yeah, most of it. Hmmm ... this is all ... names. Places. Invocations to gods to protect the soul while it travels to the realms beyond ours. This was in the guy's pocket? That's usually a voluntary thing, not something to be left behind with a sacrificial body. Of course, these specific names are significant entities and locations primarily worshiped by the Hand of the Black Stars cult, so it's likely some perversion of the usual occult rites."

"Who?"

"Bad folks. Big trouble. They are the kind of 'church' that makes LaVey's satanists look like potluck-and-PTA moms. It's a twisted derivation of chaos magic rituals with significance placed on patterns and fractals as the basis of sigils which can—"

She had come across the crime scene photo showing a close-up of the symbol that had been burned into the John Doe's back.

"What is it, love?"

"It's ... this. This sigil," Kathy said to Teagan. "I've seen it before."

"What does it mean?" Jack leaned in to take another look at it.

"I know it's believed to be very powerful, but I'll have to get back to you on the particulars of how. For now, what it gives us is a confirmation that this isn't some amateur goth kid dipping a black-painted toenail into the occult. This sigil would only be recognized, let alone used, by someone very experienced. And, I'd be willing to guess, someone with the kind of agenda followed by the Hand of the Black Stars. An indication," she said, looking up from the file, "that your John Doe is probably not going to be the only body."

Jack exhaled slowly. "Okay. I think the mayor was afraid of that. So you and I are heading up this task force, Kat. Mayor's request. My understanding from the captain is that we should defer to you on occult aspects. You let us do the heavy lifting."

Kathy nodded.

"Morris," Jack said to the young man next to her. "You dig up what you can about related deaths from exposure or animal attacks, or both. Start with just this county. Oh, and add any missing persons in the last two weeks to the search. Teagan, we need an ID on the John Doe."

"Challenge me," Teagan responded with a grin.

"Kathy—" Jack began.

She was already on her feet and halfway to the door, waving the photo of the sigil. She turned. "I've got a connection I can talk to."

"An informant?"

Kathy paused and met Jack's eyes. "You could call him that. If anyone knows what the HBS is up to or where to find them, it'll be him." She paused a moment, her expression clouded, then added, "And he owes me."

"Okay, good. If Teagan doesn't turn up anything, we'll follow up with missing persons and cold cases, see if we have any possible leads there. We'll all check in at seven p.m., back here. And gang," Jack added, "stay safe."

Kathy's drive up to Newlyn was frustratingly slow going; the snow was getting worse, coming down in thick, fluffy flakes that blurred the road in front of and around her in white. She passed by a blue sedan with a crumpled front and a badly dented tan minivan that had, ostensibly, collided and then slid off the highway and into a ditch in the wide, snowy median. Both vehicles were flanked by cop cars, and an ambulance was slowly making its way up the shoulder. The blue car reminded her of her brother's old clunker, the one he had used to pick up co-eds and—

Kathy forced herself to exhale the breath in her chest. It was hard enough to make out the lane's dividing lines without her mind scratching at old wounds (she reached up and touched her scar without realizing it) and stirring up old ghosts.

Of course, she knew herself well enough to know that forcing those memories out of her head wasn't going to work. It never had—not when her mind was made up to work through a thing. And she supposed there was still a lot about her brother she needed to work through.

She had come to find that it was common for families of serial killers and mass murderers to feel the same things she did—dumbfoundedness at the loved one's capacity for predatory viciousness, guilt that they hadn't known sooner or hadn't seen it coming—or worse, that they *had* seen all the signs, all the pieces of their puzzle, but hadn't put them together, and so had never seen the emergence of one hell of an ugly picture.

For Kathy, it had taken accidentally finding Toby's trophy box to finally understand what her brother was.

It had been a sweltering Pennsylvania summer night when Kathy had found the little wooden jewelry box, a night dense with the sounds of crickets and frogs chirping and small, furry, restless animals rustling in the tall grasses. The air hung thick with the day's unspent and relentless heat, too heavy to stir more than a sluggish breeze. Kathy remembered thinking later that the heat must have somehow gotten into Toby's brain, cooking it, blazing sense and sensitivity out of him. She'd thought then that it had to be something hot and hostile from the outside that had snaked its way in, had clawed into him and had eaten up the insides of the Toby she knew and loved. That Toby couldn't have done those things; something had to have gotten into him. It had to have been buzzing around inside him and the heat had baked it into his thoughts, smoking some kind of crazy out to the surface.

She and Toby had been close as kids, especially after Mom died. Her death had been hard for Kathy, but it had been devastating for Toby. He and Dad had never gotten along—had even come to blows, or close to them at times—and Toby, who had never been particularly good with people, had needed someone. He'd chosen Kathy with a fiercely exclusive devotion, and she had done her best to mother him in the ways she thought he needed. But the relationship grew stranger as they got older. It was wildly uneven, for one thing. His need for her seemed all-consuming at times. He could be possessive and overprotective. His looks and sometimes the casual ways in which he played around with her seemed to her an awkward and uncomfortable combination of filial and even sexual, rather than fraternal, love. At other times, he was unsettlingly cruel and angry, or utterly distracted and almost indifferent to her, a state which seemed to increase as puberty took full hold of him. She'd never been afraid of his moods before, but when he was around sixteen or seventeen, it seemed to Kathy that a switch had been flipped in him, and all warmth toward her had been shut off. It made her acutely uncomfortable. From that point on, intense anger or stony indifference alternately seemed to saturate his every move, look, and word. And it wasn't just with her. In fact, it appeared that Toby had abandoned the idea of human connection and interaction altogether. At least, that's what she'd thought.

By the time he was nineteen, she'd taken to avoiding his sullen, hulking form around the house. He'd lost his job, which had ruined his chances of moving out, a setback that seemed to stoke a barely controlled rage in him. She avoided conversation about him too, with perhaps well-meaning, or possibly just rubbernecking, friends and acquaintances who also found Toby's presence discomforting.

By the time he had turned twenty-one, he was never home. He used to tell her and Dad that he was going to the bar. She remembered thinking he spent a lot of time at the bar for someone with no known friends around town, and that maybe all that drinking was what was changing his mood and his personality. Toby could be cruel and aggressive and he could even be creepy . . . but she'd had no reason to think he was a liar. She hadn't known then about the Hand of the Black Stars cult or her brother's late-night drives around their rural little hometown. She hadn't known about his stalking, stabbing, and engaging in a host of pet paraphilias. Most of that came out at his trial.

Ironically, she had found the news stories about the dead girls from all over the county morbidly intriguing, given the unusual consistencies. There were carvings on the bodies, and each of them was missing at least one finger. Even then, she'd known about *modus operandi* and signatures from TV, although crime scenes and the people who made them were little more than a passing interest for her back then. She was only seventeen, and cute boys, books, guns, and music more often grabbed her attention. She hadn't had much reason to look further into the disappearances and murders of those girls back then. It was a problem for outside, faceless others, to be dealt with by different outside, faceless others.

It was not a jewelry box on a shelf in the back of her brother's closet—not then.

The problem had been that she hadn't done laundry. She hated it—mostly the lugging of the baskets of clothes up and down the stairs, and the heavy, uncomfortably cold weight of wet clothes as she tried to hang them up. She'd done a lot of cleaning that day, and she was hot and tired and in no mood to do a load of laundry just to have something to sleep in. Toby had T-shirts—long ones she could borrow to use as nightgowns. He'd never miss one if she took it then, while he was out. He'd never even notice.

So that hot, unbearably sticky summer night, Kathy had padded into Toby's room in her underwear and had opened the door to the closet to rifle through his clothes. She slid his dress shirts out of the way, as well as some jackets and sweaters. None of his T-shirts were hung up, which, given Toby's own laundry habits, made sense in a way. She shoved things around a bit, and suddenly there they were— a hastily half-folded pile of old football jerseys and concert T-shirts on the upper closet shelf. Perfect.

She stood on tiptoe and reached up, feeling around for a soft one, and her fingers closed around a black Metallica shirt worn thin enough to be light and comfortable. As she pulled it down, though, something sharp-edged and hard fell with it, its corner bouncing painfully off her foot before breaking open and spilling its contents all over the floor. She swore under her breath, knowing he'd be pissed. He never seemed to notice her taking his T-shirts, but if he even thought she was breathing in the direction of his other possessions, especially those in his bedroom closet, he got livid.

She crouched down, sweeping the little spilled objects into a pile. If she could put them back before—

Kathy frowned. It had taken her a moment to realize what the little ivory things were. Even after, she tried not to let the idea that Toby had what looked like finger bones cause immediate concern.

Don't overthink this, she told herself. *No reason to overreact, just because Toby has bones in a box.* But she couldn't help remembering him yanking her away from the closet the other day, one fist tangled in her hair and another digging into her arm. He'd been so angry when he thought . . . what? He'd never said why he'd gotten so upset. She'd only been looking for the box of old family photos from when Mom was alive; she'd wanted to look through them and thought he might have them. She was going to ask first. In fact, she'd already had the query half out of her mouth as she reached the closet, but he'd flown off the bed and had practically thrown her to the floor. The look in his eyes had scared her. It wasn't so much what was there as what *wasn't*. He'd had shark's eyes, dead empty, without recognition or empathy.

There are plenty of possible reasons for the bones, right? Right? She wasn't sure, but she tried to think it through. She thought the little fetishes or whatever they were supposed to be were actually made of real bone and not something synthetic like plastic. They didn't look or feel anything like that necklace of fake bones Toby had gotten for Mardi Gras last year. The texture, the color, even the weight of these bones was different—like the hip bone of the deer she'd once found out in the corn field at the edge of the woods. Even if they were real bones, though, that alone was no reason to cause that growing unease in the pit of her stomach. Animal bones, probably. Toby had always been interested in that sort of thing, animal bones and hides and hunting and all that. And okay, maybe the bones were even from an animal that had fingers, like a monkey, or . . . or a . . .

They're human bones. The certainty rooted and made itself known before she could discount it. That little voice in her brain and that unease in her gut weren't going to let her explain this away. They were real human bones, but from whom? Was Toby into grave digging now or something? Whose fingers could they possibly—

And then Kathy remembered the news articles, the ones about the murdered women. All those poor women, some of whose bodies were discovered not far from where she'd found that deer bone as a kid . . . all of them with fingers missing. And she felt sick.

A second later she had hastily dropped the bones back into the box, wiping her hands on her thighs with a vigorous distaste. Toby? A part of her resisted putting all the pieces together. It would mean Toby had done some horrible things, and well . . . he couldn't have. Sure, he was moody, and he certainly had a temper, but the person who was doing all those killings was some kind of monster. After all, these women in the paper had been raped, mutilated, carved, stabbed, and dumped like trash in the woods. And their fingers . . .

And that probably wasn't the worst of it. She'd read somewhere that police always held back some of the details of the crime so that they could weed out the crazies who confessed to things they didn't do. So there was probably more. The Toby she knew, as much of a dick as he could be, just wasn't capable of such brutal things. Okay, so he was uncomfortably weird with her sometimes, the way he stared at her, at her body, with a kind of hungry, angry expression. But people had rough patches in life where they did things, maybe wanted things, that didn't really define them, per se, that they eventually outgrew. Toby had lived most of his life in a rough patch, really. Then there was that old dog he'd said he found dead, and he'd told her he was only cutting into it to see what it was like on the inside—no worse than hunting, really, because he'd found it already dead. But people experimented, didn't they? Dad said the boy needed an outlet for that temper of his. . . .

He killed that dog, and you know it. You knew it then, the voice told her. *He killed it like he killed those women.*

No. Just no. No one related to her, with the same blood in his veins and the same DNA and the same formative childhood, could possibly do horrible things like that to other people.

So maybe Toby had *found* the box. Kathy picked it up gingerly, the tiny rattle of bones inside turning her stomach as she turned the box. Maybe he'd gone out on a long drive and then a walk in the woods and had come across it just lying there. Maybe.

Or maybe, that little voice in her head, so sure of itself, suggested, *maybe he boiled the flesh off the finger bones of each of his murder victims and kept them as trophies so he could fantasize again and again about the kills.* Maybe that was why he had yanked her so violently away from the closet. He hadn't wanted her to find his little box of treasures.

She rose on unsteady legs, her shaking hands causing the contents of the box to knock around inside, and carefully made her way back to the closet. She'd put the box back where it had been, and . . . think. She'd think about what to do next. Maybe she could talk to Toby first and tell him what she'd seen. Maybe if she just asked, he could explain everything, and maybe that explanation had nothing at all to do with the local murders. Maybe there was a perfectly go—

A sharp pain at the back of her head made her cry out. Before she could register it as fingers tangled in her hair, pulling, the box had flown out of her hand, spilling the contents again, and she was on her back on the bedroom floor with Toby straddling her. The usual dead look in his eyes had been replaced by one of abject rage, not like fire but like an ice storm, a screaming, swirling maelstrom of hate.

It took her several moments longer to see the knife. It was shiny. Clean. It looked brand new. Its polished, silvery blade caught and froze time itself for what seemed like several long minutes before Toby's distorted voice finally broke through.

"What. The FUCK. Are you doing?" His words dropped like stones from his mouth, each segmented phrase punctuated by his hand on her throat picking her up and knocking her head against the floor. He reeked of cheap whiskey.

"I—I," she croaked. She couldn't manage more than that. His hand was heavy, and she felt both words and breath forced back down inside her, causing the pounding of her heart to ache in her chest.

"Oh, Kat. Silly, stupid Kat." He brought the point of the knife down very close to her widely staring eye. "You should have stayed out of my room."

She struggled beneath his weight. "Toby, stop," she gasped, trying to keep what little of her voice she could rasp out from rising an octave in panic.

He glanced back at the little box, its spilled insides vomited all over the bedroom floor, and eased his grip on her throat, just a little. When he looked back at her, his face wore a strange expression of disappointment and excitement. "I'm afraid I can't do that."

"Toby, get off me." She coughed. "Get off me, come on! Get off or Dad will—"

Her head was rocked to the side by a blow that stung her cheek. He'd hit her. Holy fuck, he'd actually hit her. He'd taken his hand off her throat and slapped her hard in the face. She lay silent, too stunned to struggle or attempt to speak again. Her cheek throbbed, and hot tears blurred her vision.

"You know, I could do you right here. I've thought about it, you know. I could fuck you and stab you to pieces and drag whatever's left of you out into the woods. I'd hide you better than the others. Dad would neeeever find you. No one would ever find you." His voice was soft, very soft, and kind of singsongy as he drew out the word "never." He stroked the side of her breast through her bra with his free hand and grazed her bare stomach with the knife. "I could do that, Kat. I could make sure you keep quiet, so, so quiet, about the box and the finger bones and the Hand of the Black Stars—all of that. But you're my sister. I don't want to kill you—really, I don't."

He leaned down until he was lying on top of her, his groin grinding painfully against her hips, his lips close to her ear. She felt the knife point digging into her cheek, and she winced, fresh tears streaming out of the corners of her eyes.

"But damn," he said, his breathing getting heavier, "do I ever want to cut you." His erection pressed painfully hard into her hip.

"Toby, please. Please get off of me."

He sat up again and raised the knife.

"Toby, don't!"

He pressed the blade into her skin just above her left eyebrow. She could feel the sting of it, a spark of horrific bright pain, and she screamed.

He pulled the blade down, skipping over her eye and landing on her cheek just below the eye socket, a new sting that spread its venomous agony out across her face. She screamed again, all the panicked desperation inside her welling up in that one loud wail of terror and hurt.

He dragged the blade down farther, all the way to her jawbone, and now she could feel the wet heat of her own blood dripping down into her ear, her eye, her hair. Her tongue darted against the inside of her cheek and she felt it give a little, the skin there so thin, so dangerously close to tearing straight through, and she screamed again.

She barely heard the rapid footsteps on the stairs or her father and Officer Kempton shouting at Toby. She felt a weight being lifted off her and a coolness where it had been, and she began to tremble all over. She closed her eyes, bawling, and heard more shouting, but couldn't make out the words. The pain throbbing across her face had a heartbeat of its own, and she had blood in her ear, and besides, her own sobs filled her from the inside out. So she cried on the floor, cried until she couldn't hear the shouting or even her own sobs, just the furious pounding of her wound's own heartbeat, until that, too, faded, and the darkness behind her eyelids spread to her whole body.

Kathy turned up Silver Street and followed it through acres of white flatland to the visitor parking lot just outside of Parker Hall. A red brick building with narrow, barred windows and a mansard roof, it had always struck Kathy as a stern, unwelcoming place, looming in the vertical and nearly suffocating in its lengths and turns. Unlike other mental hospitals in which Kathy had found occasion to visit in order to interview staff or patients, Connecticut-Newlyn Hospital, formerly Newlyn Hospital for the Criminally Insane, was one large building with wards, dubbed "halls," extending out from Parker Hall's administrative offices in broad slants.

She parked and sat for several minutes, watching the snow gather on her windshield and slowly blot out her view of the hospital. It took every ounce of willpower inside her to make herself get out of the car. Once the cold hit her face, she found it a little easier to trudge through the snow to the front door.

Kathy pressed the intercom button and gave her full name, then flashed her credentials at the CCTV camera mounted above the front door. There was a click and a crackle on the other end, followed by a soul-jarring buzz as the front door was unlocked. Kathy left the blindingly bright cold behind and stepped into the main lobby.

Ahead and to the right, a middle-aged woman with coiffed blond hair, a tired mouth, and cool eyes magnified by thick glasses sat behind a glass wall in a small office. She waved Kathy over.

"Hey, Margaret," Kathy said with a small smile as she approached. She held up her ID against the glass between them, then slid it beneath through a narrow opening above the wooden desk. Margaret was a stickler for visitor log-in protocol despite their familiarity, and Kathy had no issue with making sure the video recordings showed Margaret doing her job to the letter. Going through the familiar motions after so long, though, brought back a surprising surge of heavy old feelings.

Margaret smiled back, or rather, offered a curl of the mouth that passed for her smile, and returned Kathy's ID, then handed her a laminated visitor's pass on a lanyard with a clip. "Hello, Katherine. Long time no see. Are you here to see our new Mrs. Dorsey?"

"No, uh . . . actually, I'm here to, um, to see Toby."

Margaret's face remained professionally placid. She nodded, scribbling something on a clipboarded form, which she then handed to Kathy to sign. After Kathy had returned it, the older woman spoke again, softly. "You'll find him in three-oh-five."

Kathy tried to smile, but it slipped awkwardly off her face.

"Want an orderly to go with you?"

"Won't be necessary," Kathy said with a tone lighter than she felt. "Won't be there long."

Margaret seemed to think on that for a moment, perhaps considering Kathy's scar. "Be careful, Katherine."

"I will."

Kathy turned before Margaret could see the pain in her eyes and made her way down the hall. There were three more doors, two that her visitor's pass unlocked electronically and the last, which was opened for her by a guard armed with a Taser, before she reached the visiting area. She sat at the end of a long table that reminded her of high school lunchrooms and waited. A few minutes later, the same armed guard brought Toby in.

It had been a while since she had seen her brother. He looked smaller somehow, smaller than when he had loomed over her, smaller than he had when he had cut her—

She swallowed hard, avoiding his eyes, which she could feel fixed on her even from across the room. His blond hair had been cut short, almost military-style, and it bristled as he tilted his head. His arms and chest, once a well-built, worked-out source of pride beneath his tattoos, looked less bulky than she remembered. She didn't suppose they let him have weights at the hospital, which probably drove him nuts. His wrists were handcuffed to each other and to a chain around his waist that also extended to cuffs around his ankles. Kathy made herself look at the youngish, good-looking face. Its pleasantness, and its resemblance to her own, were offset by a sneer of a mouth and cold blue shark's eyes. Dead eyes, she thought, behind which the blackness that had entangled itself there had swallowed whatever had been her brother. The only spark of life or passion, of connectivity to the world, was when he hurt people. Like when he had hurt her.

He sat down across from her with a careless flop and a smirk and stared down at his fingers for several seconds—just long enough to make things uncomfortable—before finally speaking.

"So, little sister. After all this time, what brings you all the way out here to see me?"

Kathy leaned back in her chair. Her movements were slow, deliberate. Her wary gaze was fixed on him, while the rest of her face remained smooth and emotionless. "The Hand of the Black Stars."

Toby's eyes shot up to meet hers, his smirk suddenly gone. "Why do you want to know about them?" Before she could answer, a look of understanding bloomed in his eyes, and he nodded. "A case. So, this is a business call. They causing trouble for you somewhere?"

"Right here in Connecticut, as a matter of fact."

"Colby?"

Kathy tilted her head, surprised. "How did you know?"

Toby smiled, but the look in those dead eyes reflected nothing but black. "The snow."

"The snow? What does that have to do with anything?"

He stood and slid around the corner of the table, and she was reminded of how frightening he could be when he stood over her. Toby had been quick and very, very strong. She didn't much like him being that close to her.

He reached out to touch her face and she flinched. He paused momentarily, giving her a small smile that could have meant a hundred different things, and gingerly traced the line of her scar with his pinkie finger.

"You look good, baby sister. Really good."

Her hand clamped around his wrist like a vise, arresting both his touch and his smile. "We need to talk. You need to sit."

They locked eyes for a moment, and Kathy was relieved to see that she'd garnered enough internal flint that even a predator like Toby recognized it and backed down. She let go of his wrist, and he retreated sullenly to his side of the table and sat.

"So let me guess," he said, staring down at his fingers again. "You have a murder case you think the HBS is involved in. So . . . what? You come to pick the brain of your slavering, psychotic killer of a brother?"

"You know members of the Hand of the Black Stars. You mentioned them the night—you've mentioned them before. I need to know the meaning of a ritual—names, places, sigils."

"Even though it's only business, it's still good to see you, Kat. Though I admit I'm surprised by this new cool serenity in you. Pleased, too. And with me in such close proximity to you. Self-help books, is it, or some kind of therapy?"

She leaned back in her chair. "I need answers, Toby. A man has been murdered."

"Only one?" He chuckled dryly. "And I should care . . . why?"

She resisted the urge to sigh. "I don't figure you do care."

"Well, you would know, wouldn't you, baby sister? Couldn't do what I did if any teeny-tiny part of me was capable of human feeling, right? But you and I both know there isn't anything so weak and pointless as sentiment in me, because the Hand of the Black Stars touched me and burned it right out of my core."

"Look, I'm not here to help you process your feelings—or the lack thereof. But whatever goes on inside you . . . it's complicated. I know that."

"Oh, do you? Well, how the hell is it, then?"

She opened her mouth to speak, closed it, and gave in to the sigh. She tried again. "It's like . . . wandering into a mirage. Or a memory. Some flat space, some echo of a moment that was or will be, but is never, ever where you are when you are. Everything—people talking and laughing, dancing, eating, working, fighting, fucking, moving along, moving through time and space—everything is happening around you and you're in the center of it, but you're not real, not really there. You're just . . . superimposed on the world. At first, you want to know the secret, why everyone seems to know how to blend in and become part of the mirage, to find and connect to its physicality, its smells and tastes and colors, and make it real. But no one seems to understand why *you* can't do it, and so no one knows how to tell you how it's done. So you watch and crudely imitate and hope you'll figure it out, but you don't—you can't—and it makes you angry. You stuff that anger down because it certainly isn't going to help you blend in, and you bury it under your own secret ideas about what life and love and happiness should be, ideas that can't help but be steeped in the anger in your head. With every social rejection, every reminder that you're just a shadow on a mirage, you accumulate more and more of that anger, which settles and compresses and turns to hate. And that hate is the only other real thing in your layer with you, just you and your hate pasted onto a world that isn't yours and doesn't want to be. And when you've spent enough time pasted into someone else's version of life with hate buoying you up most days, it starts to leak in little ways, to erupt sometimes. Whatever you were, the hate becomes what you *are*, what gives you definition and outline, and what ultimately simulates the kind of physicality you had been looking for all along. It isn't enough, though, and maybe you know it never will be, but you've tasted the world, smelled it, touched it, heard it, all through that hate, and you can't go back to being a ghost over a mirage, not ever again—not when you could be one more kill away from figuring it all out."

"Stop," Toby whispered. His eyes were wet with tears.

A cold, cruel part of her, a part that she supposed was just like him, said, "I'm good at what I do for a reason."

"What do you want from me, Kat?"

"I told you—I want some information on the Hand of the Black Stars cult. Inside information that you have."

"How do you know I have any information at all?"

She fixed a stare on him that betrayed nothing of her feelings except impatience. "They didn't make you what you are—*you* did. But they did get inside you. They validated you and your killing, facilitated it. They protected you. So you became one of them. It was a blood bond. They know your secrets, and you know theirs."

Toby sighed, scratching at his elbow. He had many long, raw red scratches up and down his forearms, though his nails were cut short. Kathy didn't want to imagine how her brother had managed those marks, or why.

She glanced at the tattoo on his right bicep, a black symbol in a rounded hexagon surrounded by runes. She had seen it countless times as a teen but had never attached any significance to it until after Toby's arrest. It was not quite as complex as the one carved into the John Doe, but it was very, very close. It had many of the same occult significations, understood only by the initiated.

The Hand of the Black Stars had been mentioned briefly during Toby's trial, probably more for sensationalist reasons than factual evidence, as a possible influence in Toby's killings. Little was proven in that regard. Little was ever proven when it came to the cult, including solid evidence of its existence. But Kathy had no doubt that Toby knew and had always known more about the Hand of the Black Stars than anyone she had ever met. They had nurtured a killer in their midst, not just because it benefited Toby to be protected, but because it benefited them, too. He could be an instrument, if guided in their ways. Kathy thought that, on some level, Toby knew that; his loyalty to them, much like their loyalty to him, went only so far as the self-serving interests of a predator would allow.

Finally, Toby spoke. "What do you want to know?"

"Where I can find them."

Toby leaned back, considering her request. "Well, there's a sect in Oregon, moved up from California. One in Maine. Alaska, Ohio, Oklahoma. There was one in Jersey, but they're all gone now." He waved a hand. "They all vanished. Not even the priests know what happened. And . . . yeah, there's one in Connecticut, but I'm not sure exactly where. Colby sounds about right." He smiled.

Kathy wasn't sure if her brother was being honest about what he didn't know, but what he did reveal matched with her own knowledge of the cult. She decided to push on. She produced the crime scene photo with the symbol that had been branded on the John Doe's back.

Hesitant to give him the satisfaction of viewing death on glossy paper, she nevertheless slid the photo over to her brother.

"What does this symbol mean?"

Her brother leaned forward, studied it a moment, finger-traced it with a kind of reverence, and leaned back again, sailing the photo back across the table to her. "It's a key."

"A key to what?"

"A door."

It was maddening, letting Toby drag out the conversation like that, just to keep her there. Still, it was, frankly, the most productive conversation she'd had with him since they'd been kids.

"What door?"

"Look, baby sister. I don't think all the visiting hours in the world are enough time to explain the ins and outs of the Hand's belief system."

"Try. We still have some time."

Toby frowned. "Okay. So you found this on a dead body, and you came to me."

"Yes."

"It's a sacrifice, obviously. The symbol is the key. The incantations ask for guidance in opening the door. The blood defines the outlines of the door. The rest—the mutilations, I mean—are how the cult members know the door is open."

"Okay . . . you'll have to walk me through this. First, what are they opening this door for?"

"You'd have to ask someone higher up in the Hand than me. It's not my place to say."

"You mentioned the snow before. Why?"

Toby smiled.

"What does the snow have to do with the cult?"

He suddenly leaned toward her over the table. Her whole body tensed.

"You can't begin to imagine, little sister."

"So enlighten me."

Toby shook his head, that small smile still hanging on his lips, and looked away.

Kathy persisted. "Is there some significance to the cult that it's snowing this late in the season? Are they planning something because of the snow? What is it?"

Toby stifled a chuckle. "You have it all wrong. It's not that they're planning something *because* of the snow. What they planned *was* the snow. It's just the beginning. Another sign the door has swung open."

Kathy frowned. "What are you talking about?"

"I'm talking about power. It's all the Hand understands, or cares about."

"And you?" she asked before she could stop herself. "What do you care about, Toby?"

He studied her a moment, seeming to calculate the urgency of her need for information with . . . well, whatever Toby balanced human decency in his head with. He glanced around before settling his gaze on her again. "Write this down."

She pulled her cell phone from her purse and opened the notepad app. "Shoot."

Toby gave her a name and address.

Kathy looked up from the phone. "Who's this?"

"An insider with information. An insider, a former Hand low priestess, as a matter of fact, who . . . likes me. Heh. She should be able to tell you what you need safely, I imagine, if you tell her you're mine. My sister, I mean." He grinned in an odd way. It would have been a boyish, charming gesture to anyone who didn't know him. "Like I said, you'd have to go higher up on the Hand food chain than me. My hands are tied, so to speak. She can give you truths. Some truths." He offered her a wink that made her skin crawl. "You can tell her I sent you. But don't tell her you're a cop . . . or whatever you do now. Although it's probably a moot point. If they got as far as calling forth the snow, then it's already too late to stop it." He stood up and signaled to the guard.

Before being led out, he looked at her with uncharacteristic softness. "You know, Kat . . . you were the only one who mattered. So much as anyone matters. And so I'll tell you this. Forget about investigating any of this. Just leave. Leave town now before you can't. Before the snow and its masters won't let you. Do that for me. Or if not for me . . . then for you. Colby is fucked, and you can't stop that." When she didn't respond, his mouth twisted into that hateful little sneer, and the softness in his eyes went dark again. Kathy fought the urge to gag as the guard led him away.

With him gone, her hand shook as she slipped the phone back into her purse. Kathy let go of a breath she hadn't realized she'd been holding, and stood up to go.

Kathy made it all the way back to her car before the tears blurring her vision finally spilled down her cheeks. The wind had picked up some, and as it blew across her face, the tears that had slid into the slender track of her scar grew cold to the point of biting. She wiped them away with a gloved hand and unlocked the car door. She grabbed her snow brush off the passenger seat, then methodically began working to clear off her car. She wanted to focus only on the mindless task, the simple necessity of it, but she found herself stabbing into the ice beneath the snow with ferocity that made the tears well up again.

Her eyes had dried by the time she had finally cleared the car and got it moving. She had work to do, and distance between her and Toby would bring clarity and focus. Besides, she had to see one Charlene Ledders, former HSB low priestess and another current resident of a psychiatric wing, this time of Colby's local hospital on the town outskirts, before the snow made travel impossible.

Chapter Three

The snow that had accumulated by morning was a formidable sight, stirring a sense of unease in those who opened their doors to the blinding whiteness. That unease only grew with the afternoon's accumulation as the sun made its way across the argent sky. Along with the heavy snow, an army of rough, dense stones of hail scratched at windows and thumped on cars as it fell.

The residents of Colby shook their heads in amazement and not a little wariness. Easygoing and hardworking people, the townsfolk of Colby generally held the belief that weather was a fickle friend, and what with the world as it was nowadays, it wasn't outside their realm of limited imagination that global warming, bio-weapons testing, and companies dumping chemicals into the ground and water might cause a change in weather patterns. One couldn't have something like the meltdown of those Japanese nuclear reactors into the surrounding ocean, they reasoned, and not think it might alter the chemistry of a sky composed of re-evaporated and re-absorbed water.

However, it was getting on toward the beginning of June, when the children ought to be getting antsy and excited about summer vacation. Parents had winter clothes to pack up. It was time for budgets to shift the household expense from heating to air-conditioning and electric fans. In town, the boutiques should have been putting out the last of their shorts and tank tops, swimsuits, and flip-flops. The pool stores should have been stocking up on chemicals and skimmers and filter parts. Targets and Wal-Marts had grills and Fourth of July picnic tablecloths and napkins to sell. The snow—and everything people needed to get through it—should have long been put away for the year.

But the snow was still here, and in thick, fluffy white abundance.

A fluke snowfall in mid-April was one thing—strange but explainable, perhaps, as winter's last yawn before settling down. But four feet of snow and counting, a week and a half before June first, was not a fluke. It was a problem, and one that set the minds of those easygoing and hardworking people thinking. Not panicking—not quite yet—but certainly wondering just on the outermost edges of their minds if maybe there wasn't something to those crazy conspiracy theories and apocalypse warnings that old man Wershaw shouted at people from the street corner outside the 7-Eleven.

It was one of these townspeople who passed Kathy Ryan's car on Main Street in the pixilated blur of white quickly smearing away the finer details of Colby. As he did so, he was cursing the snow, his premature removal of the plow, and his replacement of the winter tires on his black truck. Damn strange weather was going to set him back months, possibly. He'd have to wait not just for the snow to melt, but for the ground to thaw and the grass to grow before he'd be able to work. He grimaced at the thought that Constance would have to keep clipping coupons and dipping into their savings. She'd never say it was his fault—not even imply it with a look—but it made him ornery, to say the least, to feel like he wasn't able to support himself and his wife with good, honest work.

The side of the truck read H. CASPER, LANDSCAPING in grass-green lettering. It was an old vehicle, stubbornly strong and reliable, not unlike its driver. Riding the upward crest toward seventy years old, Casper was a mostly amiable guy. He liked his beer and ball games, he loved his wife, his son, and his little grand-baby girl, and most days, he thanked the good Lord he was still able-bodied enough to work.

Today, though, really seemed to beat all in proving that the Lord, good as He might be, worked in mysterious ways. That was if it was, in fact, the work of the Lord at all.

As he left Main Street in the rearview mirror, the maelstrom swirled against his windshield, blocking out a good portion of his view. He strained to see past the chunks of ice smeared by his windshield wipers, but could make out only streaks of gray road and the occasional telephone pole. If he could get back to the house, get to his shed, he could at least hook up the plow again. Plowing snow meant long hours of no sleep on little coffee (his doctor and his recent chest pains demanded he cut out at least some of his caffeine or stress or both) and cold hands and feet, but it also meant some decent pay to carry him and Constance through this last freak snowstorm.

A car passed him—Charlie Hines, he thought, but who could see a damn thing out there?—and honked a hello as he drove by. Casper returned the greeting, though he was feeling less and less neighborly by the minute. Folks better get their damned fool selves off the road before they got into accidents. That meant Charlie Hines of the well-oiled elbow as well.

A cold blast of wind blew by him, making him shiver. Then he frowned; all the windows were closed. Where was the draft coming from?

As if in answer, a clicking inside his dashboard preceded the heat kicking off again. It figured; if cold air could find any part of that truck as useless as tits on a bull, it was that damned heating system. In the sudden absence of warmth, a chill got in between his clothes and skin, almost between his skin and bones. He swore, giving the top of the dashboard a sound thump with the side of his fist. The heating system sputtered like a cough in a dying throat, but the heat did not come back on.

He looked up in time to see the telephone pole looming up out of the white, an impossibly large black form in the streaks of wetness that the wipers left in their wake. Casper cut the wheel sharply to the right and the car slid, the back end fishtailing into the other lane. He cut the wheel in the other direction and pumped at the brakes, but the car only wobbled, then slid suddenly into a snow bank on the side of the road. The impact jarred his bones, causing the arthritis in his knees to moan.

"Okay," he muttered. He felt his heart pounding. "Okay." He undid his seat belt and sat a moment, collecting himself. His breath was a hard knot in his chest that took a while to unravel and seep out of his mouth.

The oddly dry scratching of the snow against the windshield, as well as the jittery squeaking of the wiper blades, seemed unnaturally loud in the interior of the car—the only sounds in the whole white-washed world.

No, he thought, motionless and listening. Not the only sounds. There, just to the left, out on the road . . . a low, dull crunching seemed to be moving toward the car. *Creeping* was the word that came to mind, though it seemed silly that the idea of someone creeping toward the car should send those shivers in little shock waves beneath his skin. Why shouldn't someone move like that, slowly and carefully, easing over the ice and snow?

He rolled down the window and immediately felt a blast of cold wetness against his face. He squinted into the wind, trying to make out details of the figure—or were there figures?—approaching the car. At best he could see slivers of irregular dark shapes, possibly furry in places, trudging toward him.

"Hi! Hello there," Casper called out somewhat sheepishly. "Slid off the road. No damage, I don't think. Not sure how deep I'm b—" He stopped.

The figures—he could see now that there were two of them in thick, fur-lined, hooded black coats and heavy boots—had halted their trek and were standing stone still in the middle of the road. Their heads were bowed, ostensibly against the weather, so he couldn't see their faces. Otherwise, they seemed remarkably unperturbed by the wind whipping all around them.

"Hello?"

The figures didn't move and didn't answer. The wind shifted some of the snow away, though, and he saw at least three more figures behind those in the middle of the road. The one closest to his truck had something long and glinting protruding from its glove that Casper couldn't quite reconcile as a shovel.

"Well, yeah, I'd sure appreciate if you could help me maybe push this old heap out of this snow bank here?"

No answer. Seven of them now, he counted, still as ice.

"Okay, well, thanks," Casper said, dismissing them with an exasperated wave. Their silence left him nettled. That was the world today for you. He could remember when a fella in Colby could reasonably expect young men to be neighborly and lend a helping hand if needed. He began to roll the window up when he suddenly became aware of their presences very close to him, just outside the driver door. He turned his head in time to see the glinting thing—a knife—and had a moment to gasp before the blade was buried in his throat. Coppery, hot liquid pain filled him up so he couldn't breathe, warming him against the gust of cold as the driver door opened. He felt rough hands grab him beneath his arms and drag him out of the truck. He tried to speak, but the blade blocked the air, and the words drowned in his punctured throat. Awful pressure pushed against his chest and skull, and he fought the panic, making little choke-gasp sounds, sucking at the icy air. The effort gave no relief, but instead put an unpleasant chill on the pain.

Casper was dying. He'd been knifed and oh God, he was dying, and his body was being moved . . . where? Who were these guys? And what had he done to piss them off?

The edges of the world narrowed a little. He felt numb in his feet and hands, and that numbness was starting to travel up his limbs. He was vaguely aware of the heat inside him seeping out in longish red trails around his neck. He could also sense hard ground beneath him and an encroaching freeze from the snow drifts through which the rough hands were dragging him. Silver sky stretched endlessly across his limited view, dropping heavy flakes of snow in his eyes and down his throat to mix with and melt in the blood. Still, he sucked in greedily, fighting to take in whatever life, vibrancy, and alertness he could from the cold air. It was not enough. His lungs screamed, and his brain roared in his skull. His arthritic knees locked and throbbed, but he barely felt them. His heart pounded against his ribs, threatening to quit before his lungs could. Black haze in his vision ate into the canvas of sky.

He didn't know how long he was pulled through the snow—four minutes, forty minutes—nor did he recognize the corner of the roof or the treetop that broke the limitless silver. A light, soft part of him didn't much care. He thought of Constance, his grand-baby, his unlocked truck, the beer waiting for him at home in the fridge. Absurdly, it occurred to him that the last episode of that show he was watching on Netflix (the name escaped him now, but that Kiefer Sutherland boy was in it) had been a two-parter, and in his situation, it didn't look like he'd make it home to see the second half. That summed up his situation, he thought, and struck him as both funny and tragic. The choke sound he made fluttered between a laugh and a moan.

A hand with a strange, complex-looking tattoo he hadn't seen since the war passed over his face, momentarily blocking out the light. He was aware then of words above his head—low, chanted words he didn't understand. He didn't think the men above him were speaking in English, but it was hard to hold on to meanings of things. His brain felt weightless and empty. He found he wasn't all that worried anymore.

In fact, Casper thought as he turned his head, even that thing they were calling over to him across the field didn't seem so scary. Not all of his brain agreed—a sliver of his old strength and stubbornness, a sliver of his mind that had served him well in the war and out of it— was very worried about what was going on above his head. Mostly, it was because that thing, while big as a mastiff, was no dog, nor any kind of animal he'd ever seen. So far as his fading vision could make out, it was hairless and white, spindly, and it flickered in and out of his view, its substance one moment distinct from the snow and the next, a part of it. It made wind-chime sounds in its mouth as it crunched across the snow toward him. It bent over him, opening a gaping maw, a widening cavern lined with interlaced spindle teeth that parted like a fish bone curtain. Glassy living things, white and wriggling, moved inside its mouth. Casper couldn't quite understand the thing his eyes were showing him; it made no sense by any animal law he knew. He couldn't scream, though, and couldn't muster up enough wherewithal to realize he should want to scream. The pain had settled into a non-thing through his body. The excruciating burn of airlessness in his head and lungs had gone to smoldering. The blade in his throat felt hard and awkwardly in the way, but otherwise insignificant.

Casper tried to hold on to the last thoughts and sensations from that sliver of his mind, the ones that made him real, kept him alive, but it seemed so much easier to let them go. He didn't even choke out a cry when that odd gateway of teeth parted wider and that busy mouth closed over his face. His body twitched beneath it as his face dissolved, but by then, what had made Casper a living human being was gone.

The black-coated men continued dragging the body toward the tree. The wind howled, dragging sprays of fresh snow over the blood where Casper had been. There was a lot of blood, but there was more snow.

Across town, when Jason Houghton's shift ended late that afternoon, the snow had begun in earnest. Already, a fluffy covering of white had accumulated over all the visible surfaces outside the factory. He recognized Ed's and Carla's cars still in the parking lot, as well as Liam's Ford pickup, coated by a hardening sheath of ice onto which a new mantle of snow was steadily thickening.

Jason looked up into a cataract-clouded sky, blinking as flakes dusted his eyelashes. The cold felt good on his face. He'd been on the packing-and-stacking line today, lugging heavy boxes from the packing conveyor belts to stack on wooden pallets, and he'd worked up a sweat that the winds now cooled away. The work was nothing he hadn't done a thousand times in the last fifteen years, but he'd been on forklifts the past three weeks, so he was out of practice. He liked to think that was the reason he had been so out of breath, and not his turning forty-three next month. Twenty-six of those forty-three years had been spent as a pack-a-day smoker, the import of which was not lost on him as he popped a Camel between his lips and sheltered its tip from the snow with one hand so he could light it. Jason was short but strong, thickly muscled and mostly tattooed, with rough hands used to working. He knew he wasn't old, but some days he felt it. There were few, if any, wrinkles around his eyes but what peered out of those dark irises was an old enough soul, one that wondered more and more lately about where he'd been, and how that left him in terms of where to go next.

He made his way toward his car, a silver Hyundai nearly blotted out by the swirls of snow. He popped the trunk from the button on his key fob and took out the snow brush. It would take a while, he supposed, to clear enough snow off the car that he could drive it. He slammed the trunk lid down and trudged toward the driver's-side door, fumbling with a gloved hand in his pocket to return his remaining pack of cigarettes to safety. Wind-driven clouds cast long, dark shadows over the car and the lot around it. It was in one of those shadows that Jason, who happened to glance up from his bracing huddle against the wind, noticed something duck out of sight around the front of his car. It was the movement he caught rather than any particular identifying feature, but some quality about it raised Jason's hackles, and he frowned.

"Uh, hello?"

His boots crunched through the snow as he made his way to the front of the car. He was surprised to find that there were no footprints, no smudges of displaced snow along the bumper. Jason looked up, scanning the slope of grass and the wooded area beyond that cupped the eastern side of the factory building. It was tough to see through the snow, but Jason felt pretty sure there was no sign of movement, animal or otherwise. He glanced down at the front end of the car again.

Wait . . . there *was* a small spot at the far end of the bumper where small grooves had been imprinted into the fluffy snow. They looked like drag marks from thin, tapered fingers. Jason followed it around the far side of the car and crouched down to get a better look.

Up close, the marks struck him as even more puzzling. Not only had something dragged long fingermarks into the snow, but whatever it was had also carved thin furrows into the metal of the bumper.

"What the f—" Jason whispered, but let the final word trail off, muted by the dull, continuous thud of snowfall. There was a new shadow, suddenly darkening the grooves in his bumper. With it came a sound like glass being dragged over glass, a sound not much different in timbre from the wailing gusts of wind. This sound, though, seemed more substantial and much closer—right over his head, in fact.

Jason looked up and opened his mouth to scream, but the thing peering down at him from the roof of the car moved quickly. It was on his throat, tearing it open before the scream could surface. Still, though, the steam of Jason's heat escaped the clawed-open hole with a small whine of breath that could have been a miniature cry. Or, it could have been the wind blowing over the jagged opening in Jason Houghton. Within minutes, small drifts of snow filled the glazing eyes and the slack-jawed mouth. The ragged hole in Jason's throat still pumped a bloody spray that, against the snowy canvas beneath his body, blazed starkly crimson.

The argentine figure, ghost-like, seemed nearly translucent as it bent over the body, absorbing the blood. For a moment, it flickered a more solid outline. Had there been anyone else in the parking lot to see it, he or she would likely have thought it looked vaguely angler-fish-like, wide-eyed and scaly with serrated teeth swathed in fleshy, dull lips, big as a large dog with gangly arms and legs and taloned, three-digit hands and feet. Then it flickered out again, and was little more than the suggestion of movement as it bounded, print-less, across the ever-growing drifts of snow.

Jack Glazier was having a hell of a morning.

It had started with Katie. His ex-wife had called early, early enough to wake him. She knew he slept until six, so she'd called at 5:45, just to deprive him of those last fifteen minutes. It was one of those little passive-aggressive moves that had driven a wedge between them during their marriage and that had often swelled to flat-out aggression during the divorce. Jack didn't hate Katie, but he sure as hell had come to dislike her. It had taken a while. She was Jack Jr. and Carly's mother, and she had once been a woman he thought he could love and cherish for the rest of his life. But she liked to poke him with situational sticks, and her round refusal to ever take any share of blame or responsibility for the failure of their marriage left it squarely on his shoulders, a belief she worked into nearly every conversation. She'd been a stickler about getting what she deemed "her fair share from a neglectful, job-obsessed husband" and a marriage that, post-children, she had considered "largely a waste of [her] productive years." She (wrongly) thought he'd had an affair with Kathy Ryan, and so she also found ways to work that into a conversation at least once in a while. Worst of all, she did little to hide her animosity toward him in front of the children, and for that, he found himself often fantasizing about slapping her silly. She could, at times, be warm and thoughtful, at times easygoing and even funny. But those times had grown few and far between since the divorce, and on good days, he still groaned when her number showed up on the caller ID.

She'd called to finalize the custody schedule for the summer. In the three years since the divorce, the kids' schedule when they were out of school was to spend two weeks of every month with their dad and two with their mom, with alternating holidays. However, Katie wanted to talk at length about the snow and whether that should change their plans (he didn't see why it should) and whether anyone in Connecticut outside of Colby had been contacted about the weather, like the National Weather Bureau or whoever in the federal government was in charge of such things (he had no knowledge of that, though he reassured her the folks in the municipal building were supposedly in contact with state officials regarding potential resource help). Jack expected a state of emergency would be called, particularly if the rest of the state was also affected, but he hadn't heard anything yet in that regard. It was almost as if Colby was invisible to the rest of the outside world, and all attempts at communication in or out were being swept away by the snow. Jack didn't tell Katie that, of course. He didn't want her worrying the kids. Already she was driving him nuts, wanting to know how he was going to explain all this weather business to the children; he reassured her he would talk about it with them in an informative but non-frightening way.

It took forty-five minutes of such reassurances to finally get her off the phone, and promptly upon disconnecting, he spilled his mug of coffee across his desk. Half an hour later, he received word of Abe Maurner's mother keeling over in the snow on her front lawn, Joe Bishop's request for extended medical for his heart surgery, and Cali Richter's report on freezing deaths a block away from the local homeless shelter on Trensfer Avenue. All throughout, the phone rang off the hook with concerned citizens demanding answers, not unlike Katie, about the weather and some downed power lines that appeared to be limiting cell usage and preventing Internet access altogether, and just what the hell were the police doing about it, anyway?

What he did not get, however, was anything useful from Cordwell's preliminary autopsy report on the John Doe. He hadn't even been able to identify the animal that had left those teeth marks, and there was no forensic evidence on the body whatsoever that could help identify the killer or killers.

Jack had a headache before eleven-fifteen that morning.

Then, around 4 PM, dispatch notified him of another homicide, a multiple this time. He and his team were being asked to report ASAP to Ormann Field at the end of Woodland Road. Texts had already gone out to the CS team, Morris, Teagan, and Kathy Ryan. Responding officers noted unusual circumstances.

"Unusual how?" he'd asked Sherry at dispatch when she told him.

"They didn't say," she'd replied. "They just said to get ahold of the task force on the 'John Doe devil worship case' right away. I'm guessing there are similarities between your JD and this scene, or something in this one that connects it to the last one."

"Okay, Sherr. I'm on my way."

"Hey, you be careful out there, huh? Don't want to lose my favorite detective."

"Yes, ma'am, I will. Wouldn't want to disappoint my favorite dispatcher," he flirted back, and he could hear her smile through the phone.

"Oh, one other thing—the ROs said to bring heat lamps."

"Heat lamps?"

"Apparently, some of the evidence was deliberately frozen to the ground. They don't think it can be chipped out without possible damage to the evidence. Jars, as I understand, though the ice surrounding has kept anybody from positively ID-ing anything in them so far. Mixed reports about the state of the bodies—you're going to have a lot to sort out, I think. ROs just said there was 'Kathy Ryan kind of stuff.' You know how that goes."

"Huh."

"Yeah."

There was a pause, and then Sherry added, "Uh-oh. Oh . . . oh no."

"What?"

"Oh God, Jack," she whispered. The change in her voice alarmed him.

"What? Sherry, what's going on?"

"Calls coming in . . . ROs on two other scenes requesting your help. All multiple homicides in open spaces. All requesting your task force. You have to go, Jack. Go now. I'm texting you and your team all the info."

Jack got up, setting his new mug of coffee to precarious wobbling. He barely noticed. He grabbed his keys and coat. "I'm on it, Sherry. Tell them I'm on my way."

"It's bad, Jack. Children, too, on these . . ."

An awful lump rolled over in Jack's stomach. He hated when crimes involved children. It was really turning out to be a clusterfuck of a morning.

"What the hell's going on out there, Sherry?" Jack's question was soft, sad, and almost inaudible.

"Don't know," she answered, her voice wavering. "Maybe it's the weather."

Chapter Four

The local community college had closed its campus on account of the weather; so had nearly every business in town—at least those who employed experienced adults who knew better than to think they had to risk their lives for retail. Twenty-somethings like Dan Murphy and Jessica Florey were apparently not counted among either the experienced or the indispensable, since the Quick Mart where they had met and both worked for the last eight months or so had remained open and indifferent to their potential safety. Dan had offered to drive his girlfriend home, to see to it that she made it safely. They had left her car half-buried in a mountain of gray. Although it was in better condition than Dan's old beater, it didn't have snow tires or four-wheel drive, so he had insisted they take his. He'd meant the best; he really had.

As they passed Ormann Field on the far side of Colby, though, Dan's car shivered in the snow. They got a mile or so farther down the road and then rolled to a stop.

Dan was not inclined to panic, but feeling control of the car slip away from him in the whiteout made him distinctly uneasy; it didn't help that the snow immediately began to pile with almost unnatural quickness on the hood of the car.

"Dammit." He was also not, as inclinations go, particularly interested or skilled in the mechanical workings of cars, which he felt now was coming back to bite him. He scanned the dashboard to see if any lights were flashing, but nothing indicated a problem. The car had jerked a little as if the anti-lock brake system had detected a patch of ice, then just rolled to a stop.

He braced himself. Jessica would have something to say. She always did. It would be his fault, as nearly everything that afternoon apparently was. She wouldn't even have to voice the blame; it would be dripping all over her tone.

He tried the key in the ignition. The car wouldn't start. The engine wouldn't even turn over. He tried again: no dice.

"Dammit," he said louder, pounding a hand on the steering wheel. He sat a minute, then tried the ignition again. Nothing happened. He figured it could be the battery; maybe the cold had affected it somehow. . . .

Jessica frowned in his periphery. "Did you run out of gas?"

Dan cast a frustrated glance in her direction. "Of course not. Look—it's at half a tank still."

"Well," she returned his irritation, "maybe the battery froze. Or something is wrong with the engine. Aren't you supposed to run it to keep it going in the winter? I mean, I don't know. I'm not a mechanic."

"Obviously," he muttered under his breath, yanking on his gloves. He flipped up the hood with a switch beneath the dashboard and opened the car door. A frigid blast of air stabbed into the car's interior. "Be right back. Stay here." He slid out into the snowfall and slammed the door.

While he was gone, Jessica waited in the car, steaming the windows with her irritation. She could catch dark glimpses of Dan's coat through the blizzard as he made his way to the front of the car, brushed the snow off it with his sleeve, and popped the hood. She couldn't see him at all then, and could hear nothing but the creaking of the wind and the chuffing of the snow. It made her feel nettled. She didn't like the idea of being left alone in the passenger seat, with him doing God-knew-what to the insides of the car in some half-assed attempt at being Mr. Fix-it. She took her cell out of her purse with half a mind to just call Triple-A, but a sound outside, louder than the storm, made her jump. It had sounded like a heavy thump against the outside of her car door. She waited, listening, and thought she heard, though she couldn't be sure, something like glass scratching against metal.

"Dan?" Her voice barely broke a whisper; she shook her head and buzzed the power window down. A gust of snow-choked air smacked her face. She grimaced against it and stuck her head out the window. "Dan? Dan!"

Her hand found the door handle and hesitated. She shielded her eyes against the wind and snow as best she could and looked out into the darkness, but could see nothing. She looked down, scanning the snow drift piling up against her door for whatever could have made the banging and scraping sounds. She saw nothing.

"Dan!" she shouted, but in reply, there was only a rush of snow and ice in her eyes and down her throat, and suddenly close behind her, that metallic whine of glass on metal.

The cold formed a hard lump around the panic in her gut, and she turned her head slowly toward the source of the sound.

What she saw set loose a scream from her that the wind matched, picked up, and carried away.

Dan swore into the wind. Whatever was wrong with the car, it was far beyond his limited knowledge. No loose wires or burnt-out spark plugs. In fact, the engine was still giving off heat, so he couldn't imagine the cold had done any damage. As far as he could tell, the battery was fine, but what the hell did he know? He was no mechanic, either.

His fingers throbbed beneath the gloves, and his toes felt like they had been shoved between sharp rocks. He'd always had poor circulation in his hands and feet, and so had little tolerance for the cold weather. He'd only gotten out to look under the car's hood to get away from Jessica for a minute. She could get on his nerves like nobody else, and while he liked her in some ways, she often made him want to smack that expression of smug satisfaction in her own good looks and charms right off her face. He'd done a lot for her because of those looks and what those charms promised, and over the last month or so, it had not proved worth the headaches she caused him.

He slammed down the hood and huddled into his coat. He'd have Jessica call AAA. Hell, she probably already had the cell phone out, and if she wasn't on the phone arranging for someone to come get them already, then she was biding her time, bitching to friends over texts, until he came back and she could make a big show of calling for a tow.

Dan's overhead light was busted, so when he opened the door, it remained dark. He slid in, fully expecting an onslaught of criticism. He didn't notice the blood until he turned toward the unexpected silence.

Jessica was gone. Her purse lay open on the floor. On the seat where she'd been, the cracked screen of her crushed cell phone offered pale slivers of light and darkness as it sat in a small puddle of congealing blackness.

"Jess?" A cloying coppery smell came from the passenger seat, from that puddle. *Blood?* When a gust of wind brought snow through her open window, Dan caught a whiff of something else. It was a sour smell he couldn't place, but it reminded him of the way one's fingers smelled after touching a metallic surface in a public place—layers of other people's skin oils, dirty metal, germs, or how he imagined petting-zoo animals might smell after they di—

A high-pitched wail carried over the wind, scraping across his bones so that the hairs on his arms and neck stood on end.

Something was outside in the snow.

Outside—where he had just been, alone and completely unaware.

Dan pushed the window button just enough to buzz the passenger window all the way up, cutting off the cold, and then locked the doors. He peered cautiously from one dark pane to another, trying to make out what might be out there. The flakes of snow and ice brushed and slapped against the window like a thousand tiny fingertips trying to get in.

It occurred to him then that if the power windows had worked—for Jess when she'd lowered the window, and again for him when he raised it back up again—then that had to mean the car had at least *some* power somewhere, maybe enough to get it going again. He tried the key in the ignition. Nothing happened. Dan swore softly. What was going on? Should he go back out there and try to find Jess? He glanced again at the puddle of blood on the passenger seat, and decided a search for her would be moot. She couldn't leave that much blood behind and still be alive, could she?

He heard the wail again, closer this time, although he couldn't tell exactly which direction it was coming from. He whispered Jessica's name and realized he hadn't really made a sound. His heart pounded loudly in his ears.

A thump on the hood rattled the car, and Dan fought the urge to cry out. Through the ice-crusted windshield, he could see a shape, or at least, the occasional outline of a shape, sometimes dark and sometimes almost nonexistent. It slapped an enormous . . . paw—or claw?—onto the windshield, and Dan flinched. He could make out what looked like three unusually long, multi-segmented fingers with curving black talons.

Their points screeched against the glass as whatever those fingers belonged to moved around on the hood of the car.

Think. Think. He had to think.

He could run, but how far, and for how long? Even if he stayed on the road instead of saving time by cutting through the woods, it was a whiteout out there. It was dark now, and cold enough that if he lost his bearings in the snow storm, he could very well freeze to death even with a heavy coat.

And those circumstances ignored the most glaring and immediate problem—the one which now scrabbled up the windshield. Dan had one brief, sickening glimpse of gangly, nearly translucent legs and animal feet, each with three long, taloned toes.

A thump and steel groan from the roof of the car made him jump. Over the wind, Dan heard the thing wail in frustration as it clawed at the car.

He dug his phone out of his pocket and then swore, fighting the urge to slam it against the dashboard. It had died an hour ago. He looked reluctantly at Jessica's phone, sitting in the congealing puddle of her blood. He didn't want to touch it or, by any extension, touch the horrible thing that had happened to her. Another thump from outside, however, decided for him. He took a deep breath, let it out in a cool white puff, and snatched the phone. The screen was cracked, and when he tried to turn it on, it stuck on the brand logo for a bit and then faded to black. He tried again, but couldn't even access her password screen. Disgusted, he tossed it back onto the passenger seat. He plugged his own into the car charger, hoping there might be just enough juice somewhere in the car to power it back up. The thing on the roof wailed into the wind. Dan was going to die in that car, alone in the snowy dark. . . .

Think. His stomach lurched, and he fought the rising gorge of panic in his throat. He could stay in the car. Whatever that was out there, it didn't seem to be able to get in, so maybe he could wait it out. Maybe it would get frustrated and go away.

He glanced at Jessica's seat again, at the blood, and felt his stomach twist in fresh knots. That thing had probably been going for him, until she'd opened the window. Why had she opened it? Why had she gotten in its way? He mashed away the beginning of tears with his fist. God only knew what that thing had done to Jessica—he didn't really want to think about it. But if it had eaten her (his own stomach cramped at the thought), then maybe it would go away.

And just what the fuck was that thing out there, anyway? His bet was on some military experiment gone wrong, some kind of biological or zoological warfare that had gotten too powerful and too unpredictable to control. Shit like that was always going down in quiet little nowhere towns like Colby.

Dan shivered, clapping his hands together and blowing on the stiffening tips of his fingers. He hated the cold. He tried to think about anything else besides the dropping temperature inside the car and the nightmare thing outside on top of it. He was sure the two were related—that thing trying to claw through the roof of his car had caused snow in May, or the weather anomaly had spawned the thing, a military weather/monster experiment or whatever that had eaten his girlfriend.

Every ten or fifteen minutes that passed, Dan found himself checking the ignition. His fingers ached, and his toes felt like hard glass, fragile enough to send shards of pain across his feet every time he tried to stamp some circulation back into them. The accumulated heat from the interior had completely dissipated, and if he couldn't start the engine, he'd freeze inside the car just as easily as out on the road. He had to work at keeping his teeth from chattering. He felt cold all over.

But . . . somebody somewhere had to know Colby was screwed with snow and snow monsters, right? So, where were the police? Where were the firefighters and EMTs and the fucking National Guard? He blew on his fingers again, rubbing them futilely, and flinched at a thump above his head. No doubt people in charge of these kinds of situations, military or SWAT or whatever, were in a (warm) room somewhere planning how to make the Colby problem go away. They had to be.

Not that their deliberations would do him much good right now.

A strained part of his brain, the part that had calculated the probability of freezing to death and then being eaten in his future, found it all kind of funny. Yeah, somebody somewhere had a plan, all right. The government would come in and drop bombs and wipe Colby, its townspeople, and the military's snowbound mistake right off the goddamned planet.

Welcome to Colby, Connecticut, population negative six. A nice, quiet place to settle down. Snow here? No sir! Colby is as balmy as a paradise island, thanks to its smoking crater—all hot springs and ra-diation, a regular nuclear summer. How's that for fun? Bring the kids!

He started giggling then, and was frightened by the thin, crazed, manic quality it had in his own ears. His teeth began chattering, and he found he didn't have the strength to stop it. The chattering spread to his whole body until he was shaking. This made him feel a little warmer—not enough to be comfortable, but enough to set off an alarm in his head. He'd heard somewhere that one of the final signs of hypothermia was a kind of numb warmth, sometimes even an unbearable heat, just before death. Was this how it started? Was he starting to freeze to death?

I have to get out of here. Now.

He screamed for help into the inky emptiness all around him.

As if in answer, the thing on the roof jumped down onto the trunk, and Dan turned sharply in his seat. Puffs of its breath fogged the back window, melting the snow. For the first time, Dan saw the creature's head, and it sucked the breath and scream right out of him.

The pale head was anglerfish-like, wide-eyed and scaly with ser-rated teeth swathed in fleshy, dull lips. The body crowding the rear window was all lean muscles and angles, the scales or flesh like snow and ice. It was there one second, and then it blew away, like so many flakes in the window. Then it reformed again. It growled at him, a sound like rending metal, and for one horrific second, Dan thought the thing was tearing through the car. Then it scrabbled up the back window and onto the roof again.

It seemed like a long time passed after that. The wind blew dry, anxious whisper words of snow against the windows of the car. All around him, the night exhaled its leaden grayness, separating him further from any hope of help. He waited, his breath shallow, and lis-tened for the thing on the roof. It had been a while since he'd heard it wailing and thumping up there. Maybe it had left. He peered through the window into the swirling darkness. Everything was moving out there—it would be impossible to see where or if that thing was wait-ing out on the road.

His chest hurt from pulling in cold, dry air, and his body was shaking uncontrollably.

His phone! He scrambled to pick it up and turn it on. His fingers were numb and his first few attempts with the touch screen yielded nothing. Finally, though, his phone came on, and he laughed in relief. He was just about to call 911 when his phone went black. No amount of coaxing could make it come on again. The laughter died in his throat.

Dan swore, tempted to throw the phone out the window. Instead, he tossed it on the dashboard, disgusted.

His phone dinged, indicating a new text message. He frowned, confused, and picked it up to check the screen.

The new message was from Jessica Florey.

He looked at Jessica's phone, in the puddle of blood where he'd left it on the passenger seat. It was dark and still.

He tapped the text message to bring it on screen, and the rush of anxiety that filled his chest was the first bit of warmth he'd felt in what seemed like hours.

Run Danny Ruuunnn

The world dimmed in the corners a bit. Run? Run where? Cold and confused, he looked around the car helplessly. He had recently cleaned out his car, at the behest of Jessica. Anything he could have used to layer and keep warm was gone now—old scarves and wrinkled jackets, T-shirts balled up in the back seat . . . Hell, he thought he might have at one time even had a waterproof pair of work boots back there somewhere. Now there was nothing but an empty foam cup from Wendy's, a quarter, and—

And sweet, sweet Jesus, it was his pocket knife. He allowed a tiny smile, a slight loosening of the knot in his chest as he reached into the back seat for it. He had to force his stiff fingers to close around its handle, but he got it, and its little hard realness was something of a relief.

Run Danny Ruuunnn, the text had said. And why not? There was a good chance he would freeze to death whether he went into the snow or stayed in his icebox on wheels. His skin was so cold and it was getting harder for him to focus. Why had he wanted to stay? Was the car keeping that thing from getting to him? How long would it matter, even if that were true?

It had been a while since he'd heard the thing on the roof. A flash of panic drove him to peer out the various car windows—the thought of losing track of the thing now, just as he was contemplating escape, seemed unbearable to him.

Nothing but darkness and snow enveloped him and his car. It had to be stacking up all around him, maybe muffling the movements of the monster outside as the thing looked for ways to peel open the car like a tuna can.

Run Danny Ruuunnn

Or maybe it had given up and gone away. He clutched the pocket knife more tightly. He'd have to take the chance. He was freezing to death in that car.

His heart stuck in his chest as his hand hovered over the door handle. He counted his shallow breaths. At ten, he promised himself he'd bolt and make a run for town. *Nine. Ten. Eleven. Twelve . . .* He promised he'd go at twenty. Twenty-five.

On the twenty-sixth breath, his body made the decision for him, and before his brain could object, he was in the cold, the air stabbing his face, his eyes, his lungs, the point of the knife held out before him like a beacon. And he was mostly running and sliding, sliding and running, praying he wouldn't fall, because if he fell and that thing moved swiftly and silently through the drifts and jumped him before he could get up again. . . .

He didn't look behind him. He couldn't bring himself to. He kept concentrating on running and not falling, sliding and gliding but not falling, until dual lights rounded the corner of the road and surprised him. He stopped short. The lights kept moving, but their direction was all wrong. They were moving up toward the sky, and the sky was moving out of the way. He felt his limbs move all wrong, too, and then felt the painful, bone-shattering thud of the hard-packed snowy road beneath his back. The cold ate into his pants, his jacket. And for just a moment, a half-opaque blur blotted out the snow and that scent of unclean, over-petted dead things filled his nose and throat.

A loud bang from beyond the lights was answered with that horrible wind-wail, and the blur jerked backward, out of his line of view. He waited, afraid to get up, afraid to even breathe.

A round, somewhat cherubic face with a thatch of auburn hair sticking out from beneath a woolen cap filled his vision, and he felt a surprisingly strong grip on his arm helping him to his feet.

"Oliver Morris," the cherubic face told him. "Police. Are you okay? Is there anyone else in that car back there?"

Numbly, Dan shook his head. "Gone. She's . . . gone," he mumbled. "The thing got her." He turned slowly, looking back at the car, willing himself to look down at the lump that had been taken down by the .45 Morris was holstering. It was rapidly deteriorating into slush, which flattened and froze into black ice.

The world swam in front of him and winked out as he collapsed in the snow beside the remains of the thing that had tried to kill him.

Chapter Five

"Well, if you're Toby's sister, I suppose it's okay."
From an uncomfortable plastic guest chair left for her by a surly orderly, Kathy watched the crazy woman on the bed with no expression. She did not move. It was her experience that people like Charlene Ledders were feral things, drawn to and distracted by movement, and easily put on the offensive by loud noises and sudden gestures. She wanted Charlene to talk, to respond and not react. She waited, studying the woman.

Charlene was in her late forties but easily looked ten years older. Her sallow skin looked papery thin, as if any sudden movement of her own might tear it like tissue paper. Her eyes, a dull blue, kept darting to the corners of the room—the far corner behind the door, in particular—as if waiting for something, or watching it. What might have once been soft waves of blond hair had dulled to a bleached-bone colorlessness, hanging in frizzy dreadlocks and uneven braids. She wore a gray sweatshirt and sweatpants, as well as one sock, all of which looked like they'd seen better days. One of her wrists was in a leather cuff, bound to a metal rail that ran along the far side of the bed. The free hand, a bony, spidery thing with ragged, uneven nails, she used to scratch incessantly at her scalp. Kathy could see a crust of dried blood along her hairline. Her toenails had once been painted blue, but most of the polish had chipped away. She sat with one leg tucked under her and the other tented in front of her, occasionally bouncing on her simple, cot-like bed. Behind her, the snow beyond the barred window blocked out the sky.

Charlene's head twitched, and she sniffed, then looked up at Kathy with those dull blue eyes. "You want to know about the Hand."

"Yes."

"What do you want to know?"

"They're planning something—a complicated ritual, I'm guessing, involving human sacrifices and complex sigils—but the signs are like nothing I've ever seen. I want to know what the ritual is trying to accomplish. Toby's been . . . out of the loop, as you know, so he told me you could explain it to me." She opened the file folder she was holding and took out a photo of the sigil that had been carved into the John Doe's back. It was difficult to gauge how the woman would react to it, but Kathy had to take the chance. She handed the photo to Charlene.

The other woman's eyes grew wide, her lips working into soundless shapes, and she began bouncing lightly on the bed. "Where did you get this?"

"A friend who understands my interests. I'm told this is a key. What does that mean?"

Charlene dug her nails into her scalp and began scratching. She whispered something Kathy couldn't quite make out.

"Pardon?"

"What's it to you?" she spat with sudden venom. "Why do you need to know? You don't need to know. You can't be more than an acolyte at best. This is need-to-know."

"I need to know," Kathy said. She thought quickly. "I want more from the Hand. And let me put it this way: I intend to have it. I want to move up in the ranks. Toby is willing to vouch for me, but I need leverage. This right here—this is my leverage."

The woman gave her a sly grin. "Very smart. You *are* the right stuff. Good."

"So this . . . key, is it—?"

"It's a key all right," Charlene said. "Which means they must have found it, yes, out here in Colby. Found a door. See, first you have to find the door. Then you fashion a key. The hard part—yes, it is—the hard part is making sure the key fits the door, because not all keys fit all doors, and—"

"I'm sorry, Charlene, but you're losing me. What keys and what doors are we talking about here?"

"Some doors we open. Some are opened by others. Doors have often been opened and used by lesser gods—the Scions, the Hollowers, the Hinshing. And we can use these, sometimes on purpose, sometimes not. But doors to Xíonathymia, the Great Far Realm of Starless Space, the home of the Greater Gods who devour other dimensions, are always locked, locked, locked. And doors to the places where those who serve the Greater Gods live—those are locked, too. They need keys."

Kathy had, in her extensive work in the field, come across those names of the "lesser gods" Charlene had mentioned, and their supposed invasion of and influence on parts of the United States, Great Britain, Mexico, Africa, and South America. She had studied the legends of comparable beings from this very dimension, this very planet, which indigenous people all over the world had worshiped and feared for thousands of years. But the symbol that had been carved on the dead man's back had nothing to do with any of those. She was confident now that any murder in relation to that symbol would be only the first of many in a string of atrocities in the name of the belief system connected to it. This was not a key meant for the common realms and passage of lesser gods. There were bigger things at stake here. Kathy pressed on.

"So you're saying one of these doors, I'm assuming one leading to this Xíon—Xíona—"

"Xíonathymia." She pronounced it *Zy-on-ath-EE-me-ah*.

"Yes. Xíonathymia. So the Hand found one of these doors, specifically a portal of some type to Xíonathymia or someplace similar, right here in Colby?"

Charlene nodded. "Town was probably built right on top of it."

"So what is the purpose of opening it? What does the Hand expect will happen when they cross through to the other side of the door?"

Charlene scratched at her scalp and looked away from Kathy, her jaw cracking as she stretched it. "No one goes through the door, Toby's sister. No one in her right mind would dare go." She shook her head, amused. "Besides, most doors only go one way—from there to here. And so, so many others come through . . . first spirits and forces, then legends and lesser gods, then the mighty minions and then their masters. Only the most devout ever discover what is on the other side, in the other places beyond the Convergence, and they only know stories based on stories based on dreams of ancients who were given the secrets. No one has actually been to Xíonathymia."

Kathy had expected the woman to go into a little esoteric philosophy, but it didn't make wading through it to get useful answers any less exhausting. It was all about asking the right question, but that was sometimes a trial-and-error kind of process. Most of the time, what the actual belief system was didn't matter beyond what it meant to the cultists and their plan of criminal action. But a ritual of this level meant a belief in the need for human sacrifice, and it was crucial for Kathy to ascertain the extent of the sacrifice.

"Charlene, I need you to focus for me and tell me what the Hand of the Black Stars hopes to accomplish by opening this door in Colby. It's very important."

"We—the Hand of the Black Stars and I—believe, or believed, or have maybe just proven, that these god-doors, lesser and greater, open to . . . other places. Other worlds, other planets, other universes—it depends on the type of door. How to do it is in some book they have. A book of doors. And of keys, because a door is of no use without a key to open it. Keys require sigils and sacrifice, different types for different doors. Different rituals to open different gateways and commune with different beings possessing knowledge of life and death and everything between—"

Kathy slapped the picture of the sigil down on the bed in front of Charlene, causing the woman to flinch and then giggle nervously. "Focus. I need you to tell me what happens in the ritual that uses this symbol. I need to know what I'm looking at here." She changed tactics. "Toby told me you could help me. He recommended you to me specifically. Was he wrong?"

She blushed. "Of course I can help. I—well, I mean, the Hand in particular worships a pantheon of greater and lesser gods from Xíonathymia the Great Far Place, like Iaroki the Swallower of Suns, Imnamoun the She-Beast Mother of the Spheres, Xixiath-Ahk the Blood-Washed, Okatik'Nehr the Watcher, Thniaxom the Traveler—"

"I get it," Kathy broke in. She was losing patience.

Charlene nodded and continued. "To bring them here would create a commixture of worlds, an Interverse through which we would have access to the Greater Gods and lesser gods and all their power. It is the One Purpose of the Hand of the Black Stars. It takes a complex ritual, see." She pointed to the photo of the sigil. "That ritual. And it happens in monumental stages, a chain of events. All these door-opening rituals are like that. First, there is an awakening, like cold blood splashed on the face, usually when one identifies a door. The first of the sacrifices must then be made. Then there is a cleansing with fire or ice, with screams and death, with the rendering of humanity to viscera, meat, and waste. Then, a seeding and a spawning and the growth of a new world. The faithful believe that enough open gateways will bring about the Interverse. It will be a glorious and chaotic intersection of supremely powerful and ancient beings from the outermost edges of space where there are no stars, from far points of the universe and from worlds beyond it, in other universes. A tumultuous end to everything, and a beginning unfathomable to mere human minds. There will be no need for doors or keys, and the faithful will be powerful and knowledgeable beyond imagining. The dimensions and the Convergence will bleed into each other.

"Of course, this ritual, the one to open the portal to Xionathymia, has never been completed successfully. Sometimes the wrong doors were opened, or opened in the wrong order. Sometimes the rituals were incomplete. Sometimes keys were fashioned incorrectly or incompletely. Sometimes, the Ones Who Come Before cannot be summoned. And of course, there are others—many of those lesser gods, in fact—who come through instead, who are too powerful to be enemies, but too indifferent to our One Purpose to be allies. They cannot be harnessed or cajoled to work toward the One Purpose. So you see, so very much can go wrong. So very much is left to chance, to providence. And worthiness—you need to prove yourself worthy of the favors of the Greater Gods before they will deign to protect you from the fallout of their coming. From what I've heard, they've tried twice in New Jersey and once in Massachusetts, but these attempts were miserable failures."

She leaped toward Kathy then, and Kathy braced herself for defense. The restraints held Charlene in place, though, and only that haggard face came close, those dull blue eyes sparking with little flashes of excitement as she talked.

"But not this time. No, no. Not this time, not in Colby. The Hand has summoned some of the Ones Who Come Before—the Blue People. See, see," she went on, her one free spider hand reaching for Kathy's sleeve, "this winter, this snow and ice and those that hunt in it—they're all part of the cleansing phase."

"The Blue People? Who are—"

Just then, something scratched at the outside pane of her window. Charlene started as if jabbed with a pin, her eyes now wide and shining with genuine fear. A tight knot of anxious surprise sat heavily in

Kathy's stomach. On the heels of what Charlene had said about cleansings and the winter, Kathy felt uncharacteristically afraid.

She followed Charlene's gaze to the window. A dark shadow passed over the frosted panes. Charlene began bouncing again, but this time with a rhythmic slowness, as if her body was keeping itself occupied while her mind was somewhere else.

And somewhere else her mind most likely was; all Charlene's restlessness and nervous tics had halted. Her attention was riveted to that window, and she was whispering something about the winter.

"Charlene?"

The shadow passed over the window again, and this time Kathy heard a high-pitched whine like pieces of metal scraping together and a kind of scratching against the side of the building.

"Go," the other woman whispered. "Go now."

"What is it? Tell me what's out there."

"The winter has come. More sacrifices make the fingers of the Hand stronger . . . much, much stronger. Get out of here, Toby's sister—go! Go NOW before it gets in!" While she talked, her voice rose, and her last words thinned as they reached a near-hysterical pitch and volume that rivaled the sounds outside. She sounded both terrified and ecstatic, and it made Kathy's skin crawl. There was a wild desperation in her eyes, though, as if she knew something inevitable and terrible was going to happen, which finally got Kathy up and moving. Those eyes burned with some awful knowledge that seemed at once both painful and orgasmic, and the woman shook and twitched as volts of emotion wracked her worn-out frame.

Then Charlene started screaming. It might have been hysterical laughter or crying—at that breaking point, they looked and sounded the same—but the overall effect was horrible to witness.

Kathy thought she finally understood what others must feel around *her* sometimes. She wanted to get away from Charlene, away from the crazy-sickness spreading through her as a reward for loyalty to her beastly gods, before it infected her as well.

As she backed away from the woman, she went to knock on the door, but it was already swinging outward. Alerted by Charlene's screaming, three orderlies pushed past Kathy to their patient, who was now thrashing against the restraints and laugh-crying with wild, hysterical abandon. The orderlies attempted to sedate her, but her body bucked so wildly that their efforts were lost amidst a fog of grunts and swearing.

Kathy couldn't watch any more. Unnoticed, she slipped into the hall and hurried toward the elevators. She'd gotten all she was going to get out of the crazy woman, crush on Toby notwithstanding; even if there hadn't been such conviction in Charlene's dismissal, she was right that it was time to go. But that conviction, that desperate and elated certainty in the Hand of the Black Stars' theological tenets, had been present in every facet of Charlene, and in Kathy's experience, that usually meant something. Possibly even something big enough to blot out feeble moonlight as it scrabbled across the hospital window.

She pushed the down button on the elevator panel, and when the doors slid open, she slipped inside. Already, the part of her that functioned on pure animal instinct was on high alert; she sensed something she couldn't quite put a finger on, a kind of dread whose source was still unknown. She didn't like it.

She noticed in her periphery as she hurried across the lobby that there was no nurse at the front desk. It was weird, but fine with her; she felt a distinct need to avoid human interactions at that moment, even of the most passing kind. She had to get out of there, back to the familiar boxy security of her own car. She'd had enough of hospitals and the dangerous ends of crazy people for one day.

That animal part of her knew, though, that the day wasn't over. Her gut feeling might have been based on nothing more than shadows and the earnestness in Charlene's voice, but Kathy trusted those gut instincts.

There *had* been something at the window—something obviously not human and probably not even animal. Something *big*.

She thought about what Charlene had told her about the cleansing phase and the servants of the greater gods. Part of Kathy's job was to weed through what people like Charlene said for strands of truth or fact. She sifted for useful tidbits of occult belief that corresponded to actual things or events, or that guided and therefore helped predict pathological behavior. That Charlene was such a shell of a person now compared to what she must have once been was both a tragedy and a relief; it was unsettling to watch anyone die slowly of intellectual malnutrition in the deserted wasteland of a broken mind, but if there was even a speck of truth to what the HBS believed, then thank whatever good God existed that there was one less competent person to bring their plans to fruition.

And just how much of it was true? Kathy had always thought that what passed for HBS occult theology was mostly mumbo jumbo, the usual flawed nihilistic philosophy mixed with folklore. But . . . maybe not all of it. Not this time. Despite Charlene's obvious limitations, she had held a position of some power in the HBS and knew what she was talking about, at least so far as their gods and monsters went. Charlene understood the motives of the cult because she believed in them, and knew the practices of the cult because she'd once led them. She believed on good authority, then, that the cult intended to wipe out all of Colby with . . . entities from some other dimension. And frankly, the whipping icy wind and snow outside bore out her story. Kathy had been in the occult business long enough to have had the occasional brush with the unexplainable, the unarguably supernatural, and, once in a while, the flat-out evil. And as she rushed through the double doors, which whooshed open and then closed behind her, cutting off any last warmth or fortress-like security, she shivered. She was fairly certain that whatever had been outside that hospital room window trying to get in, whatever had sent Charlene into such a frenzy, was going to fall into one, if not all, of those categories.

She had to see. She had to know.

When she swung out into the snow blanketing the empty grounds, she made her way around the building to the side where Charlene's room was. It was out of view of the street for the most part, facing a barren lot that had already accumulated a thick carpet of snow. It had grown dark, but surprisingly, there were no doctors, no patients making their way to and from the building, no EMTs in ambulances. There was nothing alive as far as she could see, except for her . . . and the giant creature scaling the side of the hospital's mental health ward in the moonlight.

"Oh fuck no," she whispered.

It was big, easily the size of a pickup truck. Its body reminded her very much of scorpions, with dark, shiny segments, like large plates of black ice, forming the better portion of its back and the upward curve of its pick-like tail. Four pairs of jointed legs moved the thing with surprising speed over the ice and snow that clung to the side of the hospital. But that was where the similarity to anything Kathy had ever seen ended. A number of muscular, waving tendrils snaked out ahead from the front of the body, seeming to somehow sniff or feel the air. Above and behind them, the body curved upward in a stalk-like neck banded with the same slender muscles, surmounted by a head like a floral bloom knocked on its side; the rather elliptical bulb tapered into tightly entwined petals. When it sensed her, perhaps hearing her footsteps, those petals unraveled with disconcerting speed and bloomed open to reveal a deep, ruddy interior studded with silvery teeth spiraling down into the yawning chasm of the throat. It screamed, that high-pitched sound reminiscent of metals scraping together, and one of those long, silvery-black tentacles snapped with an electric white spark in her direction.

She flinched. The biting cold scraped across her skin. The snow around her boots sank its wet and cold into her feet.

Every part of her wanted to run, to scream, to draw some other human's attention to the thing to prove that what she was seeing wasn't some stress-hallucination. But some primal instinct, perhaps tinged with training or experience with predators, kept her still. The creature's feelers waved and snapped over her head as if blindly groping for her. It could smell her, perhaps, with those odd feelers, but it didn't seem able to locate her. She took a chance of glancing quickly back toward the front of the hospital to gauge the distance to her car in the parking lot. When her head snapped back to the thing sloughing snow as it moved across the wall, its feelers were reaching closer but were still off course. Slowly, she sank straight down and scooped up a handful of icy snow. She packed it into a hard little ball as she rose again. The muscles in her legs and back strained to move as imperceptibly as possible. The thing didn't seem to notice. With a quick flick of the wrist, she tossed the snowball as far from her as she could. Immediately the feelers strained in that direction, the petals of its mouth parting just enough to release a steely whine.

So that was it, then. It could likely sense sound or movement, and maybe even smell the presence of something, but it couldn't see her, at least not in the way she thought of seeing.

Still . . . how fast could it move? What were the odds she could outrun it to her car or, having accomplished that, outdrive it?

It was then that she heard laughter. Immediately, the thing on the side of the building twittered and spidered its way a few feet along the wall toward the ground. The moonlight rippled over the plates of its back.

Oh God, no, nonono, she thought.

She turned slowly, aware that the feelers, reaching for the source of the voices, were waving right over her head now. Across the street, a twenty-something with a blond bun and a conservative blue dress was walking arm in arm with a young man who looked to Kathy like a member of the Young Republicans.

Kathy made a move in their direction, and immediately the feelers snapped back toward her. She stopped, holding her breath and then letting it out slowly. She had a .45 in her car; even though she was no longer with the Bureau, she had kept up her firearms license. But her car was a good sprint away, and the snow would slow her down. And a gun was no guarantee anyway; those back plates looked pretty thick. Maybe its underside was a vulnerability, but—

While Kathy was considering her options, the thing on the hospital wall skittered around to the front of the building.

"Shit!" she whispered, and loped over the snow drifts after it. When it came into view, she froze again, glancing slowly across the street to the couple. The man held out his key fob as they were walking, and the *boop-boop* of the unlocking mechanism was followed by the flashing of headlights from a car about two hundred feet away.

The creature let out an ear-piercing whine and jumped down onto the snow. Its feet, Kathy noticed, didn't sink as she would have expected with the obvious weight of the thing. Instead, it skittered across the ice and snow as easily as it had scaled the side of the hospital building. Fixated as it was on the couple, the thing paid no attention to Kathy, and so she detoured toward her car, grasping for the driver-side door handle just as the thing reached the middle of the street. The couple had reached theirs as well, and it was when the woman opened the passenger-side door that she saw the creature bearing down on them. Her scream echoed down the empty street.

Kathy dove across the driver's seat to the glove compartment and grabbed her gun as the man's screams joined the woman's. She opened the passenger door, aimed as best she could at what she thought was the underside of the thing, and fired. It wailed, a bloom of white opening up where she hit it, and the feelers lashed out wildly in multiple directions.

The wound didn't slow the creature down, though. It climbed partially onto the hood of the car and shattered the windshield with a leg, spearing the man through the chest as he cowered behind the wheel. Kathy fired again, but the creature moved and the shot glanced off its back plates. Another bullet tore into its leg, and for a moment, Kathy had hope as the thing wobbled and slid along the car hood. Then it regained its balance. The woman cried out as the creature's tail dove straight for her. When it rose again, Kathy could see the woman dangling from the spiked end of the tail like a limp rag doll, the blood surrounding the hole in her gut soaking her top, raining down, and staining the snow beneath her.

Kathy yanked the passenger door shut and sat up, then slammed the driver's door closed as well. She started the car just as the creature down the street managed to shake the woman free of its tail. It withdrew its leg and turned toward her.

"Let's go, bitch," she muttered, half to herself and half to the thing as she threw the car in drive and peeled out of the lot. She tore down the street, fishtailing at the corner as she made a left, but she barely let off the gas. Behind her, the thing screeched, and that screeching kept up with her, though she could make out no crunching of snow. It had to be practically flying over the drifts, closing the gap between them. She glanced in the rearview mirror and saw it leap into the air. She slammed the gas pedal to the floor, and the car jerked just out of reach as the thing landed behind her. The tail came down, breaking the ice-crusted layer of snow along the curb behind her. Kathy fixed her gaze on the road ahead. She turned off on one of the country roads, a back way to get to Colby, along which she felt fairly certain she could keep the thing away from anyone else. The creature followed. The road, flanked by thick woods on both sides, was a strip of darker white amidst growing mounds of glistening snow. Occasionally, the thing behind her grabbed hold of trunks or branches and swung from one to another, closing the distance between them. She couldn't see the center line or even a good portion of the pavement. There were no streetlights on the road, either, so only her headlight beams, twin arms of amber-white glow, reached into the darkness ahead of her. Occasionally, the overhanging tree branches pulled back and the moon reminded her that she had not fallen off into an endless void. That, and the metallic squeal of the thing gaining on her.

A tail or leg—Kathy had not seen which—shaved the side of her car, furrowing through paint and metal and jerking her to the left. She nearly lost control of the wheel but compensated quickly, swerving toward the left to put space between her car and the creature.

Then she hit a patch of ice. The tires slid, tractionless, toward a snow bank ahead and to the right. Panic welled up into her throat, threatening to choke her, but she swallowed it down. She pumped the brakes, cut the wheel into the skid, and regained control, pulling the car back onto the road just seconds before it would have buried its front end into the snow drift.

The creature behind her wailed into the wind and dove forward.

A half-obscured sign that swam up in her headlights told her the center of town and the police station were seven miles away. Almost there . . .

A terrible rending sound, followed by the sudden descent of a leg into her back seat, sent her on another skid. The creature was above her now, on the roof of the car. She could hear the groaning of metal and the scraping sounds of its other legs as it sought a way to hold on. Feelers smacked against the windshield; one took hold of a wiper blade and wrenched it free. Kathy screamed, as much out of anger as fear. She hit the brakes, hoping the sudden stop would throw the thing, but this sent the car spinning in circles. The feelers clamped down on the frame of the car; against her windshield, she could see small suckers like tiny, hungry mouths slurping at the glass.

She cut the wheel again, trying to stop the spin—hoping, even praying a little, that she could get the car moving forward again.

The back end of the car hit the post of a sign that said the police station was now only three miles out of reach, and miraculously, the car righted itself, nose pointing in the direction of the town center. *Thank the universe,* she thought, *for small favors.* Within seconds, she was moving again, but the thing was still latched on to the roof of her car like a barnacle

The car was coming up on a bridge over a small pond, not terribly high but high enough to warrant care when crossing. The county had never gotten around to replacing the wooden guardrail with a metal one. It was a lonely bridge on a county back road hardly anyone ever took; that it had even been kept up with as well as it had was enough to let county officials sleep at night.

It was pitch black over the side of that bridge, and the water cold enough, Kathy imagined, to stop a heart. A glance down at her steering wheel, though, and a scream from above her as another leg tried to puncture the roof made the decision for her. She clicked on her seat belt.

With its leg firmly embedded into the back seat of her car, Kathy floored it and cut the wheel. The wooden guardrail splintered on impact with her bumper, and as the car sailed off the bridge, it hit a patch of moonlight in midair and then slammed through the first layer of ice on the pond.

Chapter Six

When Teagan found him, Jack was standing stone still amid the bustling of uniformed officers cordoning off Chandler Park, white puffs of breath making tight little clouds in front of his face. Beneath a canvas tent, half-frozen bodies, minimally clothed and illuminated by park street lamps on old-fashioned iron poles, were laid out atop the rows of picnic tables, attended to by Cordwell and Brenner and CSIs who were taking pictures and measurements and poking and prodding. There were a lot of bodies—eight or nine—and Jack stood in the center of them, amid the rows of tables, staring up into the snow-smeared night. Occasionally, flashlight beams arced through the tight circumference of the scene's darkness, followed by mumbled comments carried on frosted breaths. So far as Teagan could tell, Morris and Kathy weren't anywhere on the scene.

"This is one of three," Jack said without looking at him.

"One of three what?" Teagan asked, joining him among the bodies. He took an unlit Camel from his flannel shirt pocket and popped it between his lips. He'd quit three years ago, but the presence and taste of the little stick, even just hanging there unlit, was both a comfortable affectation and personal challenge, a reminder of a vice he'd conquered. He blew on his hands to warm them up, then shoved them into the pockets of his jeans.

"Three crime scenes just like this. Ormann Park, the Colby Public Library parking lot, a baseball diamond behind the high school on Fremont Ave. Information's still trickling in, but estimates quote twenty-seven dead. Nine each at the three crimes scenes, which I'm sure Kathy will tell you is of occult numerological significance. All Colby townspeople. Business owners, bums, teachers, hairdressers, landscapers, cooks, carpenters, bus drivers, factory workers, retired folks, even cops. Kids, Teagan. Little kids. Third body from the left, that little one there, is a kindergartner. Gracie Anderson. She was five fucking years old." Jack's voice never rose above a tight, strained monotone.

Teagan knew the man well enough to understand the incredible restraint it must be taking for Jack not to break, especially regarding the child. He felt much the same way at the moment. "Jaysus," he said. "What the fuck is going on in this town?"

"Well," Jack replied, "Cordwell says at least three people at each scene were murdered by other people—our Hand of the Black Stars cultists, I'd say. And on those nine vics, Cordwell found evidence of manual strangulation, use of bladed implements—knives, straight razors, that sort of thing—and gunshot wounds. But the rest he swears are some kind of animal attacks, like our first John Doe."

"Chris Oxer," Teagan said.

"You ID'd him?"

"Aye. He used an ATM card at that convenience store, and the bank gave us a name. Family confirmed the identity. And here's a biteen of news. They say the lad had taken up with some new friends—no one the family had ever met. They said Chris was almost superstitious in not talking about them."

Finally, Jack looked at him, then nodded. "Well, it looks like Oxer's new friends had a field day this afternoon. And turning on him wasn't enough, apparently. Most of these vics went the way of Oxer. Ripped apart, half-eaten, bones gnawed and snapped . . . and those damned symbols carved all over them still. But the killers made it easier to sort things out this time. Wallets and cell phones were all left behind. Like covering up the murders doesn't matter anymore."

"Well, that was a sound bit a help, that."

"Yeah. And the uh . . . jars . . . are over there," Jack added, nodding in the direction of a cordoned-off park bench with a row of mason jars on it.

"Jars?"

"Eyes. Mostly eyes. Some tongues. A couple of fingers and an ear."

"Fuck," Teagan said.

"I think the sigils bother me the most. Every one of these bodies has that same symbol as Oxer's carved into it, or one like it. Damned if I can tell the difference, but they look pretty much the same to me.

And apparently it's the same deal at the other scenes. It's like they're being tagged, marked somehow as belonging to the cultists. That gets under my skin, ya know? They're flaunting their sickness all over this town—bodies, jars. But no footprints, Reece. For all this fucking snow, not a single damned footprint, no animal droppings or animal prints, despite all the animal attacks that supposedly happened, and no evidence of snow brushed aside or out of the way. No weapons. No hairs or fibers. It's like ghosts killed them all."

"What do Morris and Kathy think?"

"Don't know. Morris was supposed to be at the high school, but he texted that he was detained, whatever that's supposed to mean. Don't know the details yet. And I have no idea where Kathy is. But you know . . . that's Kathy. She can handle herself."

The two men stood in silence for a few moments. Teagan frankly wasn't sure what to say, and sensed that Jack hadn't quite found a way to look objectively at the crime scene all around him. It was a struggle sometimes to do that. Teagan knew the feeling of having to fight the personal and professional fear and insecurity in one's soul to regain composure and do his job. Rapists, child molesters, murderers, torturers, terrorists, the sad, the lost, the widowed, the orphaned, the insane . . . Sometimes it was a heavy, monstrous job, and it could get inside of a person, if one wasn't careful. The various everyday evils and their aftereffects could find a way inside the less tangible substances, the "cells" of the heart, mind, and soul, injecting its icy blackness and sucking out the life and light. It could make a person feel weighed down and even monstrous, too. Take this case, for example. . . . What was *wrong* with these cultists? He had seen hate before—had, in fact, been in the thick of hate that had hardened and grown stronger over hundreds of years. But what kind of hate could drive someone to jar up the parts of other human beings? To carve them up like hams and feed them to wild animals? And was it even hate? The thought turned his stomach that it could be simple indifference to other people's suffering . . . old people and children. . . . Sometimes the scope of evil, plain and simple human evil, was overwhelming.

But the catch-22 of it was in the alternative. Teaching yourself to feel nothing or next to nothing was too easy—too damaging, Teagan had found—to allow it to become the quick and convenient defense mechanism against all of life's pain.

However, standing there waiting for the old habit of swathing oneself in indifference to kick in might not be the best option in this case. Maybe a little outrage was needed to match the senseless indifference of the crimes surrounding them and spur them to action. Furthermore, it was cold out, and Teagan's fingertips were getting numb. So finally he spoke.

"Jack . . . what's the plan?"

"Well, I think the first thing to do is—" Jack stopped abruptly, mid-sentence.

Teagan followed his gaze to a dark spot at the corner of the park, where the hiking trails began. "What is it, Jack?"

"I . . . I don't know yet. Come on." He started off toward a far dark corner across the field that was devoid of all police action. If Teagan remembered correctly, the beginnings of the hiking trails were over there. It was an odd move, to be sure—Jack was not usually the type to walk away from the heart of a crime scene. But then again, maybe diversion was what he needed to get his head right again.

Or maybe Jack's gut was telling him something connected to the scene—or worse—was out there in those woods.

"Jack, wait up, mate." Teagan dropped the Camel back into his shirt pocket and did his best to sprint in the snow drifts after the senior detective, his hand on his gun's safety.

Jack had made his way nearly to the tree line, his .45 drawn, when he stopped. The snow coming down around him in the moonlight formed a kind of halo of shimmering movement and shadows.

"For the love-a God, mate, what're we chasin'?"

On the hiking trail, a pale blue shadow—*a shadow of blue light*, despite the contradiction of terms, was exactly what Teagan thought it was—passed from a bank of charcoal night behind one tree to another. It was human-shaped but missing any discernible detail, a semi-transparent thing moving through the surreal shade of unbroken, wooded stillness. He drew his .45.

Jack motioned silently for them to flank the grouping of trees behind which the phantom had disappeared. They crept to the tree line, parted, and submerged themselves in the gloom. Teagan tried to breathe shallowly, afraid that even the puffs of his breath would put him somehow at a disadvantage to the stealthy thing in the woods.

Once Teagan stepped into the forest, all sounds from the crime scene were suddenly muffled, as if he'd closed a door or window. But he felt something, all right—not quite a sound or smell, far less than a physical touch, but something that stirred the hairs on his arms and brushed cool non-fingers across the back of his neck. He'd spent time camping one college weekend with friends at Seafield House in County Sligo, the allegedly haunted ruins of an old Irish mansion overgrown with trees and ivy, and the feeling on the grounds had been similar—the feeling that energy was moving around him, anxious, even hostile, crowding and closing in.

His gut told him to step out of the area, to back away from it and not turn his back on it, to go back to the crime scene. That's what his gut said, but his brain told him he was being a right savage tool. There wasn't anything in here, in the snow and dark, that hadn't been here any of the countless times he'd come through before, running or hiking or bringing a bird on a romantic nature walk. He set his jaw, narrowed his eyes against the rising wind, and began searching for the figure. If it was a cult member, it better hope that Teagan found it before Jack did; Jack was bulled enough to lamp whoever it was but good.

As he crept slowly over the underbrush toward the hiking trail, he listened. It made sense that the figure (he couldn't quite conclude to himself, for reasons unknown, that it was anything quite as tangible as a person just then) must have hit upon the hiking trail. There was no crunch of shoes breaking branches or rustle of trudging through foliage, and no visual evidence of it, either. Not that Teagan was a tracker of any kind, but he didn't hear or see much of any sign of life, human, animal, or otherwise. The cold was seeping into him. His toes felt like hard, painful little rocks in his boots, his fingers stiff and raw around his gun. He wished Jack would emerge from behind some tree or other and call off the search. Maybe what he had thought was a figure had been a strange effect of the moon glancing off of an icy tree trunk, or maybe some animal with its winter coat, bounding away back to the cover of the woods.

A glint of bright silver from the corner of his eye caught his attention, and he looked toward his left. He just caught darting movement beneath a swish of soundless blue-white fabric before it ducked behind another tree and was gone. Teagan hesitated, considering a quick shout to Jack, but decided there was no time to wait for the other detective. He took off after the figure. The graceless hopping and pounding of his half-frozen feet over the uneven terrain sent bolts of pain right up to his shins, but he kept running, picking up the hiking trail where he could.

Teagan's pursuit was arrested by a root-glutted ridge of dirt and rock, and he looked up to see a figure standing motionless on top of it. Moonlight backlit it in a halo of bluish light, obscuring its features in shadow, but so far as Teagan could make out, there was nothing like a condensing breath escaping into the air.

He aimed his weapon. At the clicking off of the safety, the figure's bent head rose into moonlight and turned in his direction.

Teagan whispered a string of Irish Gaelic swears that would have made his old granddad blush. He backed away from the thing on the hill, but couldn't take his eyes off the face.

It had no eyes. Empty black sockets seemed to swallow up the dark around it. The skeletal face was blue—corpse blue, frost-bite blue, a blue of things that had never seen warmth or sun. It opened its mouth, and Teagan was blinded by the light that poured forth from its throat. When the light finally faded several seconds later, the figure was gone.

Teagan ran. Blinded by the snow and the afterimage of the light from that thing's mouth, an odd shaft behind his eyelids of shifting colors that made the near-lightlessness of the woods somehow more impenetrable. He stumbled, scraping arms and hands as he flailed against trees to stay upright, stay moving.

He had just about reached the spot where he'd first taken off after the figure when he heard rustling to his right and skidded to a stop. Someone was heading toward him through the overgrowth that had retaken a giant fallen tree. He swung his gun around that way, sure for several irrational seconds that whatever was making its way toward him was not human, cultist or otherwise.

A pale hand reached over the massive trunk, its fingers curling slowly on the bark.

Teagan steadied the gun at it.

Moments later, a head emerged—Jack's head. Teagan sighed with relief, replacing the safety and re-holstering his weapon.

"Reece," the detective breathed.

"Jaysus! You put the heart crossways in me, mate," Teagan said, reaching a hand out to help Jack over the trunk. "Hey, you'll never belie—" When he got a good look at Jack, he frowned. "What the fuck happened to you?"

Jack's hair was peppered with clumps of dirt and twigs. His tie was askew, he had long streaks of snow and dirt on his normally pristine dress shirt, and the hem of his jacket was torn. His coat was missing, and his teeth were chattering uncontrollably. A gash in his forehead had dribbled blood into his right eyebrow, and his nose, if not broken, had certainly taken a bruising wallop. His right foot was twisted at an ugly angle, the swelling visible even beneath his boot.

"We have to go," Jack muttered.

"Come again?"

"We have to get out of here. There are . . . We can't—we need backup." He swayed where he stood, and Teagan moved to keep him upright, helping him toward the hiking path and in the direction of the tree line.

"Who did this to you, man?"

"They did."

"The cult?"

Jack shook his head. "The snow . . ." He shook his head, unable to verbalize it.

Teagan carried him back toward the crime scene. About halfway there, they were met by a uniformed officer that Teagan knew in passing, Sabas Moreno Jr. Moreno had been with the force for a little over a year and a half. He was amiable, hardworking, a dark-haired, dark-eyed man in his late twenties with a warm smile and a swagger buoyed less by arrogance than a simple blessing of good health, good looks, enjoyment of his job, and enjoyment of his life.

His usually jovial expression, however, was immediately replaced by one of concern when he saw Jack.

"Shit, Detective Teagan, what happened to him?" Moreno rushed over to help guide Jack across the field.

"He thought he saw someone in the woods—maybe one of those cultists. So we split up to surround the git, and Jack came out of the brush like that."

The two men maneuvered Jack back to the picnic tables, waving over Cordwell to attend to him.

Jack accepted a blanket but brushed any other help away. Cordwell gave him a skeptical look. "I'm fine," he said with labored breath, and Cordwell shrugged, backing off. Scratching his forearm absently, Jack glanced over his shoulder, then added, "Really, I'm fine. I just—I fell in the snow, and—and I think the wind got knocked out of me."

Teagan exchanged glances with Moreno over Jack's head. Teagan clamped the Camel back between his teeth again and gestured for the officer to wait a minute, to hold off asking any questions until Cordwell and some of the other cops hovering around them in concern had gone back to trying to bring order to the scene. It didn't take long; the news crews had finally made it through the snow and were just at the line of police tape, jostling each other and jockeying to get a better view of the carnage. By then, a fluffy layer of snow had accumulated across the benches of the picnic tables and buried most of the blood splatters. The steaming viscera of the butchered had already been bagged and tagged, and Cordwell had begun instructing the CSI team in loading the bodies onto trucks. Many of the bodies had been inspected by Jack already, before Teagan had shown up. There wasn't much for the news crews to see, but it didn't stop them from crowding the officers who had jogged over snow drifts to keep them from crossing the tape.

Teagan glanced around and nodded, satisfied. He pinched the cigarette between two fingers, inhaled its unlit flavor, and pointed it at Jack, saying, "Jack, mate—tell us what really happened. Nothing about falling in the snow, now. Did that—whatever that was in the woods, the figure—did it do this to you?"

"I told you guys—"

"You fibbed," Teagan said quietly, replacing the Camel between his teeth again.

"And you know that how?"

"Your tell. When you fib, you look over your shoulder, like you're waiting for someone to be walking up on you and catching you out. And you scratch at your forearm like you're doing now."

Jack looked down, stopped scratching, and sighed. "Okay. But I don't expect that you'll believe what I have to say."

"Try us, sir," Moreno said.

"Okay . . . well, that hiking trail there . . . I saw someone, like Teagan said. I thought maybe it was someone who'd come back to the scene. They do that sometimes . . . come back to the scene to admire their handiwork, see the chaos they caused. We don't know a damned thing about these cultists, other than what Kathy's told us so far. We don't know where they are, how much more killing they're planning on—nothing. So I thought if we could nail just one of them . . ."

The rest of the sentence was carried away by a sigh, and his gaze trailed off toward the woods. "Something wasn't right, though. I . . . I think I knew it. The snow, the wind, my being tired—I'm willing to lay this story at the feet of any of those things, but I tell you, I knew in my gut that whatever Teagan and I were trying to get a jump on was just wrong somehow. It was too quiet. It moved too fast. No shadow, no footprints. Like the snow was helping it escape. I don't really know how to explain it better than that."

"So . . . not a cultist, you mean?" Moreno sniffed, shifting his weight uncomfortably from one frozen foot to the other.

"Yeah," Jack said. "Yeah, I guess. Anyway, I had moved around this tree and I saw him . . . it . . . whatever. I couldn't make out much. I mean, it was sort of camouflaged with the snow and all, so I wasn't even really sure what I was seeing. But it moved. It was the movement, see? It didn't move like a branch or bush in the wind. It moved deliberately. Fast. But then I caught up to it."

"What was it?" Teagan asked. He wanted to hear Jack say it, to give confirmation of what he himself had seen.

Jack looked up at the men, a look of genuine bewilderment on his face. "I . . . I honestly don't know. A man . . . sort of. Maybe. It looked more like a corpse. Blue," he said, gesturing to his face, "like it'd frozen to death or something. No eyes."

"You . . . didn't see his eyes, sir?" Moreno asked.

Jack leveled his gaze at the younger officer. "They weren't there."

"Ah."

"I approached the man . . . or whatever . . . and told it to freeze. Heh heh, 'freeze,' I told it. That's funny."

"Sir—"

"And it just . . . well, it didn't stare at me. It had no eyes, like I said. But it knew I was there. It knew, and I could feel its disdain. Its disgust. It was like standing so close to a fire that the waves of heat are painful, you know? Except there was no heat at all—it was cold and sharp. And then . . . then there was a blur of snow and it lashed me across the face. It rose up off the ground and twirled into this rope of ice and snapped at me. All around me, the snow did that—swirled into little ice-storm whips. They yanked at my coat, wrapped around my arms and legs, lashed my back and face. It wrapped around my ankle and twisted. . . ." He was shaking now, though it was not easy for Teagan to tell whether that was from the cold blowing under and through the ambulance blanket wrapped around his shoulders or from horror.

"I managed to pull a hand free, and I shot at the figure. I shot it twice. *Boom, boom.* And . . . nothing. But the snow fell away from me and I ran."

Teagan suspected from Moreno's expression that he was thinking the same thought: *There had been no gunshots, at least none that he'd heard. Could Glazier have only imagined he'd fired his weapon?*

Moreno coughed politely. "Sir, I think maybe we should get you—"

"Don't," Jack said, holding up a hand. "I'm fine. Look, let's just all get back to work, okay? We have a crime scene—a massive fucking crime scene—to process. Get back to your CO, huh?"

Moreno nodded and headed off. Teagan supposed the young officer had questions he'd kept to himself, perhaps none he thought it wise to ask or that he believed Jack could or would answer. That Moreno recognized the wisdom in staying silent instead of pushing the issue affirmed Teagan's faith in him.

"You know," Teagan said, glancing around the crime scene, "the blue lad—"

"Teagan, please—" Jack put his head in his hands.

"It had light in its mouth."

Startled, Jack looked up.

"I saw it, too, mate. Just for a minute, but . . . yeah."

Jack searched his face. Finding truth rather than placation, he nodded. "We can't go back for it now. Later, maybe, but . . . these people need us. These . . . little Gracie. She and the others deserve our attention first."

"Aye," Teagan replied, and crossed to another picnic table. Gracie Anderson's body lay in the body bag already. Her little eyes were closed, and flakes of snow blown around on the wind had settled lightly on her eyelashes. Her lips were blue. A symbol like the one found on Oxer, carved post-mortem into the little girl's forehead, made him look away for a moment; a kind of clear gel had been rubbed into the bloodless track. She was wearing a Barbie undershirt; the rest of her had been zipped into the bag, as if tucked into bed.

His tenuous mantle of indifference wavered. The tears that formed in his eyes grew cold and began to freeze to his lashes.

He almost missed the scaly clump of white she was holding between small, frozen fingers. Evidently, Cordwell had missed it, too. The cigarette fell from his lips, unnoticed, to the ground.

"Jack, look at this."

The other detective joined him at the body. Teagan gestured at the clump.

"Is that skin? From what?"

Before Jack had a chance to answer, Teagan, who had noticed something odd, reached out and yanked it free of the wound in Jack's head.

"Ow! What're you—?"

Teagan held his hand out to Jack. In his palm sat another clump of white, scaly skin, melted a little around the edges. From its center protruded a sharp little tooth like the one Cordwell had found at the Oxer crime scene.

"She grabbed one of . . . whatever attacked you," Teagan said quietly, and dropped the clump into the snow. "Whatever made the animal attacks."

Jack didn't respond, but Teagan supposed they were both wondering the same thing—what the hell (or from it) was out there in the snow?

Moreno had managed to reach the tree line at the start of the hiking trail without anyone, least of all Jack Glazier, seeing him. The scene was winding down, and more cops were standing around stamping cold feet and cradling cups of warm coffee than actually doing anything productive. It seemed like a good time to slip away.

He didn't know Jack Glazier any better than the reputation which preceded him, one of level-headed efficiency, stoicism, and an understanding of logic and reason that had closed more cases in his nine years in the detective bureau than in the last fifteen or so prior without him. Moreno admired the man's professional career in many ways, and had been happy to find himself under the man's wing, so to speak, and in his confidences earlier that night. Obviously, Jack's perception of events had been a little skewed. Corpses darting through the forest? Snow dervishing up into weapons wielded by unseen hands? But then, who could blame the guy? It was bad out there. Freak snow, bodies piling up like the drifts, no one getting any sleep and everyone on edge . . . plus something very well must have given him that gash on his head. So . . . hallucination, maybe. Hypothermic hallucination.

He didn't really know if such a thing existed, but hell, it sounded far more reasonable to him than what Glazier had claimed happened.

Still, he felt a kind of obligation, having been a party to the immediate aftermath of Glazier's incident, to vindicate the man by finding something to explain what actually had taken place in those woods. If it was a Hand member who had attacked Jack—and the possibility was good that it was—then maybe there was something left behind. A footprint protected by an overhanging tree limb and, as yet, unburied by the new snow, or a torn piece of cloth caught on a jagged branch . . . anything. It certainly couldn't hurt his professional aspirations to find evidence of the cult, either.

He turned on the flashlight app in his cell phone and shined it along the trail from which he'd seen Teagan and Glazier emerge. There wasn't much to see, he noted with some disappointment. Massive mounds of snow covered most of the ground; it had started to pile up along the side of the tree trunks too, giving the bark an odd, almost luminescent glow. He let out a long, slow breath and stepped onto the hiking trail, shining the light over the snow. The tiny ice crystals caught the light and sparkled. It would have been kind of pretty, almost sort of peaceful, if not for the circumstances. He followed the trail, examining pockets of darkness between and around the trees, occasionally glancing back at the waning bustle of the crime scene to see if he was missed. It was more of the same: blankets of white enfolding and obscuring blankets of white, piling and spilling over onto more white. It all started to blur after a while, the horrors of the park and the white and the cold and the long hours he'd spent wading through all three. He almost missed the movement to his left, a blue-gray shaft of something sparkling pistoning up and down. He paused, a shaky glove finding the handle of his gun and drawing it out, only to point it at . . . empty snow.

He had a moment to sigh in relief before a muffled thump at his back made him jump. He wheeled around, nearly slipping. A large clump of snow had dislodged itself from the tree behind him.

"Mother of God," he breathed. He was about to abandon the whole idea and head back to the car when a rustling from the branches above got his attention. He made his way over to the tree, swearing as he sank a leg knee-deep into a frigid drift, and squinted at an inky hole in the pine needles. The branch of needles shifted and from that hole, a glistening, scaly white hand with one extremely long, taloned finger reached out. It disintegrated to flakes that an unfelt breeze picked up and carried a few inches before they melted away. A few seconds later, it reformed again.

"What the—"

A pale head like an anglerfish emerged, baring serrated teeth behind its fleshy lips. Moreno opened his mouth to scream, but the sound died before it could escape him. He raised his weapon to fire at the creature, but in the next second, the thing was on him, tearing at his throat. The heat of his blood melted the snow in a semi-halo in front of him as the thing ravaged its way down his chest. His body dropped.

The snow surrounding the cooling form of the police officer surged up around him, and it took an unusually short amount of time for the snowfall to cover what remained of him completely.

Chapter Seven

Morris was on his way to drop off half-unconscious Daniel Murphy at the hospital when a woman stumbled from the darkness out onto the road. Her blond hair obscured most of her face, but something about her frame and her movements, despite her obvious injuries, seemed familiar to him. She lifted her head at the oncoming headlights and waved her arms, and Morris saw the scar on her face. Kathy? It was Kathy! He skidded to a stop, leaping out of the car and over a mound of snow to help her.

Her nose was bleeding, she had the swollen beginnings of a bruise near her temple, and there was an angry red mark high up on her chest reminiscent of a restraint. The way she held her wrist, he suspected that it was either sprained or fractured, and she limped, favoring her left knee.

"What the hell happened to you?" he asked as she collapsed against his chest. "God, you're half-frozen. Are you okay?"

"Car accident," she whispered hoarsely. "Can't feel my legs. Are they there?"

"You're walking on them," he answered softly as he helped her to the back seat. Once he'd slid into the driver's seat and shifted to drive, he said, "Kathy Ryan, meet Dan Murphy—car accident, too, of sorts. Dan Murphy, Kathy Ryan."

Kathy waved halfheartedly in the direction of the passenger seat, and Dan moaned back.

"Right, then," Morris said. "Busy night."

He drove in silence the couple of miles back to town.

"Thank you," Kathy said suddenly as they crossed the town border.

"Don't mention it," Morris said, glancing in the rearview mirror at her.

She tried a smile, but it seemed to bring pain to her face, and she winced. "So what's his story?" she asked, gesturing at Dan. "Something attack him out in the snow?"

"Yeah. Took his girlfriend, he says. Something, ah . . . I'd say some kind of animal, maybe, but it wasn't like any goddamned animal I ever saw. I don't know what to call it, to be honest. But I saw it and I shot the thing. Kathy, I shot it, and I don't even know what the hell I shot, because it *melted*."

"Funny coincidence," Kathy said flatly. "Monsters attacking cars. Must be going around."

The term "monster" made Morris uneasy, but he supposed that's exactly what it was. As crazy as it sounded, there were *monsters* out there in the dark of Colby.

After a few minutes, Kathy asked, "How big was the thing?"

"About the size of a Greyhound, I'd say."

"Bus or dog?"

"Dog."

"Hmm. Look kind of like a scorpion?"

Morris shook his head. "More like a rabid fish-monkey. Or one of those, what do you call them, uh . . . anglerfish."

"I'd laugh at that description, but it hurts enough to breathe, let alone laugh."

"Want to talk about what happened to you?"

"Not especially," she said. "I want to sleep."

"How about you sleep after the doctors confirm you don't have a concussion?"

Kathy grunted.

The car's interior settled into silence again. Morris checked the rearview and saw Kathy's eyes fluttering closed, so he spoke. "Kathy, what's going on out there? I mean, really, what the hell is going on? I've been trying all day to radio out, send an email, hell, even post a call for help on Twitter and Facebook. Nothing's going through. I tried four different computers in different parts of town. Nothing. It's snowing in June. Dead bodies are turning up ritualistically mutilated all over town. And now we've got what? Yetis? Abominable snowmen? Monsters?"

She didn't answer. In fact, the silence stretched out so long that Morris was worried she'd slipped into shock when Kathy said, "They're part of the snow."

"Pardon?"

"Those . . . things. The creatures out there. They're part of the snow. And the cultists caused the snow."

Kathy must have caught Morris's incredulous expression in the rearview because she sighed and added, "I know how it sounds. I know. Ten years ago, I would have had much more trouble believing it myself. But what I've seen . . . what you shot . . . it's not so hard to make the leap that the usual explanations just don't work. Or that crazy, evil people who plunge head first into the strange and unusual might very well have caused something strange and unusual to happen."

"Guess I can't argue there," Morris said earnestly. "But why? Why are they doing it?"

"The ex-cult member I talked to today told me it's part of a bigger ritual. The snow, and everything in it—it's just the beginning. There is going to be a lot more death—a *lot* more—if we don't stop them."

"So what's the next step?"

"We need to fill in Jack and Teagan. And then some research. If there's a ritual to start all this, then there's likely a ritual to stop it, too."

Morris didn't answer.

"Can I sleep now?" she asked, resting her head against the car window. "I'm so tired."

As dawn found police and crime scene investigators wrapping up their grim work in various parts of Colby, the cleansing by snow and ice had been well under way for hours.

The streets of the town were nearly silent, except for the faintest crack and tinkle of icy tree branches swaying in the wind and the muted crunch of snow beneath the feet of the occasional desperate or unbalanced person, dead-set on getting somewhere, anywhere. These latter apparitions would appear from the swirl of snow, pass by the darkened window of a survivor's house, and then disappear, hunched over and trudging through the drifts, back into the endless white. Sometimes, screams would follow.

Every neighborhood was a still photo of frozen moments, abandoned by the people who had made and should have owned them. Invisible movement driving the pathways of wind and water over object and pavement alike had been caught and held in frozen streaks. In some cases, old bones had taken on a new kind of flesh, a translucent mantle, cold and inflexible.

The entire town was coated in shades of blue and white, silver and gray. Crystalline sheaths of ice lent a surreal, somehow haunted quality to cars, park benches, fences, telephone poles, and signs. Houses bore rows of long, sharp icicles in a snarl above people's heads. The heavy snowbanks that ate sound, burying it beneath mini-avalanches from roofs and eaves, reminded the few survivors that terrible silent things were still out there. And the wind, the low and mournful moaning and wailing, was always around the head, in the ears. It got into buildings (and people) through any opening available—every unsealed crack, every hole that weather had worn through, every raw throat despairing of ever feeling warmth again. It drowned out the mortal sighs and creaks of the body and stole words from right out of mouths.

Dominic Gasbarro, one of those remaining survivors, had been a teacher of freshman biology at Colby High School for almost twenty-five years. He had a master-of-science degree in animal biology and had spent eighteen months in South America studying rare and exotic wildlife. He had even done a three-week cryptozoology research expedition.

None of that prepared him for what he'd seen the night before.

There had been the scorpion things with the tentacles and the blooming mouths—he'd come to think of them as fat-tails, after the scorpion species, even though the creatures' tails and backs were really the only similarity. They were big and brutal, but not as quick and deadly as the anglers, who wavered and shimmered in a way that sometimes hurt the eyes, disappearing or deconstructing in one place and, seconds later, reforming somewhere else. The anglers were on people in seconds, tearing them open all over the snow and shoving chunks of flesh into those ugly anglerfish mouths with long, clawed single-fingers. Those creatures—the anglers and the fat-tails—terrified him, but they hadn't been as bad as the spider/hand-things that ate Mrs. Mueller.

For Dominic, the pandemonium in the snow had started earlier the night before, when he had been awoken by barking dogs at 11 PM. He was much more of a morning person than a night person, but even so, it had taken him a long time to fall asleep. Too many bad dreams of sad, broken people in run-down, broken places. It was withdrawal from the Effexor; he couldn't get the damned pharmacy on the phone for a refill, damn the snow, and the lack of antidepressant in his system always gave him surreally bad dreams.

It had thus put him further out of sorts when the mournful howling and angry barking of Bettie from the house behind and Sir Lawrence from next door managed to penetrate the storm windows of his bedroom and shatter his long-awaited sleep. He padded to the window and looked out on his backyard, but could see nothing but the muted gray of night layered over the snow. A wail and a yip were followed by a throaty growl before the barking of one of the dogs—Bettie, he thought—ceased. The odd suddenness of it jarred him enough to wake him fully, and he went to the other window in the room, the one facing his neighbor Emily Seeger's and Sir Lawrence's house. Dominic knew Emily's husband was a local cop and worked most nights, so she was usually home alone.The motion light on her back porch had been triggered, and Dominic could hear the little Pomeranian scratching frantically at the back door. At first, Dominic thought the hulking white thing with the gangly limbs sneaking onto the porch was a large dog; it was too big to be a raccoon or even a fox. The thing was, it didn't move like any of those animals. It had a predatory fluidity of silent motion, but it seemed more comfortable moving on its hind legs alone, its massive head and front legs sweeping low to the ground ahead without touching it. It didn't walk in the snow but rather *on* it, so Dominic could see the length of those limbs and the shape of them were not right at all for . . . well, any animal that he knew of.

Sounds from within the house next door suggested Emily had been awoken by Sir Lawrence as well. Her scream, returned by the thing on the porch before it wavered, disappeared, and reappeared on the porch railing, was the beginning of the chaos. The Pomeranian leaped through the doggie door and the thing was on it in a flurry of white, followed by a frenzy of steaming blood and mangled fur. Then it went after Emily through the same means. . . .

After that, all up and down his street, he could hear shouting and unnatural animal sounds. There had to be dozens of those things out there, judging by the chaos. A few times, he even thought he heard gunshots. He called 911, but the line was busy. That astounded him. Could 911 even *be* busy? Shouldn't he have been rerouted to another call center or something? He kept trying, all night in fact, as the carnage raged around him, heard but mostly unseen. It was busy every time.

His doors, he thought with a modicum of relief, were all locked. They were always locked, a habit which his Colby neighbors thought an amusing personality quirk. Colby was a small town whose people were, for the most part, decent, law-abiding, honest folk. Most people saw no need to lock their doors all the time. But Dominic had grown up in an urban part of New Jersey, and locking doors was as much a nightly ritual as brushing his teeth. He was glad just then for that, because whatever was wreaking havoc out there didn't seem able to break in—though not, as evidenced by the commotion from his neighbors, for lack of trying. Maybe they were drawn to sound and porch or interior lights; Dominic had none of those on and had kept as silent inside his house as possible, and nothing had attempted to enter.

By morning, he had begun making serious attempts to block out what he had managed to see and hear all night from windows all over the house. A car had been stopped in the street by a fat-tail's stinger and had overturned. A small posse of jeans-and-winter-coat-clad men who had the group sway of poker-night drinkers and the group resolve of scared husbands and fathers had almost made it to the end of the street when the lot of them had been swallowed whole by the terrible blooming maw of a fat-tail's mouth or thrown against telephone poles and dashed on driveways by its tentacles. A group of teenagers tramping along the snowy sidewalk, possibly to party destinations unknown, had been scattered and hunted down one by one by an angler.

Watching all those people get butchered was almost more than his sanity could take. One of them, a girl of about sixteen with a bob of black hair and glasses who reminded him of his niece, had made it as far as his own front porch. He'd unlocked the door and opened it a crack, motioning for her to come inside to safety, and the look of relief on her face was powerful. That, in the next moment, the expression turned to indignant horror followed by genuine fear as bloody claws suddenly appeared through the gory mess in her abdomen, broke his heart. He slammed the door shut against that look, bewildered and helpless but pleading all the same, and locked the door again. When he'd managed to stop the world from swaying and the gorge in his throat sank, by degrees, far enough for him to breathe again, he peered out the front window.

The girl was gone. Most of her blood, which had spattered the railing and puddled on his front porch, seemed to be seeping into the snow as if being drunk in by something underneath.

And then there had been Mrs. Mueller. She was eighty-seven, a dancer in her early life and a volunteer at the local library in her present one, a sweet but fiercely independent little firecracker who had taken a mildly maternal interest in Dominic's well-being over the last few years. He was quite fond of her, and looked in on her often. He had, in fact, been bolstering up the courage in the pink and gray hours of dawn to venture out and check on her when he saw her emerge, bundled up head to toe in winter clothes, from her house. He went to the door and flung it open, intending to warn her to get back inside and lock her doors. She was a little hard of hearing, a condition that she only grudgingly acknowledged, and Dominic figured it was possible, however incredible it seemed to him, that Mrs. Mueller hadn't heard what was going on outside all around her. Maybe she didn't know the danger. And Dominic couldn't let her walk right out into death's jaws.

His slippered feet hardly felt the snow on the front porch as he ran out. "Mrs. Mueller! You need to go back inside!"

The elderly woman looked up and waved. "Oh, hi there, Dominic! Some crazy weather, eh?"

"Mrs. Mueller," he shouted, aware of how singularly loud and attention-drawing his voice was in the neighborhood's silence. He didn't see any blood, no bodies or prints or even snow-sloughed signs of struggle. There was just the eerie quiet, broken only by him and the old woman, and it made him feel exposed. Nevertheless, he risked raising his voice and speaking more slowly and clearly, but his gaze darted toward anything in his periphery that seemed like movement. "You need to go back inside. It's not safe out here."

She paused, then waved away his concern with a gloved hand and a smile. "Oh, I'm fine, dear. Just getting the newspaper before the snow swallows it up. Got to keep up with what's going on in the world, eh?" And she made her slow and careful way down her steps.

If anyone in Colby was more of a morning person than Dominic or Mrs. Mueller, it was Mr. Chavez, their newspaper delivery man, and so it was not unusual for other early risers to find the tightly rolled and bagged paper waiting for them at six or even five in the morning. However, Dominic was fairly sure that given the circumstances, delivery service was probably suspended for the day.

"No paper today," he shouted back. "Trust me. You need to get back inside. *Please.*"

"Oh? I guess it's this snow, then, is it? Okay, then. Thanks for letting me know, dear."

Dominic was relieved when she waved a thanks and turned to climb up her stairs again. He was about to call out to her to stay safe and warm over there when he saw the spider things.

They were creeping across the length of front lawn next door to him, half obscured by the gray mounds of snow crowded between the houses. They were the size of small cars and reminded him of spidery hands. It was a crazy thought, he knew, even in the midst of the impression, but no other idea suited those things better. The bifurcated bodies looked like withered, emaciated palms. Each had five extremely long, segmented fingers, three shorter ones in front and two longer ones farther back. Each "finger" ended in a shining black talon, serrated along the edges like a ragged fingernail stabbing into the snow. The surface skin of the spider things was a dead white-gray, and looked rough and flaking. *Like chapped lips* was the crazy thought that came to his mind, though he supposed it was no crazier than the idea of giant spider hands. There were eyes, set between the knuckled joints where the finger-legs met the body, and these were also a kind of gray. At first, he thought they had the cloudy appearance of cataracts, but as one passed closer in its erratic path across his lawn, he could see a hundred, maybe a few hundred, pulses of dull red that could have either been irises or blood vessels. Either way, they seemed, so far as he could tell, to serve as the primary physical sensory organ of the things, and gave the distinctly disturbing impression of a constant awareness of several directions at once.

Dominic froze. He wanted to warn Mrs. Mueller, but he couldn't get his mouth to open. He'd never seen one of the snow creatures up close, and now that they were moving into the street toward the old lady's house, he was overcome with a terrible sense of awe and dread.

They moved fast. They moved so fast.

The pain finally seeping in from the cold snow in which his feet were partially submerged broke the paralysis. He hopped backward into his door frame, leaning into his front hall to grab his boots from the mud tray. As he kicked off his slippers and yanked the boots on, he heard the first of Mrs. Mueller's screams.

He swung back out onto the front porch in time to see one of the hand-spiders skewer Mrs. Mueller in the chest, knocking her to the ground. It seemed to make the spider-thing glow. The white was dazzling, almost blindingly so, and Dominic had to shield his eyes. When the glow subsided, he could see the bloody tatters of Mrs. Mueller's winter coat. At least, that's what he thought he saw, until those tatters moved feebly, deliberately, and a desiccated arm reached up and grabbed at the black talon pinning it down. Dominic blinked, bringing the scene into better focus, and saw what was left of Mrs. Mueller try to sit up around the talon. Her shriveled skin had turned a dirty shade of gray, her swollen tongue lolling out over shrunken lips. Her eyes were gone—the withered lids hung limply over empty sockets. Dominic couldn't imagine any life was left in the woman, and didn't want to imagine what was animating that husk. He sank back through his doorway, closed the door, and locked it, then bolted to the bathroom and threw up in the toilet.

He'd spent the rest of the morning leaning against his front door as if his bulk provided an added measure of security against the elements. He counted his breaths and tried not to think about anything at all. When he finally stood up, he tried 911 again. This time, instead of a busy signal, the line was dead. He was on his own.

From the front hall window, he could see his car in the driveway. The snow had piled up around it to the tops of the doors. He wasn't going anywhere that way. He considered walking to the police station for help, but it was at least a mile and a half in about four feet of snow, with God only knew what out there. He tried getting onto the Internet through his phone, and when that didn't work, he made a frantic attempt to log in on his computer. That didn't work any better; every time he tried, he got an error message saying his network couldn't connect to the Internet. He didn't know much about troubleshooting those kinds of things, and within fifteen minutes, he'd given up on the verge of tossing the damn thing out the window.

He'd have to stay holed up in the house, at least for the foreseeable future. He had plenty of food and water, and as long as the heat—

A heavy thump upstairs broke into his thoughts. He stood still, listening at the foot of the stairs. His heart pounding filled his ears with a rhythmic roar, but he could still hear dragging, a thump, more dragging, and a faint chirping on the floor above him. He went to the kitchen and got the biggest knife he could find, then made his way back to the stairs. He took each step slowly, one at a time, trying to step only on the parts of the risers that would creak the least. Above him, the dragging continued, like something heavy was being hauled across the bedroom.

By the time he reached the second-floor landing, he could not only hear but feel the movements in the bedroom through his tightly wound frame. Each jerk and drag caused him to flinch. His sweaty palms made the knife handle slippery, so that it no longer felt like much of a weapon. As he crept down the hall, the sounds in the bedroom got louder; it sounded to Dominic like the thing in there was knocking over furniture.

He had almost reached the door when the floor beneath his feet creaked. He froze, a wave of hot fear washing down over his body. The sounds in the bedroom stopped. It had heard him.

Please oh please, God, don't let it come out, please. . . .

He counted out each second of silence. The thing did not appear in the hallway.

Dominic reached the bedroom doorway, and wiping his palms as best he could on his sweatpants, he clutched the knife more tightly and peered around the door jamb.

He was met with a blast of cold. Snow was blowing in through a ragged hole where his window and part of his wall had been, dusting his bed and hardwood floor with flakes that had begun to accumulate as the heat of the room dissipated. In the center of the room, with its front legs propped up on the bed and its back legs crowded against the closet door, one of the spider-things sat. It really was big, fully the length of the bed and at least twice its width. It must have been a feat for the thing to squeeze its bulk through the opening in his wall. And that close to it, he could smell it, the way packages of fish fillets smelled when left too long in the back of a freezer. That same paralyzing fear overtook his limbs, almost a palpable, physical thing.

It moved its bulk in awkward little shifts to maneuver around the furniture, and Dominic pulled back into the hallway. He entertained the hope that maybe it had wedged itself but good in the room. Maybe he could outrun it, down the stairs, and—

And then what? Run out into the snow with the rest of them?

Maybe he could get a good stab in, kill the thing before it could kill him. That seemed like the only real option. He took a deep breath, counted to three, and swung around the door frame to confront the beast.

He found himself within inches of a fleshy cluster of pulsating red eyes. The black slit-like centers of each gelatinous orb grew wider. Without thinking, he shoved the knife forward, plunging it into that mess of red and black right up to his fingers. A silvery fluid ran over his hand, biting into his skin with a terrible cold. The thing staggered back, letting loose a wail that shook the walls.

He turned and took off for the stairs. The pain in his hand was immediately enormous, the skin waxy, red, and swelling. He took the stairs two and three at a time, trying to wipe the silver stuff off onto his pants, but smears of blood and flaking flesh, now blue-black, came off instead.

When Dominic reached the first floor, three of his fingers fell off. A wave of nausea caused him to skid and nearly trip on his way to the front door, but he made it, his good hand closing on the knob. He was just about to pull it open when a sharp, cold pain in his back and a sickening tug on his spine yanked him backward. His legs went numb, collapsing uselessly beneath him. He fell to the floor, aware by slow degrees that something was in his back, something big, filling him with ice, freezing his blood, crystallizing all the water in his body. Then he felt that pulling everywhere, in his head, his chest, his limbs, like his insides were being drawn out. The front door swam in front of him, and his gaze fell on the crack beneath the door. He could see a bright line of white through it, and feel the cool air from outside. He tried to reach for it, but his arms wouldn't move. His jaw fell open when he tried to scream, but the sound had been sucked out of him. His vision blurred. Something burst, first warm, then cold, in his chest. It hurt at first, but then the pain was sucked away, too.

The line of white under the door faded to gray, then black, as the last of Dominic was drained into the spider-thing above him.

The following morning, Jack and Teagan came back to Jack's office to find an essentially empty bullpen, with abandoned desks stacked with papers and file folders, computers in sleep mode, and coffee mugs of cold, stale black ichor. It was eerie, seeing the department like that, when usually it was so full of animated chatter, ribbing, jokes, ringing phones, and detectives interviewing people or going over the details of various cases between each other. It was like a giant hand had come down from the ceiling and scooped them all up. The echoes of their work lives were faint and fading into non-being, but still present enough to put an ache in the hearts of the two men, who could only begin to wonder what had happened to their colleagues.

Perhaps because of their long hours at last night's crime scene, in the presence of the bulk of Colby's armed police force and in a location whose chaos had moved on to other parts of town, Jack and Teagan had been spared the true extent of the carnage of the night before. However, a lot of it was explained to them in a flurry of messages forwarded from Sherry at dispatch. Whatever information came back to her, she had sent it to Jack and any other available officer still out there. Apparently, those few officers who had made it to work in the snow had been run ragged all over town answering distress calls.

One voicemail contained the recording of an emergency call between Sherry and a stranded motorist. It began with wind blowing, followed by a tentative male voice speaking into the receiver, "Uh, hello? I think I need help." When Sherry asked him what the nature of his emergency was, he told her, "I . . . I don't know. It's too dark to see under all this snow. I think . . . I think I've been buried alive. I can't see anything but snow, but . . . I can hear things. The most awful things. I think there might be . . . something. Something out here in the snow with me." This had been followed by some incoherent mumbling to himself, which Sherry tried to clarify. She kept asking him for his location, but it was like he had forgotten she was there. He was talking to the terrible things making the sounds. He was talking to the snow itself. But he wasn't talking to Sherry. Eventually, he hung up.

In another call, a frantic woman kept screaming over and over into the phone about her kids. It was hard to make out. Her high-pitched cries were cracked and raw, and she was crying pretty hard. But it sounded like she said a snowman had eaten her children.

One caller reported a break-in at his address on 1741 Ashwood Road. On the recording, Sherry repeated back the address for confirmation and then asked the man to describe the intruder. He replied, "I—I can't. It's . . . I don't know what it is. It's big, though. It came through the window . . . crashed through. It's downstairs, in the kitchen now. Oh . . . oh no. No, no, no! I think . . . I think it's coming upstairs!"

The man's voice dropped to a whisper on the recording. It was hard to make out everything he said, but it sounded like he kept asking, "What do I do? Oh God, what do I do?" until there was a loud crunching sound and screaming. Then the call got disconnected.

A man told Sherry that his girlfriend had disappeared. One minute, she had been there, walking home from the supermarket beside him, and the next, he turned to see why she was so quiet and found only one of her gloves in the snow a foot or so behind them.

The one that was perhaps the most unnerving was nearly all static. It sounded more like a broadcast than a phone call, with periodic moments of silence punctuating long crackles. About fifteen seconds in, when Sherry had evidently gotten tired of saying, "Hello, Colby dispatch, what is your emergency? Hello? Hello?" and was about to hang up, a child's voice, thin to the point of barely contained hysteria, said, "End the imagination game. Cover your ears and understand the thirteenth principle. Sixth of Nine is open. You cannot stop for bread or wine. You cannot write your name on the stones. You will not be remembered or saved." The voice, as the speaker was talking, dropped from a child's to registers below human range, then rose again into an impossibly high falsetto, but it never faltered. The words, however chilling or nonsensical they were, remained perfectly clear. Then there was a tiny giggle, and the caller hung up.

And there were many more of the same. People from all over town had reported break-ins and murders, stranded motorists disappearing, people trapped in their homes, and general chaos. The common thread, Sherry had been careful to note, was the prevalence of reports involving claims of monsters in the snow—spider things, scorpion things, and some kind of ghastly faced demons that reminded the old folks at the tavern on Green Street of anglerfish. Morris and Kathy arrived to find the detectives screening voicemail message after message of screaming, crying, desperate people begging for help, while in the background there were sounds like splintering wood, rending metal, and howling winds. Many ended abruptly, as if something had swept away the callers.

Teagan noticed with concern Kathy's bandaged wrist, the bruise on her head, and the way she limped to a chair. He leaned over between messages to ask Kathy quietly, "Are you okay? You come across one of these things yourself, love?"

She nodded, trying to smile around a slightly bruised lip. "I'm fine. It looks worse than it feels. Nothing ruptured, broken, or sprained. No concussion. The rest is just . . ." She waved her bandage dismissively.

"Doctors said whatever happened to you, it was a miracle you weren't killed," Morris said. "You better be okay, because I don't think they'll take you back now." To the others, he said, "She gave the hospital admins hell when they tried to admit her for the night."

Kathy waved him off. "If I was doing so badly that I needed to be admitted overnight, that orderly wouldn't have backed off as quickly as he did."

"Well, a crazy woman waving a badge and flashing a gun will do that to a guy," Morris said with a small smile. Kathy gave him a look.

"Well, I'm glad you're okay, Kat." Teagan gave her a reassuring squeeze on her shoulder. Normally, she would have found such a gesture annoying, even patronizing, but from Teagan, it spread a pleasant warmth through her. A brand-new Camel cigarette seemed to materialize between his fingers, and he clamped it in his mouth.

"How you doing with that?" she asked, gesturing at the cigarette with her bandage.

He grinned around the Camel. Kathy found it both sexy and endearing. "Smoke-free three years last Thursday," he offered proudly. She squeezed his shoulder back with her good hand.

"Glad everyone's living clean and mostly unbroken," Jack said. "But there are more messages to wade through. I think we need to listen for anything that could identify any of the cultists."

It took about forty-five minutes to field all the messages. When the last voicemail clicked off, they spent another two hours debriefing each other on what they'd experienced the night before, and what had been learned about the cult and the ritual and how it related to the snow. The growing picture, as each contributed his or her piece to it, implied terrible proportions and portents that none of them seemed quite ready to talk about yet. But it hung there among them, all the same: this was the beginning, not the climax of these horrors. These cultists were crazy—there was no doubt about that—but they weren't operating on delusions, not these people. They had brought their own horrible belief system of gods and monsters into the real world, a world of Netflix and cell phones, farmer's markets and local pubs, Kiwanis Club and PTA and potluck dinners and fourth of July fireworks and high school football. All of that—security, normalcy, the escape from the broader horrific through the mundane—was gone now. Kathy had never had much faith in those things as permanent fixtures in her life anyway. Her brother had seen to that. But she knew people—fathers like Jack, for one, and earnest do-gooders like Morris, for another—who still very much believed in them. Needed them. And it made that small part of her heart, where she let such things be felt, hurt for them.

"Jesus," Morris said when the conversation had finally waned, each detective lost in thoughts of the coming days. "It's real. All of that end-of-days shit out there, it's all real. How the hell are we supposed to stop the apocalypse? A snow-pocalypse. For Christ's sake, what the hell are we supposed to do?"

No one answered him.

Teagan rolled the filter of his cigarette between two fingers. Morris stared out the window.

Jack tapped a pen absently on his desk. He was staring at a picture of his kids—little Jack and Carly, probably six and eight by now, Kathy thought—and she could tell he was worried about them. They had moved out of Colby proper to the edge of town after the divorce, and Kathy suspected that with all the increasing cell phone problems in the last day or so, Jack probably hadn't been able to get ahold of them and make sure they were okay. Kathy didn't think much of Jack's ex-wife, but she knew he loved those sweet little kids like crazy.

"Jack?" she asked.

He seemed to come back then from where his thoughts had taken him, and he looked up.

"I'm sure they're fine," she said quietly.

"Yeah," he answered. "Yeah, I'm sure, too. They're smart kids. And Katie's too bitter for one of those things to eat." He tried to smile, but it faltered and fell off his face.

"Go out there. Check," she said. "We can do without you for a few hours. In the meantime, we can work on this, a piece at a time. Identify the cultists. Identify their leader, and the ones specifically involved in the ritual that caused all this. Find a reversal spell. I'm confident there is one—any spell or ritual as monumentally big and complicated as this is likely to have a way to stop it or disrupt it at the very least. I have literature at home that might give us some leads."

"I can't believe this is happening," Morris muttered.

"I wouldn't believe it either, mate," Teagan said, "if I hadn't've seen what I saw."

Kathy cleared her throat. She had never been forthcoming about the things she'd seen in her line of work. Some were just too hard for the average person to believe and impossible for her to prove, and she'd come across nothing of the magnitude of Colby's current problem. Still, believing in evil was easy; what was hard was accepting that most of it could be attributed to humans not so different from anyone else. Kathy knew that better than even the men in the room. Having something supernatural, something monstrous, to blame Colby's evil on was, in a way, a kind of relief for her. At least it wasn't an aggressively indifferent father or a psychopath brother, hell-bent on destroying anything even vaguely reminiscent of their mother . . . or her.

The men looked at her with a mix of curiosity and expectancy. She hadn't ever shared her experiences of evil, the human or non-human kind, with any of them except Teagan, and he only knew very vague and limited details related to past cases she'd advised on. However, if she were inclined to share it all with anyone, these men would have been the limited few. It wasn't that she worried what they'd think, not exactly. Rather, she was well aware that she carried around so much of the world's ugliness inside, and it ate at her, scarred more than her face. She didn't want to heap that particular set of albatrosses on anyone she cared about. She wasn't afraid they would *not* share the burdens of evil with her; she was afraid that they *would.*

With this case, though, she thought with dismay, it was out of her hands. Not only was this world's ugliness everywhere she looked in this town, but other worlds' ugliness had burst through, as well, and it had touched every one of them in the room.

"Waiting on you, Jack," she prodded softly.

"Okay. Kathy's right. We tackle this on multiple fronts. Kat, go see what you can find on reversing the ritual. Take Teagan with you. Morris, stop by and see Cordwell. Maybe he's finally got something we can use to hunt these bastards down. I'll go check on my family. We'll meet back tomorrow morning unless we get a break in the case first. Keep your cells on you. Local calls and texts seem to get through okay sometimes, so . . . you know, just in case. And any problems, you shoot first, got it?"

The detectives rose to go.

"I mean it," Jack said softly as the others reached the door. He had on his coat. He held his car keys in one hand, and the other hand rested on the framed photo of his kids. "This is not your average criminal investigation. You run into any kind of trouble out there, you kill as many of those . . . those *things* as you can. Nothing standing."

"Nothing standing, boss," Morris said, and solemnly, the detectives made their separate ways out into the cold.

Chapter Eight

Getting anywhere in the snow was going to be easier said than done. By the time Kathy and Teagan reached his car, it was half buried in a snow drift up to the bumper, and by the time they returned with borrowed shovels from the department, the snow had reached the hood of the car. All the cars in the lot were similarly buried, although the snow was not nearly so high in the empty spaces, nor in the street. It seemed the more they dug, the more tightly the ice clung to the car and the snow blew up to fill in the freed spaces.

Still, it was time spent with Kathy. Teagan had not been afforded many opportunities to be alone with her or to talk about anything unrelated to a case, but in the number of instances where he had, he'd come to find he very much cared for her. She seemed to relax around him, open up a little. He knew Jack had reservations about her bouts of maniacal and almost suicidal dedication to the job and her drinking habits, and Morris, well, he was afraid of her, but Teagan thought they saw what she wanted them to see—the scar, and the walls she'd built up around it. He, on the other hand, caught glittering glimpses of all the things behind that wall. She was beautiful, somehow even more so with the scar, as if what made her physically attractive had a power and shine all its own, unable to be marred. And when they talked, it was easy to see how witty, smart, driven, insightful, and charming she was. He learned more about her, though, in what she said *in between* the things she said, the words *under* her words, the whole vulnerable realness of her that he wasn't sure even she was aware of sharing. And that was what he had fallen in love with.

The current situation, though, had them both on edge. Neither spoke until they were in the car and pulling out onto the road. The silence in the lot—in that whole area of town—was eerie and all-encompassing, and neither was inclined to break it. It was something instinctive, something difficult to put into words—a vague but insistent feeling that the snow itself was watching them, listening, waiting for a chance to swirl up and bury them, too. In the car, they felt a little safer—not much, but enough to speak to each other in furtive, low voices.

They spoke of little things, stretched thin to the point of breaking over the big things just beneath. Then the silence fell there, too, for a time.

"You know," Teagan said after a while of listening to the windshield wipers, "when I stopped by the bullpen while working the ID of the John Doe yesterday, I saw the oddest thing. Put a Santa hat on it and called it Randal, this."

"Oh? You saw something weird in the last twenty-four hours?" She winked at him.

He chuckled, poking the Camel between his lips. "Yeah. 'Tis the thing, I guess. But this . . . this was some shit. See, these two uniforms had picked up an eighty-four—two missing teens, a brother and sister, this was—out at the edge of town. Their mum said they were of a mind to leave Colby, that the snow was only here, and that if they could just make it over the border. . . ." He paused, remembering what Detective Owen Ford, the lad on the case, had told him about the sad state of the kids' mother. "So these two uniforms go looking for the kids before they catch their deaths out there. Two hours go by, and nothing. No check-in, no kids brought home to their poor, worried mum, nothing. So they send another two lads out to check on the first, and those find the first ones' patrol car, empty. Door open, snow blowing in. No footprints, no signs of struggle. No officers. And of course, no kids."

He glanced at Kathy, but her gaze was fixed on the road ahead. There wasn't much to see; the sun reflecting off the icy patches in the road was blinding.

He continued. "The second pair radios in another eighty-four, then brings the car back to the station. They search it for some sign of what happened to the first lads—the slightest hair or fiber, a print, anything. Know what they find?"

"Nothing," Kathy said.

"Not quite. They have, what do you call them here? The dashboard cam video. Caught the whole thing."

Kathy looked at him, startled. "What was on the video?"

Teagan exhaled slowly. "Well, see, that's the odd thing. First, it shows the two officers riding up on the kids as they were walking. *Walking*, in snow like this. Had to be gone in the head, them. But our first set of heroes, see, had actually found the kids—so far, so good—and they pull up behind the kids and one gets out. It's dark and the snow is blowing across the camera, but you can mostly make out what's going on. That officer—the lads at the station watching the video told me his name was Aleski—approaches the kids. They're just trudging along in the snow, their backs to the car, and they don't appear to notice the police cruiser or Aleski at all until he taps one of them, the young lass, on the shoulder. The camera catches their faces when they turn around. The light isn't great, of course—headlights, scant moonlight, odd shadows—but Kat, I swear it, they look... poisoned. Like something... something gone *wrong* had touched them, tainted them, and it'd spread all throughout them. Or maybe like a shadow had passed over them, but... underneath their skin. And in the video, Aleski backs away from them, like he knows it.

"Now you could argue that it could have been a trick of light or a quality issue with the video. I thought the same thing, and so did the officers viewing the tape. After all, here are two kids practically half-frozen, probably hungry and tired. That they look off is probably nothing unexpected. But then there was the wall."

"The wall?"

"Oh, aye, the wall." He exhaled slowly. "When the kids stop, Aleski says something to them. There's no sound with those things, so no one knows exactly what he said, but you can imagine it was probably something like, 'It's fucking freezing out here! Why the hell aren't you kids at home?' Anyway, he's talking and the other cop—Seeger, his name was—gets out and moves around the front of the car to join him, and as he does, the wind starts blowing and all these ice crystals start knitting together. When he moves out of the shot again, you can see in the video that there's suddenly a wall behind the kids. Time stamp says elapsed time was three seconds. Three seconds, and this ice wall was just... *there*. So Aleski stops talking and walks past them to examine it. He reaches out and touches it and his hand gets stuck. Freezes right to the wall. And the ice starts forming over his hand, don't you know, and around his wrist. Starts climbing up his arm. And it looks like he's screaming, thrashing around, and Seeger goes to help him, and . . ."

Teagan looked away, remembering what he had seen. It had been partially off-screen, but Teagan could see enough—the way the ice took hold and sank into the flesh of the officer's arm, freezing it, killing it, turning it black, and the soundless, frantic struggling, the desperate attempt of Seeger to pull Aleski free. It took less than a minute for the ice crystals to swarm over both the officers. It happened so, so fast. One minute they were tugging at appendages half-melded with the wall, and in the next, the wall surged out and devoured them.

"Reece?"

"Next thing," he went on, "the wall swallows up Aleski and Seeger. The ice just . . . washes over them like a wave and pulls them into the wall and they're gone. And those damned kids . . . they don't look scared at all. They just stand there . . . watching. Just watching it all happen. They look more curious than anything. Aleski and Seeger, their faces were twisted and they were obviously screaming and trying to pull themselves free. They were even reaching out toward the kids, looking for help. And the two kids just *stand* there. It's a fucking awful sight. And when the cops are gone . . . the kids change. They get all wavery for a second, like if you try to look at something through heat waves and smoke. They get all shimmery and then they stretch and their hair falls out and their eyes roll back into their sockets and fer the love of Jaysus, Kat, they were snow, just *snow*, with just the right light and shadow to create the impression of faces, hair, clothes. . . .

"One of them reaches out toward the wall and both the snow-figures and the wall turn to powder and blow away. The kids, the wall, the officers, they're all gone. Just . . . gone." He shook his head. "Not one lad in that room, including me, could say anything. All we could do was stare at the storm of static at the end of that video, just like those kids stared. We just had nothing."

Teagan stopped. Kathy wasn't looking at him with disbelief, exactly, but there was something there.

"Why are you telling me this?" she finally asked. It wasn't an accusation, but rather an earnest question.

He thought about it a moment, then replied, "Because this problem—none of us, except maybe you, have the faintest idea what to do about it. Because underestimating the scope of it is unwise, and communicating as many of their tricks as possible strikes me as a good idea. Because I couldn't bear keeping it to meself and carrying it around anymore. And because none of us have really talked about the very real possibility that we can't get out of Colby, and no one from the outside can get in. If, that is, there even is an outside anymore. We don't know how much area this storm has covered. We don't know if it's just Colby, or all of Connecticut, or all of the East Coast, or more. And none of those messages we listened to before mentioned any of that, either. We can't email, can't seem to make calls outside of local numbers, and can't access the Internet. I haven't gotten mail in almost a week now. It can't be that no one here has thought to leave, and I find it hard to believe that no one from the outside has tried to make it in here, even if just for deliveries or whatever. So . . . if no one has, maybe it's because no one can."

Kathy was quiet a moment, then said, "Jack's family is just on the edge of town." She didn't say more, but she didn't need to. The full implication of her words hung between them. Jack might not be able to make it as far as his family—if his family was even still there to make it to.

"Does Jack know about that, about the video?"

Teagan nodded. "He's going after them anyway."

"Of course he is. Wouldn't you?"

Teagan looked her in the eye and said, "Aye. Aye, I would."

They turned into the parking lot of Kathy's building and parked near the door of the place where she crashed when she was in Colby. It was a rent-controlled apartment complex, and one of three Kathy kept up the rent on, given her almost phobic distaste for hotels. It was the only one that anybody had ever heard Kathy speak of fondly, though she spent no more time there than anywhere else. It suited who she was; there was no place she could love and trust enough to call home.

Teagan pocketed his smoke again, and as he went to get out of the car, Kathy grabbed his arm. She had a second-floor apartment near the end of the unit, and she was staring warily at her illuminated bedroom window.

"What's the matter, love?" he asked, looking up at the window, too.

"I didn't leave the light on," she said.

Both withdrew their weapons and clicked off the safeties as they got out of the car. Kathy tried the front door and found it open. He pointed to her apartment and gave her a nod, then silently followed her up the stairs.

The door to her apartment was slightly ajar, the lights inside all off except for the bedroom. Kathy gestured to Teagan to go in on three, then silently counted off. They slipped into the foyer and started searching the rooms, one by one. Teagan stood to the side of the coat closet door, braced himself, and flung it open, counting off a second or two before swinging around to search it. It was clear—just a few coats, a jumble of shoes, and some cardboard boxes marked DAD'S HOUSE.

Across the apartment, he saw Kathy gesture him over to the den. Her desk, standing in the corner of the room, had been thoroughly rifled through, papers torn and scattered all over its surface and on the floor around it. The chair cushion had been cut and the stuffing pulled out. The lamp by the couch had been knocked over, and the couch cushions had been slashed and tossed off the frame. It was clear of people, though, and anything that might identify who had done the damage.

Kathy gestured that she was going to move on to the kitchen, and Teagan pointed to the open bathroom door. He squeezed her arm and mouthed out the words, *Be careful.* She mouthed back, *You, too.* Then they moved off to their respective rooms.

Teagan cautiously approached the bathroom, peering into the mirror from the hall before slipping through the doorway. The shower curtain was drawn back, and the shower was empty. He let go of the tight breath in his chest. He glanced in the mirror, and the face looking back at him was tired, a shade too sallow. He ran a hand through his hair, then moved back out into the hallway.

Kathy jumped when she saw him, and he mouthed, *Sorry*, then offered her a smile. She winked back at him, a tiny little return smile on her mouth, and gestured toward the bedroom.

The door to the bedroom was closed. They paused, listening. Teagan watched the sliver of light beneath the door for shadows of movement. After a minute or so of no sound or movement from within, Kathy turned the knob slowly and eased open the door.

The bedroom, too, had been trashed, the sheets pulled off the bed and tossed in a careless heap on the floor. The mattress had been upended as well, and had been left half-leaning against the bed frame. The drawer of the night table had been pulled out and thrown across the room, its contents—a notebook, an old issue of *Forensics Journal*, and assorted odds and ends—spilled across the floor.

Kathy frowned, reholstering her gun. It was the most reaction from her that Teagan had seen since they'd arrived. He supposed it was possible that she had encountered her share of threatening behavior from cultists and other criminals trying to shake her up, throw her off their trail. Maybe she'd even had her apartment broken into before. But there was likely to be something more upsetting about knowing they'd been in the bedroom, her private space, than anywhere else in the apartment.

Teagan moved off and checked her closet. It, too, was clear. "Did they take anything?" he asked, putting his own weapon away.

"No," Kathy said with a sigh. "No, it doesn't look like it. I'm guessing the HBS were tipped off by my visit to Charlene Ledders. Now that their precious, delicate ritual of destruction is in motion, they probably don't want us doing anything to upset it."

"What about your occult research? I'm guessing they were intending on taking it?"

Kathy went over to the bed frame, pulled it with a grunt of effort away from the wall, and gestured toward a slightly worn patch of plaster. She dug a nail under the upper left corner and a slab came away in her hands. "I hid it," she told him, "in the event that something like this happened." She pulled a small notebook-sized laptop from the hole, as well as some papers and a thin book. She dropped them on the bed.

"Before we do anything else," she said, reaching into the hole again, "let's lock this place up again, shall we?" She produced two large mason jars that appeared to be filled with powders or tiny grains of something.

"What are those?" Teagan asked, gesturing with the Camel before he put it back in his mouth.

"This one," she said, holding up the jar in her left hand with orangeish powder in it, "is mostly turmeric. It is usually more powerful if ingested, but it'll do for now as a means of warding off whatever watchdogs the cult may have left behind to keep an eye on us. There's also some sea salt in here, a little powdered chalk, and, if you can believe it, some pulverized black tourmaline that I got as a thank-you gift from a client on one of my cases. This jar's kind of like a combination of a security system, barbed wire, and an electromagnetic field."

This other one"—she held up the purplish one in her right hand—"is mostly sage. We can burn that. I've found it helpful in clearing out whatever's in the air that entities of various types can latch on to."

Teagan's expression must have betrayed his skepticism because she smiled sheepishly at him, putting the sage down on the night table to unscrew the cap on the other mixture. "You'll just have to trust me that it works, Reece." She handed him a scoop of the mixture, which smelled kind of funny, though not unpleasantly so.

"Oh, I trust you, Kat, regarding those particular things that go bump in the night, but what about keeping the human intruders out? Assuming they were the ones who broke in here, how are you going to keep them from coming back?"

She patted her .45. "I'm a light sleeper. Besides, past behavior of the Hand suggests they won't be back tonight. Leaving aside that they have the next phase of the ritual to plan for, it would be too risky now for any one of them to return here. They're like lightning, like that. Now let's get to work."

Teagan helped her sprinkle the powders around all the doorways, windows, vents, and every other conceivable opening in the bedroom, and then likewise, throughout the apartment. When they were finished, she set out a glass candleholder in each room, sprinkled the sage from the other jar in each, and, with a long-necked kitchen lighter, she set each on fire. The sage smoldered, creating a fragrant smoke that over-ran the smell of the other stuff she had used. Nevertheless, Kathy opened a few of the windows in the apartment just enough to let the smoke out to prevent it from becoming cloying or setting off the smoke alarm in the hall. When they were done, Kathy closed the windows, then scooped up the laptop, papers, and book from her bed.

"Ready?" she asked him.

"Lead the way into the realm of darkness, my lovely," he said, grinning, and was pleased to see it elicited a grin back.

Teagan followed her and her research into the den. She righted her chair, dropped the papers and book on the desk with a thump, and then flipped open the cover of the laptop and turned it on.

"I keep everything in an encrypted file on here. I have it saved to one of those password-protected cloud things, too."

"Smart, that," he said, impressed. She'd often professed to be an utter Luddite when it came to computers, but it didn't really surprise him that she'd downplayed the extent of her technical skills. She was a little bit like Columbo like that, letting people believe whatever preconceived limitations they formed, and occasionally encouraging those notions so that she would be underestimated. Teagan thought she took a certain pleasure in swooping in on a case with a victory that stunned those who had judged her.

After what felt like several long minutes of clicking and typing, clicking and typing, a PDF popped up on screen.

"Here we go," she said, sinking into the chair.

"What is it?" he asked, leaning in over her shoulder. This close to her, he could smell her perfume—something light and floral—and it pleased him immensely.

Some of the document was in other languages. Teagan recognized Latin, Greek, Japanese, German, and Egyptian hieroglyphics, but there were portions in a language he had never seen before. It looked like a cross between complex pictographs and cuneiform. Interspersed between these sections and wrapping around diagrams and other graphics was the English text.

"Well, not a counter-spell, *per se*, but a pretty good idea of where to find it. See, these passages here"—she pointed to the language he didn't recognize—"are in a special sort of secret language of traders—people in, uh, my line of work, I guess—who need to exchange information from forbidden or banned grimoires. It looks like nonsense, a made-up language, right? It's not. It's designed so that sensitive information isn't accidentally accessed by the uninitiated, and so it can pass without trouble under the noses of most gatekeepers. There is an underground compilation series of books in this language—I have a copy of every volume except the most recent—that contains accumulated knowledge from all of the most important books, scrolls, and documents on the occult in the world—*The Munich Manual, Codex Seraphinianus, The Voynich Manuscript,* the *Heptameron, The Book of Doors,* the *Libro Novem Saecula, The Picatrix,* the *Oera Linda Book,* oh, and *The Red Dragon Grand Grimoire,* of course . . ."

Seeing Teagan's polite but confused nodding, she moved on. "Anyway, if there is a spell to counteract the one used by the Hand of the Black Stars, one of these PDFs will have it, or tell us where to find it."

"Right then. Ah, anything I can do to help? Other than try to read that?"

"Pour me a drink?" She winked at him, then turned back to the computer. "Glasses are in the kitchen cabinet all the way to the right. Bottom shelf. Vodka . . . that should be on the counter by the sink."

Teagan headed toward the kitchen. The occult aspects of the case were, frankly, beyond him. He'd grown up in a strictly, stiflingly Roman Catholic family, and he had shirked most aspects of religion, anyone's religion, a long time ago. While his upbringing had given him some understanding of a worldview on supernatural evil, what Kathy was talking about was different. It was science and science fiction and magic and religion and physics and mathematics all sort of rolled into one. That somehow made it more terrifying. It wasn't just a matter of simple faith, but also of invasive and immutable truths that belief systems of pure faith and no proof sought to bury under layers of condemnation.

He found the glasses and poured out two vodkas, and was set to carry them back into the den when his cell phone rang. The sound was jarring. It had been days since he'd gotten so much as a text message, and the ringtone seemed almost unearthly and out of place in that little kitchen. He put the glasses down and took the cell out of his back pocket. It was Morris.

"Hey there, mate," he answered the phone.

"Teagan! It works! The cell, I mean. I had my doubts I'd be able to get through. I couldn't reach Jack at all."

"Aye, I was a bit surprised meself to hear the mobile ring," Teagan admitted. "How're you holding up out there in the snow?"

"It's . . . quiet. It's kind of how I imagined a nuclear winter might be."

"Spend much time imagining such things, do you?"

"In this line of work," Morris said, "I imagine a lot of ways the human race will ultimately fuck itself over."

Teagan smiled thinly. "Not much left to the imagination these last few days."

"Tell me about it. How are you and Kathy?"

"Fine. We're at her apartment. She's looking for the counter-spell to the one that caused this mess."

"I hope she finds it," Morris said. He didn't sound all that confident.

"So what's going on?"

"Well, I found out about that figure you and Jack described," Morris said.

"Really?"

"Yeah. Took some leg work, by the way. Not the kind of thing you can just Google, even if the Internet were working right now."

"You're a prince among men."

"No kidding. Just left the home of a local college professor to ask about it. Their theology expert, Trina Majoram. She's a recognized authority—right here in town, no less—on obscure ancient religious symbolism. The rituals, mythologies, gods and goddesses, all that sort of thing. I guess you could say she bridges the gap between the church of my Sunday school days and the cults of Kathy's, uh, devil worshippers."

Teagan balanced the cell between his ear and shoulder and brought the glasses of vodka into the den. He handed Kathy hers, and she nodded a thanks, then mouthed out *Who?* and gestured at the phone. Teagan switched the phone to his free hand and responded with *Morris*. To Morris, he said, "Did she recognize the description of the figure? I'm putting you on speaker so Kathy can hear."

"Yeah." Morris's voice came through a little tinny on the speaker setting, but he was audible. "She confirmed that such descriptions historically have been found in relation to ritualistic torture-sacrifices offered to gods of other worlds. Almost exclusively, those rituals were attempted by that Hand of the Black Stars cult Kathy mentioned. She said there isn't much written about them, but she did know they were a bad, bad group of people. They're into some pretty freaky stuff. Cannibalism, piquerism, necrophilia, cryptozoophilia—hell, some of this stuff I don't know the meaning of, and I don't want to know. But they've been doing these things a long time. There's evidence of them at least as far back as the Nineteenth Dynasty of ancient Egypt. Old-school, pissed-off, violent group of psychos, as if we didn't know that by now."

"Aye, that's what our Kathy says about them. What about the figure? How does it relate to this ritual?" He took a healthy swig of the vodka. It burned a little in his throat—Teagan was more of a whiskey man, himself—but it warmed his chest.

Morris cleared his throat. "Well, Majoram told me—" There was a sound like papers being shuffled on Morris's end. "Geez, it's complicated. Okay, so according to Majoram, they're scouts of sorts, I guess. They're mentioned as demons in other religions, but she recognized them all right. If evidence points to these Black Stars nut jobs finding a door to a dangerous alternate dimension, like Kathy said, a portal between worlds, then they must have found the keyhole, too. Fashioned a key and unlocked the door—you know, in a metaphysical, supernatural sense, I guess. When it opened—the door, I mean—the snow and everything in it came through. And those figures, the scout-demons or whatever, control it all—the snow and ice, the monsters, probably even the cultists at this point. Majoram called them the Blue People."

"The Blue People? Charlene mentioned them," Kathy said, then turned to the PDF to check for the phrase.

"Yup. They're . . . cleaners, I guess you could say. Interdimensional fixers. They and the monsters and the snow are meant to wipe out everything. All life, anything that might complicate the arrival of . . . others. Apparently, the cultists think that once the Blue People are done making Colby an empty, frozen wasteland, the conditions will be right for these 'others' to come through that door and take over."

"Sounds like that's bang on with what that header told Kat."

"That's what I thought, too. And why go to all this trouble destroying Colby, you ask?"

"I did wonder," Teagan replied with a small smile to Kathy.

"Because in exchange for preparing the way, these cultists will get their rocks off on being the new favorite pets of whatever 'others' come through that door. Those 'others' would, and I quote, 'provide knowledge of the universe, of other universes, and of the forces which create and destroy, cure and kill, forces which bend time and fold space. Bodies would be changed to withstand the powers unlocked in the mind.'"

"So wait—" Kathy began.

"There's more." Morris flipped through papers again on the other end. "These ancient beings were 'formed in and of the pure dark of starless space from which all of creation and destruction springs forth.' Sound like those Greater Gods Kathy's nut job mentioned?"

"Aye." The smile slipped from Teagan's face.

"I think we might be fucked here, guys."

It was a difficult point of view to argue with just then. Teagan could see the grim consideration of what Morris had told them in Kathy's expression as she scrolled through her document. The light from the screen reflected in her eyes seemed to magnify her determination. But it was a lot for Teagan to swallow. He managed with great effort to shake his head. "Nah. We'll stop it. You'll see. We'll stop it."

"I wish I had your confidence," Morris said quietly, then, "but I'm up for a fight, at any rate. Gotta jump off. Snow's getting bad up here, and—"

A pause followed by a high-pitched scream caused both Teagan and Kathy to exchange alarmed looks.

"Morris? Hello? Morris?"

"I'm okay," Morris said. "I'm fine. But I gotta go. I'll call you back."

The phone disconnected, and for a few seconds, the two detectives just stared at it. Finally Teagan put it in his back pocket and took another swig of vodka.

"I'm sure he's fine," he said.

"Sure," Kathy agreed, taking a healthy gulp of her own drink. "It's Morris."

"Aye, it's Morris," Teagan said. But the knot of worry in his gut was reflected in Kathy's eyes. "Any luck finding anything?"

"A reference to the Blue People in the *Libro Novem Saecula*— that is, the *Book of Nine Worlds*. I happen to have a copy of that one on here, but it's an abridged version. Let's hope we have enough."

Morris hung up the cell and slipped it into his pocket, drawing out his gun. It seemed like he was doing a lot of discovery and rescue these last two days. His newest distress call was coming from a tan SUV across from his parked car. The driver-side door was open and a middle-aged man was half sprawled across a snow drift that had risen up to meet the tops of the tires. His legs appeared to still be in the vehicle, while his arm was draped over his down-turned face. A little blond girl of about eight was screaming and pounding on a back window with tiny mittened hands.

Remembering the beastly thing he'd seen when he'd come upon Dan Murphy stranded the night before, he opened his car door, grunting against the efforts of the wind to push it closed again, and cautiously got out. The wind bit into his cheeks and sailed beneath his clothes, making him shiver as he scanned the immediate area for signs of monsters, human or otherwise. The abandoned car appeared to be alone, collecting snow and losing heat by the minute.

Morris flashed his badge to the girl so she would know he was a police officer, and that seemed to calm her a little. She stopped screaming and her pounding on the window faded to muted little thumps, but Morris could see that she was shaking badly, probably from both the cold and from fright. Whatever she had seen was likely something no little kid should ever have to see.

He reached the open door of the SUV, and crouched by the man's head. Enough snow had blown in under the car that there was no space beneath for anything to hide, but no way for the tires to move. From the color of the skin on the man's neck, he could tell the man was dead. He touched a shoulder and found it stiff. When he tried turning over the body, he saw that the blood that had spilled from the man's head had frozen into crimson ice and adhered to the snow beneath. It took some tugging, but Morris got the man free and turned him over. Then he cried out and fell backward into the snow. The man's face was missing. Instead, a blood-soaked mess of fleshy frozen shreds of butchered meat and white protruding skull bones had replaced anything even vaguely resembling facial features.

With a quick glance at the girl in the back seat, who now sat quietly, apparently numb with shock, Morris hastily turned the body back over into the snow. The rest of it slid out from the car, and Morris gagged a little as the tattered stumps where the man's legs had been thudded against the door frame. He rose with some difficulty; it felt like the snow had been trying to bury him under, just in the few minutes during which he'd been on his ass in it. He brushed it off as best he could, instinctively repulsed by the hard clumps of ice which clung to his coat and gloves. He unlocked all the doors from the panel on the driver-side door and went back to the girl.

When he opened her door, he was surprised to find that although she was bloody and a little bruised, she was not seriously injured. She was a tiny wisp of a thing, doll-like in her features. Her long blond hair had clumpy streaks of crimson in it, just under her wool hat, and a small cut on her cheek had trickled a tear of blood that had almost made it to her jaw before drying. Her mittens had dark brown smudges on them. Similarly colored stains on her light blue parka looked unnervingly like smeared handprints.

"Hi," he said in what he hoped was a soothing voice. "I'm Oliver. What's your name?"

"Jill. My family calls me Jilly."

"Hi, Jilly," he said.

She looked up at him with round, haunted hazel eyes and in a monotone, replied, "You're not my family."

"Uh, yeah, of course. You're right. I'm a police officer, and I want to help you, Jill. I want to get you out of here."

"It took my mom," she whispered. Then, a little above a whisper, she added, "My brother, too. Kenny. And my dad—it killed him, didn't it?"

"Was that your dad that was driving?"

She nodded, tears forming in her eyes.

"I'm so sorry, honey," he said, and then fell silent as she bent her head and cried softly. It broke his heart to see her crying, this little blond angel, an innocent little child, over a loss too big for words. But indeed, no words came out; nothing seemed to do justice to that kind of pain, that kind of horror. Nothing would adequately explain the terrible wrongness, the impossible strangeness of having her mother and brother taken away from her and her father torn apart by the very monsters she had spent the first few years of her young life being convinced were not real. He just let her cry, because sometimes tears were stronger, safer, more powerful, more honorable than words could ever be. And when her crying had reduced to sniffles, he squeezed her shoulder.

"We should go, Jill," he told her. "It's not safe here."

"I know," she said, and exhaled a shuddery breath.

"Do you have someplace I can take you? Some family, or a family friend?"

She looked up at him with big hazel eyes still shining with tears. "Ms. Harper. My mom always told me that if anything bad happened and she and my dad couldn't get to me"—fresh tears spilled down her cheeks—"that I should go to Ms. Harper's."

"Okay," Morris said, helping her out of her seat belt (she was still dutifully buckled in) and out of the SUV. "Do you think you can guide me there from here?"

Jilly nodded. She felt like such a small thing, so fragile, as he steered her by the shoulders to his car. She went around and got in the passenger seat, buckling the seat belt again. The gesture made him smile softly as he got behind the wheel and buckled his own seat belt.

"Okay, Jill, lead the way."

She directed him back toward the center of town and down a few side streets to a dead-end cul-de-sac of large houses and landscaped lawns. She pointed at a brown cedar-shingled three-story Dutch Colonial house numbered six, and he pulled into the driveway.

Morris put the car into park. "Come on. I'll walk you up to the house and explain everything to Ms. Harper," he said gently.

The little girl nodded, allowing him to lead her to the house.

Morris listened to the surrounding stillness as they walked up the driveway. It was unnerving, how quiet it was. Even the sound of snow, which should have crunched beneath their feet and blown dustily about in the wind, was muted. There was something about snow, especially that much snow, that deadened everything, darkened it even in the day. It created a perception of being isolated, alone in a world of feathered white crystal. It was a dangerous thought in its all-encompassing pervasiveness, the kind of thought that made a person sit amid all the silence, let it surround him, deafen and silence him, weigh down his limbs, lull him to cold, shadowed sleep. . . .

He shook his head. Deep down, the beginning waves of unease were washing back and forth inside Morris, but he kept walking. It was far more likely that whatever was wrong was out here with them instead of inside that house, but to be sure, Morris kept a hand on the butt of his gun.

When they reached the front door, he knocked heavily. There was no mail in the mailbox, he noted. It was just another little jolt of reality, of the disconnect between Colby and the rest of the world. It made him shiver.

"I don't hear Hunter," Jilly said.

"Sorry?"

"Ms. Harper's dog. Usually, he barks like crazy when someone knocks on the door."

Morris frowned. He didn't say anything, but those waves of unease were beginning to crest.

He knocked on the door again. From within came sounds of movement, and a soft and somewhat elderly-sounding voice said, "I'm coming."

The door opened a crack and the muzzle of a shotgun peered out. Immediately, Morris shoved Jilly behind him. Grasping the stock and trigger in a death grip were two bony white hands with neatly manicured and pink-painted nails. The sliver of face visible in the doorway was equally as bony and white, with one sharply intelligent brown eye and the corner of a firmly set and delicately thin-lipped mouth.

"Uh, Ms. Harper?"

"Who's asking?" The barrels of the shotgun didn't waver.

"Detective Oliver Morris. I have someone here I think you know." He gestured for Jilly to come around, and when she did, Ms. Harper immediately lowered the shotgun and opened the door. She leaned the weapon against the door frame and swept Jilly up in a hug. The little girl started to cry again.

"Oh, Jilly, my baby, my baby," she cooed into the girl's hair, stroking her back. Over her head, she asked, "Her parents? Kenny?"

Morris shook his head, and the old woman's face fell. She smoothed an errant strand of silver-white hair back toward the bun from which it had escaped and sighed.

"It was the men with the glowing mouths," Jilly said in a small, flat voice. "They came out of the woods. Out of the snow." A sudden thought seemed to seize her, and she turned to Morris, as if really aware of his presence for the first time. "The snow brought them. Or they brought the snow. I don't know which. But they had monsters, and the monsters hurt my dad." The girl sniffled, and Ms. Harper took her by the shoulders and said, "Jilly, honey, do you want to lie down?"

"No," the little girl replied in that same small, flat tone.

"Okay. Why don't you help yourself to some milk and a snack from the fridge, okay? I have to talk to the policeman."

The girl gave them both a hesitant glance but headed off down the hall. Ms. Harper watched until she was out of sight and then turned back to Morris.

"My apologies about the shotgun," she said, extending her hand. "What with everything going on, I couldn't be too careful. Julianne Harper. I've been a friend of Jilly's family for years."

"Not a problem, Ms. Harper," Morris answered, shaking her hand. "Frankly, I'm relieved to be able to bring the girl to someone I can feel confident will protect her."

Ms. Harper gave him a small smile, then slid gracefully around him to relock the front door. "Those . . . things out there, whatever they are, got my dog this morning. I couldn't . . . I just couldn't get back to him fast enough with the gun." The woman's eyes glistened with tears that she seemed determined not to shed. "And Jill's parents . . . her poor dear brother . . . I take it those same things got to them as well?"

"Looks that way," Morris said. "I found Jill there in the back of the family SUV. Her mother and brother were gone. Her father, what was left of him, had, if you'll pardon my language, spilled out into the snow."

Ms. Harper shook her head. She was a fit, attractive woman for a late sixty-something, and moved with a kind of grace and elegance that Morris immediately admired. She gestured for him to sit on a plump easy chair in the sitting room. Behind them, Morris could hear Jilly clanging around in the kitchen.

"Those poor people. Evan and Bernadette were good parents. They loved their children so much. She was a radiology nurse, you know, and he did something with computers for a non-profit organization. Genuinely good people." She sighed raggedly. "And Kenny. Good God. He was only eleven. I can't . . . I just can't imagine what Jilly's been through this morning."

"She's a brave little girl," Morris said. After a pause, he continued. "Ms. Harper, I know this is an unconventional request, but . . . well lately, we've found ourselves in an inarguably unconventional situation, so . . . I was wondering if Jill could stay with you? I don't know for how long, but I'd wager we'd all feel much better having her stay here with you than in some foster system. Truth be told, there aren't many systems in Colby that haven't broken down anyway, as you may have noticed."

"I have," she answered. "And Jilly can stay here for as long as she likes. She's always welcome. I love her like my own. I'll keep her safe."

Morris patted her arm. "I know you will."

"Oh, forgive my manners, Detective. May I offer you something warm to drink? Something to eat, perhaps?"

"Thank you, but no. I have some business to attend to."

"I understand completely."

"If it's okay, though, I'd like to come back and check on her when things settle?"

"Please do," she said, offering him the first genuinely warm smile since he and Jilly had arrived.

They both rose, and she showed him to the front door. That was when they heard a wailing like a harsh wind, followed by the heavy thud of footfalls on the porch.

Jilly came running in from the kitchen and clung to Ms. Harper. "What was that?" The panic in her voice was heartbreaking.

"Stay here, ladies," Morris said. He went to one of the front windows by the door and positioned himself so that his body was next to the glass rather than in front of it. He drew his weapon and peered out the window. Outside, mere inches from the front door, three of those things like the one that had attacked Daniel Murphy were pacing the front porch. Occasionally they stopped in front of the door, swinging those massive heads back and forth, those needle-lined jaws gaping, as if they sensed the humans on the other side but didn't know how to find them. Often, they flickered or turned in such a way that they all but disappeared from view. In the next second, they would reappear several inches away. To Morris, it was perhaps one of their most unnerving qualities.

Morris gestured to Ms. Harper and Jilly to be quiet, and then he turned back to the window.

The creatures growled, nipping at each other and occasionally swiping at the front door. Behind him, he heard Jilly whimpering every time one of those large, taloned paws pounded on the relatively thin boundary between them.

He considered opening the windows a crack and firing at them from the house, but he feared it would make too much noise. They were close—very close—and he suspected the key to killing them, if gunshots would even work, would be to have the upper hand, the element of surprise. Drawing their attention before he was ready would be an extraordinarily bad idea.

"Ms. Harper," he said in a low voice, "do you have any other weapons in the house?"

"You mean like more guns? No, I—I don't. Just the one shotgun. I have kitchen knives, I guess. A baseball bat that used to belong to my husband."

"Okay, okay good. Knives can be . . . messy, but the bat is good. What about, like, blow torches? Battery-powered tools?"

Ms. Harper looked flustered. Her mouth opened to answer, but closed again. She shook her head.

"Okay, no problem. How about nail polish remover?"

"Oh, that I have! But why?"

He turned back to the window. "I'm betting we can burn them."

Ms. Harper and Jilly exchanged worried looks, but the woman said, "Whatever you think will kill the bastards."

"Okay," he said, keeping a wary eye on those things pacing outside. "We'll need the nail polish remover, some rags—whatever you have that we can tear up, uh, corks if you have them, a lighter, and . . . glass bottles. Beer bottles, Coke, whatever."

"Gotcha. Come on, Jilly. You go through Frank's closet and get whatever T-shirts are in there. I'll get the polish remover."

As the two climbed the stairs, Morris grimaced at the window.

Fire. It could work. He hoped to God it would work.

One of the things that Jack noticed about the snow as he drove out toward the west edge of town was its unnerving capacity to take the shape of forms and faces, even in broad daylight. Many of the roads to and from the outer parts of town were surrounded on either side by woods, and the way the wind swirled the snow between the tree trunks gave Jack the impression of being watched by pale faces with hollow eyes and crooked, slashed mouths. Tricks of light and shadow, maybe, but it was unsettling to Jack, who was already grappling with a growing certainty that the Hand of the Black Stars cult was a far more organized and well-informed organization than he had thought. He suspected they had eyes, human and otherwise, everywhere.

Or, to be more accurate, he supposed, *they* were now functioning as the eyes for something else, something that could, by unnatural means, root him out wherever he was and wherever he went. These things were, after all, here to level Colby to the ground, and they were just the grunts. Whatever was coming through to this world (if Jack and his team couldn't stop them) would be much worse. The devastation in Colby would spread, if it hadn't already. The whole state. The East Coast. The country, and beyond. . . .

What was one little planet to beings who destroyed whole universes?

There was something so infuriatingly horrific about that idea: not just everything Jack was and had ever done, but everything the human race had ever been or accomplished since the beginning of civilization, would be gone. Not just humans but humanity itself would be erased, relegated to an old folk tale, a lost chapter in an endless book of tragedies.

And in that moment, as his car sped over patches of ice and cracked street pavement, Jack felt sick in his heart for his children. He couldn't bear the thought of their being afraid at the end, or worse, of them watching a world they had only a tentative grasp of so far just slip away from them before they found a good reason to fight for it. Children, in Jack's mind, were so newly minted from that pure place where beautiful little souls originally came from that they had less trouble letting go of life and physicality in this world. He had, unfortunately, seen it time and time again in his line of work. He'd seen it in the last seconds of Gracie Anderson's life when her little hand let go of his, just before the cold and blood loss made her blue eyes glaze over. It wasn't that children gave up life willingly; no, Jack thought, it was simply that children instinctively knew that there was some place to go after this world because they could still, on some subconscious level, remember that there had been a place from which they'd come before. It didn't make him any less enraged when children's lives were taken, but it allowed him to put that rage on a kind of mental shelf and do his job to catch their killers.

It wouldn't be possible for him to do that where his children were concerned. He wondered how easy it would be (or *had been? Oh no, no no*, he wasn't going to think like that, not now) for his children to give this world up.

And as for doing his job and hunting the killers in Colby? He frowned to himself. The worst murderers he had ever encountered in the course of his career had committed some pretty monstrous acts, but they were still human. Many people seemed to forget that—*wanted* to forget it, as if the thought of these killers being human somehow tainted others' humanity. People didn't like to believe that they could share any traits with child-killers and molesters, cannibals, necrophiliacs, rapists, serial murderers, and the like, because it meant that, deep down, they would have to acknowledge that anyone could be that kind of monster, even a loved one. Even oneself. To Jack, however, the fact that the worst criminals he had ever come across until now were still just human beings with human weaknesses and flaws was somewhat reassuring. He didn't want to chase phantom boogeymen. He wanted to catch bad human beings doing bad things and lock them up in a cage using irrefutable but utterly human forensic proof.

With this case, Jack wasn't sure anymore that even the cultists were human. Lord knew nothing else out there in the snow was.

He wondered where his children were right now. Were they in the house they had grown up in, the one Katie had gotten in the divorce? Had they gone over to Katie's on-again, off-again boyfriend's house? Jack didn't believe *that* guy was any great shakes as a protector. In fact, if he'd have allowed himself such an uncharitable thought, he would have hoped one of those spider things had already eaten the guy.

The kids wouldn't be at school, so he could eliminate searching there. Classes at the grammar, middle, and high schools had been canceled the last few days, and there was talk of cutting the year short and adding the missing time to the beginning of the next school year. That there was no promise that things would be righted by then had not been publicly discussed.

Around him, the faces in the snow looked like they were laughing. *Fixed? Not at all, sir! Oh, we have big plans for Colby—big plans! Come September, this little fleck of human loss will be an iceberg, and there won't be a school to go back to, or any children to attend it.*

Jack shook his head to clear those thoughts from it. They didn't feel like his thoughts. It sounded crazy, even in the confines of his own head, but they felt like the *snow's* thoughts. Or maybe they were the projected ideas of the things in the snow. Still, he couldn't help feeling that the snow itself somehow had a mind of its own, that it was a thinking, calculating thing waiting to exploit the weaknesses of those who made the foolish attempt to trudge through it.

He was almost to Katie's house, and the tightness in his chest suddenly felt crushing. He was afraid, frankly and starkly afraid, of what he'd find there.

As quickly as he was passing them, the snow faces disassembled and reassembled between the next two trees, and the next, and the next . . . the snow was, indeed, following him, tracking him.

As he reached the town border, he slowed to a stop. No one else was on the road. The drifts of snow had formed an odd snow-fort kind of wall across the length of road just a few hundred feet beyond the town limit. It would have been, under normal circumstances, a fairly easy thing to plow, but Jack had doubts about making any attempts to drive over or through it. He thought briefly of the dashboard cam video of Aleski and Seeger that Teagan had told him about earlier. That hill of snow probably ran around the entire perimeter of the town, through the woods and everything. He could see beyond it now, and although the snow appeared to continue out toward the next town, Jack couldn't be sure if that was an illusion.

The left turn onto Maple, which ultimately led to Katie's street, was on his side of the border. He thought some of the subsequent roads might cross the town limits proper, but he had to try to navigate it. His kids needed him.

He tried Katie again on the cell, but was met with the same frustrating busy signal he'd been getting since yesterday afternoon. This close to the outside world, the snow was wreaking havoc with cell reception. He tried to text her for the third time that morning, and again, the text bounced as undeliverable.

"Dammit," he muttered. He glared at the border. A gust of wind dusted up some of the snow and the faces were immediately there in bas-relief along the border. Indents the size of fists formed eyes, mounds formed sharply jutting facial features, and small, sharp icicles hung from sunken mouth areas in various sardonic smiles. Winter had always bothered Jack, but in that moment, he hated it with a renewed and seething passion. He was tempted to take his snow brush and beat those faces down to disfigured, half-melted lumps.

Instead, he stayed behind the wheel, feeling the feeble heat from the dashboard vents and listening to the idling engine growl low, like a threatened dog.

"You are not going to get in my way," he told the faces in a steady, even voice. "You are not going to stop me."

The aspect of the faces changed. Maybe clouds had shifted to cover the sun or the wind had shifted the shape of the bas-relief, but instead of wicked amusement, the expressions were now soaked in hatred. The carved, almost chiseled animosity was far clearer than just an impression. There *were* faces in the snow now, and they were snarling at him, baring those icicle fangs. Beneath the faces were the beginnings of ice—taloned paws, as well.

Jack eased the car forward toward the turn, eyeing them warily. Could they move? Could they form bodies as well and pull free of that ice wall? And if so, how fast could they bear down on his car?

The faces watched but made no move to stop him. He gunned the engine, his tires kicking up an albescent spray, and peeled into the turn. In his rearview, the faces at the border and the claws beneath seemed to be reaching out of the bank toward the car, a chilling ice-and-wind effect of motion caught and frozen mid-reach.

He focused on the road ahead and pushed down on the gas pedal even harder, until he had put enough distance between him and that wall of snow that he couldn't see it anymore. He turned right onto Cloverlane Road and then made a left onto Piedmont. If he wavered back and forth over the town border, nothing hindered his progress, but those snow faces followed between fence posts, against tree trunks in backyards, or wedged between parked cars.

They were watching, but waiting.

Finally he reached the right turn for Katie's street, Shillham Drive. His body tensed as he rolled down the road toward the house. It was on the left, a white bi-level, and Katie's car was there.

The car doors were open, the interior silent and still.

Jack felt his chest tighten. He put the car in park, pocketed his keys, and took his gun from the glove compartment. As he got out of the car, the wind picked up, slicing across his face and biting his ears. In it, he thought he heard the whispering of many voices on the verge of forming discernible words. It felt invasive, having those voices so close to his ear, furtively pushing the suggestion, if not the statement, of mockery at him. He shook his head and strode purposefully toward his ex-wife's car.

He braced himself for blood. His heart pounded so hard he could hear the silent rush of his own blood in his head, even over the wind. He took a deep breath and looked inside the car.

The interior was empty. No ex-wife, no kids, no blood. He exhaled with relief. His attention turned to the front door of the house. It was shut, and looked undamaged—both good signs . . . provided that Katie and the kids had made it inside.

He had a key to Katie's house on his key ring, and as he approached the door, he took it out of his pocket. Behind him, the wind blew snow at his back. The scratching of the tiny pieces of ice against the fabric of his coat felt like fingers clawing at him, trying to divert his attention.

Jack tried the knob first, turning it easily and swinging the door inward. The foyer ahead was dark. He stepped inside, closing and locking the door behind him.

"Guess I didn't need these," he mumbled to himself, putting his keys down on the small wooden table by the door. He dropped his gloves next to them and then made his way through the hall to the kitchen at the back of the house, peering into the empty den and dining room to the left and the even emptier bathroom and sitting room to the right. The kids' overnight backpacks, he noticed, were leaning up against the couch in the den. Odder still, their winter coats and snow boots had been tossed carelessly by the back door. It didn't add up. The house was swathed in empty stillness; he hadn't checked upstairs yet, but his gut told him they weren't there. Still, for all Katie's flaws, she was a good mother, and she never would have let them out in the snow without coats and snow boots.

Jack frowned. Where the hell were they?

He opened his mouth to call out, then closed it. If they were in the house, he'd find them. But if anyone else—or any*thing*—was in the house, he didn't want *it* to find *him*.

Instead, he went back down the hall toward the front door and climbed the stairs. His hand rested on his gun as the steps creaked beneath his weight.

He caught a whiff of Katie's perfume when he reached the second floor. It seemed to be coming from Carly's room, so he looked in there first. Her favorite little stuffed white unicorn sat on the bed. He picked it up, turning it in his hands, looking at the innocent blue eyes, the rainbow yarn hair and tail that he'd learned how to braid just for her, the smudge of blackberry juice that subsequent trips through the washing machine had only reduced to a faint purple patch. He inhaled the smell of his daughter's shampoo, the scent of her soap, in the fur of the little guy. Just thinking about her formed a lump in his throat.

He put the unicorn back down on the bed and moved on to his son's room across the hall. Jack Jr.'s PS3 was on. Jack frowned. He picked up the controller. It was warm; if they had left the house, they'd done it very recently.

He shut off the PS3 and the TV and made his way toward Katie's bedroom. It had been his bedroom once, too, but he felt nothing of nostalgia stepping through the doorway. The room, the house, the woman who ran it—they were not his anymore, and that was okay. Very little of it even looked the same, but more than that, it didn't feel the same.

What hadn't changed was how he felt about his kids. He had to find them.

Suddenly seized with desperation, he searched the room in a flurry—under the bed, in the closets, in the adjoining bathroom, calling out to them, monsters be damned.

"Jack! Carly!"

He went back to the kids' room and searched the closets and under their beds, too. He looked in the kids' bathroom tub, on the off chance they thought it might be safer to hide inside it. He ran down the stairs, rechecking behind the couch, in the coat closet, any place he could think of where people could hide.

They were gone.

Jack returned to the back door in the kitchen and looked out at the yard. The aluminum swing set he'd put in for them when Carly was three stood like a pale silver and blue monument to their childhood, their little ghosts haunting the curve of the swing seats and the worn-shiny spots on the slide. Both the swings and slide were piled high with small mountains of snow, weighing them down, and they creaked when the wind blew. He could hear it somehow, even in the house with everything closed up to seal out the cold. It was as if the weight of whatever had happened to the children was an unbearable burden it needed to share with him.

He remembered the message from the woman who'd claimed snowmen had eaten her children and shuddered.

On the back porch, the barren sticks of an old raspberry bush Katie had started that spring poked up through the snow gathered in the clay terracotta pot. A diminutive patio set consisting of a metal-framed pair of chairs and a small alfresco-style table practically blended into the drifts around it. There were no footprints, but he didn't really expect there to be. Whatever drove the faces to form in the snow also swallowed up any trace of humanity that was left out there. It would not be imprinted; it only assimilated. The returning idea of the snow as a sentient, absorbing kind of creature in and of itself made sense, a lot of terrifying sense, and did nothing to soothe his fears for his family.

Where could they have gone? He pulled out his cell again and tried Katie's and cursed as her voicemail picked up for the umpteenth time. He'd done some information gathering on Katie's new boyfriend when he first learned of the guy's existence, which he justified to himself as due diligence on a man who would be spending time with his children; as a result, he had the boyfriend's address, but there was no cell or landline phone number associated with him, so he couldn't call. How a person functioned in this day and age with no way to be reached was beyond him, and seemed unwise given that he may, at some point, have Jack's children at his house. And no criminal record and essentially positive employment performance reviews didn't mean the guy was smart or financially responsible. He'd just have to go over there then, he thought as he turned away from the back door. It was a ten-minute drive to the guy's house, and—

Then Jack saw the note.

"What the—?" It was a small white envelope whose bottom corner was frozen in a jagged line of ice that ran along the counter. He would have sworn it hadn't been there before, but there it was, with his name written in Katie's graceful, looping handwriting. A fine fuzz of frost ran the length of the flap.

With a little finagling, he managed to wriggle the envelope out of the ice. The whole thing was cool to the touch and it made him uncomfortable. It was as if something perpetually arctic had held it, had wrapped its fingers or tendrils or whatever around it and imparted its unceasing frigidity into the fibers of the paper itself. He had this semi-irrational thought that maybe the cold would pass into his fingers, through his hands, and leave some part of him permanently frostbitten.

He opened the envelope and took out a piece of white paper the size of a note card. On it, four words were printed in a block-letter handwriting he vaguely recognized but, frustratingly, couldn't call to mind. Not Katie's, and not the boyfriend's, but . . . dammit, he couldn't place it. Still, the words most certainly had a freezing effect on his heart:

YOU'LL NEVER FIND THEM.

His stomach bottomed out, and for a moment, he thought he might get sick right there on the kitchen floor. He had to pull it together, though. He had to find his kids.

He took several deep breaths, forcing down the upheaval inside him, blinking the world back into focus. He slipped the envelope and note into a paper bag. His fingerprints were on the note, but he hoped forensics could find other prints as well.

Kathy had mentioned once that the identities of Hand of the Black Stars members were a very closely guarded secret. Well, fuck that—he'd get names, addresses, their fucking pants sizes. He would find his family, and the cultists who took them. They had to be alive, just had to be, because the need to find them would be one of the surest ways to manipulate Jack and his team. So be it, if it got him closer to them. He *would* find them, one way or another.

And if those crazy sons of bitches got between him and his family, he'd kill them.

Chapter Nine

"So," Teagan said as he finished off the last of the vodka in his glass. "There's been something I've been meaning to ask you."

"Okay . . . shoot, I guess," Kathy replied.

"How in hell did you manage to survive driving your car off a bridge into freezing water with a monster speared through the back of your trunk?"

Kathy turned around, flustered. "What? How did . . . how—?"

"Magic Irish intuition." Teagan smiled, looking at the empty bottom of his glass a moment before meeting her surprised eyes. "That, and dispatch picked up a report about your car frozen halfway in the river just outside of town, front end smashed to hell, with a big, silver spike rammed through the roof. Bridge's railing was busted. Weird thing is, ice is unbroken right up to the paint job on your car. I know the river's not that deep, but . . . m'girl, you beat some savage odds."

Kathy smiled uncomfortably. "Okay, yeah. I drove my car off the bridge. I calculated the odds of survival considering my seat belt, air bag, the shallowness of the river, the ice barrier on top of it, the monster that was tearing into my roof . . . and I took the chance."

"Incredibly dangerous, that."

"Yeah."

"So then what happened?"

"Well . . . a lot of the finer details are a blur. We bounced around a lot going over the edge. I hit my head. I think the impact with the ice knocked us both out. I remember sort of waking up, though I can't quite reconcile how much time I was out. It couldn't have been long, because only the front end of the car had sunk, and I think it struck the bottom, or maybe a big rock . . . I know it took a few minutes to really bring awareness back into my body and remember what happened. By all accounts, I should have been killed, but I wasn't. A freak stroke of good luck. I don't know if it was the seat belt or air bag or the angle or what, but there I was. Anyway, I remember the dark went away a little, and when I looked out the windshield, that thing was on its back on the ice. The ice . . . it was weird, but it looked like the ice was . . . holding on to the thing. Like it had sort of climbed up all around the creature, or it had sunk and the water beneath had splashed up somehow and frozen . . . I don't know. My head hurt and I couldn't see so well. But I thought I saw the thing struggling to pull free of it. It was still alive, and the ice was trying to swallow it up. . . .

"Anyway, like I said, I couldn't see so well, and I couldn't feel the cold. In fact, I couldn't feel much of anything; my legs felt like a dead weight and it scared me. I wasn't sure if I was paralyzed." She shook her head and sighed. "But I could hear creaking—the back end of my car balancing on the ice, I think. I was afraid to move, to even breathe, for fear of the whole thing just sinking flat under the ice. I wasn't even sure I could move, but I did, very slowly at first. I don't know what even got me moving. Maybe it was the way the ice was all over that scorpion thing, like the snow was cannibalizing something of its own, eating its child. Or maybe it was the creaking. But my body knew before my brain that it wasn't just going to lie there and die.

"So I turned around, and you know, I think that might have been the hardest part because I had to turn my back on the thing out there. That, and I had to make my legs move. That took a while. It was probably only a few seconds of me sitting there thinking they were shattered, that I must be broken to pieces from the thighs down and paralyzed for life, but it felt like hours. Hours of my brain screaming at my muscles and nerves to move, *move, dammit.* But I did it. I got them moving, and I climbed into the back seat as carefully as I could, with the car rocking and creaking all around me. I moved that stinger aside and climbed out the hole in the roof onto the trunk, then down onto the pond. Then I managed to make it across the ice to the shore. I skidded and slipped a lot, but I made it without falling. Then I limped to the road and flagged down Morris, of all people."

"Jaysus, that's something else, Kat. Almost like something was looking out for you. Protecting you." He swirled the ice around in his glass.

Kathy looked away for a moment before answering. "Maybe. I'm inclined to believe that the balance of worlds means that there are good forces out there as well as bad. And if there is a God or gods, a force of good . . . it doesn't seem willing to let me die, despite my best efforts."

"I'd guess it's wise that way," Teagan said, winking at her. "This world needs you."

Kathy's mouth formed that lopsided smile again. "Thanks, Reece. You know, it's funny. Most of our law enforcement colleagues—Jack and Morris included—perpetuate these funny ideas about me. That I'm, you know, reckless. A liability to other officers because of an . . . indifference to danger or death. But they never seem to remark that despite my many run-ins with both, I'm still here. I don't know. Maybe I am a liability to others, but no matter what happens, I come limping or crawling back from that brink."

"Aye, you do. I never got the impression you had a suicidal streak, for what it's worth. If anything, and I'm hoping you'll not take offense, Kat, I always thought of you as more, well, evenly matched with death. That you and the Reaper see eye to eye, have an understanding. You dance together, but you don't leave together, if that makes sense."

Kathy gave him a look that indicated she was both moved and surprised. "Yes, it does. Very much so. And . . . I appreciate that you see something they don't. Now, enough about me. Let's get back to work. I—oh! I think I found something."

"Really? Is it the spell?" Teagan finished off the vodka in his glass and set it down. He had been poring through some of the printouts Kathy had given him, but it was like reading a secret code. Even when the passages were in English, they still made little sense to him—references to names of places and beings he had never heard of and couldn't pronounce. Still, he had diligently searched each page for one or a combination of symbols Kathy had sketched for him that would indicate reversal spells. So far, he'd found nothing.

"It's . . . no, nothing." She grunted, turning from the screen with her vodka. "I'm starting to think Morris is right. We're just fucked. Us, Colby, the whole human race."

"Maybe," Teagan said noncommittally. "Some days I believe that. I look at this fucked-up bloody world and see we don't be need-

ing the likes of monster-gods with unpronounceable names to come
and do the job for us. We do just fine screwing ourselves, don't we?
It makes me wonder just what, exactly, we were put here for. Like,
what are we supposed to prove? What are we looking to accomplish?
We're so many tiny anecdotes, linked together in a chain that tells a
story of . . . what? It seems like so much fuss and trouble for such a
small, small element of the universe to make such a big deal of being
a part of it. Or, even more laughably, of trying to master it. But those
are usually whiskey thoughts, and usually I think right then, 'Ah, but
whiskey is a beautiful little thing.' A little thing, like we are. I've
many moments I can recall where I've had me whiskey and sat looking at stars and felt comforted by being held in the palm of something
bigger. Maybe we're just here to listen to a babe giggle, or feel a
woman's kiss, or understand in an exchanged look everything words
never could express. And so I figure that we aren't here to conquer
the universe, but to experience all the facets of it, one moment at a
time—good, bad, indifferent, amazing. It's not petty and insignificant
to count the accumulated little things any more than it is insignificant
to count wealth dollar by dollar. What else do we have in this life, if
not all the little things that make us stand out, or stand out to us? All
the little moments—and when it comes down to it, the most important are usually such fleeting wisps of moments—are not only the
things that remind us of what we were and where we are, but why it
matters to look forward. And I tell you, love, despite what others
seem to think is your suicidal streak, no one fights so hard for the
rights of others to experience every moment due them than you. And
you make me want to fight for them, too."

Kathy was quiet for a bit, and then asked, "Is this one of those
moments you mean?"

He grinned. "Aye, love. I think it is."

Ms. Harper returned with Jilly in tow. Between them, they were
carrying three bottles of nail polish remover and armloads of rags—
torn T-shirts, old dress shirts, frayed washcloths and towels.

"Perfect," Morris said as he took the items from the girls and put
them on a nearby side table. "Now, would you happen to have some
glass bottles we can use, as well? And maybe some wine corks?"

Ms. Harper gestured toward the kitchen. Her voice shook a little when she spoke. "I keep some beer in the fridge for guests. Lord knows I certainly don't like the stuff. We can dump it out in the sink and use those bottles. Now, I do have wine, and I keep the corks in a little basket. Would that work?"

"That would work just fine," Morris said, offering what he hoped was a reassuring smile.

Ms. Harper nodded and led Jilly into the kitchen. He could hear the clinking of bottles as they were retrieved from the fridge, and the smell of hops wafted into the front hall. Morris kept an even gaze on the things on the front porch. The creatures outside flickered as they paced like caged animals, making their strange wind-noises and snarling at each other.

One of them shouldered its way to the door, shoving a second out of the way. The latter lashed out at the one that had displaced it, slicing a deep blue wound on the thing's shoulder. The wounded creature bellowed in pain and rage, wheeling around to confront its attacker. It swiped at the other creature's throat, opening a slash that spilled thick blue iciness onto the porch. Where it puddled on the wooden boards, they crystalized and cracked.

The creature with the throat wound, meanwhile, staggered backward, nearly slipping down the front steps, swayed on unsteady legs, then fell over at the edge of the porch. Immediately, the other two descended on it, tearing it open and shoving tattered chunks of it into their mouths. Three more flickering shapes grew solid, and they, too, joined in the frenzy. His instinctive unease about the things on the porch was catapulted into nauseated loathing, but he couldn't turn away until the lump of shreds that was left finally flickered and melted, blending with the disturbed snow on the steps.

Finally, Ms. Harper and Jilly returned with the rinsed-out, dried beer bottles, a small basket of wine corks with their ends tinged pink, and a kitchen pilot lighter. Morris thanked them and took the bottles, pouring nail polish remover into each one. He counted out seven of them. That was good; there were five of those things out there, which would give him two extra Molotov cocktails in case . . . well, just in case.

He dug into the pile of rags and found a T-shirt, which he tore into strips, dipping one end of each into the bottles. He shoved the corks into the bottle necks, leaving enough of each strip to serve as a fuse.

"Ms. Harper, I think it would be best if you and Jill got away from here—maybe went upstairs? This stuff is deadly, and I don't want you two breathing in the fumes. Take the shotgun . . . you know, just in case."

"No problem, Detective. Jilly, come on." Ms. Harper grabbed the shotgun and led Jilly toward the stairs. At the first step, Jilly turned back to Morris.

"Detective Morris?"

"Yes, hon?"

"Will you kill them? All of them? My family . . ." Tears formed in her eyes. "Please kill the monsters that took my family."

Morris felt a twinge in his chest. "Sweetheart, I'm going to do my level best. Now you go on and get someplace safe, okay?"

The girl nodded, and she and Mrs. Harper climbed the stairs.

Once they were out of sight, Morris peered out the window again. The trees across the cul-de-sac were blowing back, away from the street. That meant the fumes would be blowing away from the house. He had to get moving before the wind direction changed.

As quietly as he could, he opened the storm pane of the window and eased up the screen. The snorting and snarling stopped, and the things on the porch froze for a moment. Morris had already touched the lighter flame to the rag of the first bottle, and he swiped and tossed it practically in one fluid move. It flew a little wide of the mark, skidding past one creature's leg and shattering on the porch. Immediately, that area of the porch burst into flame. The acrid smell of the polish remover burned his nose, but thankfully, the wind was carrying it away from the house. Still, he held up a sleeve to his face before slamming down the window pane.

He could hear the creatures screaming outside, skittering away from the flames, and quickly, he lit another. He unlocked the front door and pulled it open just enough to aim at a creature distracted by the fire. He hurled it with all the strength in his arm and it hit the creature head-on, shattering bright yellow-white fire all over the wailing monstrosity. He slammed the door closed.

Cheering came from upstairs, and it made Morris smile to imagine Ms. Harper and Jilly watching his progress.

Morris checked the window again and saw the creature on fire vigorously shaking its massive head. Its jaws gaped as it bellowed, loping around the porch. Morris repeated a silent mantra to himself that those things would remain too stupid to try to put the flames out with snow.

The burning one, at least, hadn't caught on; it dropped in a shuddering heap that even the others wouldn't try to devour. One of those others roared, swinging an overlarge paw at a corner of the dead thing that wasn't in flames, sending it sailing off the porch and into the snow. The flames sputtered, mostly going out, but a fringe of blue and orange still spilled across the exposed parts of the creature's body.

Before the creatures could swarm back toward the door, Morris lit two more and opened the door. The creature that had cleared the path immediately advanced on him, and when Morris tossed the next bottle, one of the large paws batted it away. The bottle sailed backward, shattering against the edge of one of the porch balusters and raining fire down on the creature behind. That one wailed and thrashed, flickering in and out of view. It brushed against another creature, which leaped away in pain.

The second bottle Morris tossed just as the creature leaped at him. The bottle collided with the thing's underbelly, bursting into flame, and the creature dropped out of the air. Both burning beasts flailed wildly, too panicked to put themselves out.

Morris coughed as the fumes reached him. He felt light-headed and slammed the door, stumbling over to the window. The wind was still with him, but the porch had caught fire in two places now. He didn't think it would spread over the ice and melted snow—fervently hoped, in fact, that it wouldn't—but if the wind shifted or one of those things caught fire and charged the house. . . .

He counted the bottles. There were three left. There were two of those things that weren't flaming clumps of melting scaly flesh. Morris looked out the window. The two creatures stalked toward the door, growling low before pawing at it and finally hurling their bodies at it. The door rattled against its hinges with every *thump, thump, thump*, and Morris flew to lock it.

Then he heard a crack as the wood on the outside splintered a little.

"No. Oh no, come on," Morris muttered to himself. He lit the next bottle and threw up the window. One of the creatures turned to Morris and when he threw the bottle, the creature backhanded it out of the air. It landed, unbroken, in a snow drift.

"Shit." Morris picked up another, lighting it, but the thing was on him, its large, taloned paw wrapped around his wrist. Instant pain shot up his arm and down into his hand; he was pretty sure the thing was crushing the bones of his wrist. It unhinged its heavy jaw to roar at him in a polar, rotted-meat rush of air, and Morris saw his chance. He dropped the bottle into the creature's maw. Startled, it let him go, gagging a little on the bottle in its throat. Then it swallowed the lump of flaming glass, and for a moment, the creature turned back to Morris and began to advance. Then it began to tremble badly. Morris coughed, breathing through the sleeve of his damaged wrist, and with his good hand, he slammed down the window just as the creature exploded from within, pelting the window glass with lightly burning chunks of blue-blooded monster flesh.

Morris sank to the floor, breathing hard. His nasal passages and lungs burned painfully, despite the care he'd taken not to inhale the flames. He was bleeding from the corner of one eye, though he couldn't remember how he'd gotten cut. And his wrist throbbed. He looked at it, and saw that a white, scaly substance lined the marks of the thing's finger. Panicked, he rubbed his wrist hard to try to flake it off, ignoring the pain screaming through his forearm.

A loud crack nearby made him flinch, and he turned in time to see the front door bow inward. Outside, the remaining creature bellowed. Morris rose shakily and grabbed the last bottle. He lit it, and clumsily opened the window. The creature galloped toward him. He threw the bottle, but the ache in his wrist threw off his aim. The bottle crashed against the steps, the fire crackling quickly along the length of the tread. The creature's leg stepped easily over the flames as it made its way to the window.

"Dammit!" Morris slammed down the window again. What was he going to do? He was out of Molotov cocktails, and that thing would be able to break down the door with one more blow. He was pretty sure its blood was deadly, and if it got to him . . .

He thought of little Jilly and Ms. Harper upstairs, and made a snap decision. He leaped for the door and threw it open. The creature, still by the window, looked startled. He ran out the door and leaped over the blazing steps into the snow, landing on his back near the last errant bottle. When he looked back, the thing was already just behind the curtain of flames, snarling. It leaped onto the balustrade not on fire and then into the snow across from Morris. His fingers closed around the neck of the bottle and he threw it high into the air above the creature. Then he drew his gun and as the bottle descended, he shot it, sparking the contents within. Fire came down full-force on the creature, and for good measure, Morris opened fire on it. Three shots and the thing fell over in flames, and Morris sank back into the snow. He couldn't move, and found he didn't really want to. The crackling of the fires and the cold both seemed faraway, as did the muffled voices somewhere above his head.

"Detective Morris? Detective?"

Ms. Harper's face swam into view over him, followed by Jilly's. Each of them had a rag from the pile they'd brought down tied over their mouth and nose.

"Detective, are you okay?"

"Did I get them all?"

"Yes, and if I may be so bold, in a very cinematic, Clint Eastwood sort of way." Ms. Harper offered him a hand and pulled him up and, with Jilly's help, got him to his car. The heat of the nearby flames had melted the snow around the tires. In Morris's state, he would have sworn the snow seemed to be shying away from it.

"Your house," he said weakly. "I'm so sorry, ma'am."

"Hush, now," Ms. Harper said. With his keys, she unlocked the passenger-side door and helped him into it. Jilly got in back and Ms. Harper made her way around to the front seat.

"Where to?" she asked, starting the car.

Morris blinked, pulling himself together. "County coroner's office, on Hyatt Street. I've been trying to get there all day."

When they reached Hyatt Street, Morris directed Ms. Harper toward the lot. The tan stucco building was imposing in its authority, with its modern angles, mirror-glass windows, ice-ridged aluminum railings, and official county seal on each of the doors. By the time they had parked and gotten out of the car, Morris felt much more himself. He shouldered into the wind, which had picked up again, spraying abrasive snow filled with tiny sharp ice particles in their faces and chests.

Morris was relieved that the county coroner's office was still up and running. His appointment with Cordwell aside, he supposed all the incoming bodies were keeping the coroner busy. Jackson, the guard, was another welcome sight. It was a sign of normalcy, of business as usual—or, at the very least, of order amid all the chaos.

Morris led them through the doors and to the guard station, where he showed his ID and signed and time-noted the guest book. The elevators were just beyond, and Morris paused before heading toward them. A morgue was no place for a little girl. He looked at her, then Ms. Harper, before finally turning to Jackson.

"Jackson, would you mind?"

Jackson looked confused, then caught Morris's nod in Jilly's and Ms. Harper's direction. "Who, me?"

"Yeah," Morris said. "If you would. The girl's been through a lot today, and she does not need to see anything down there. Ms. Harper is her guardian. If you could keep them company while I talk to Cordwell . . ."

Jackson sized them up. He was a big, round man with an appealing sense of humor and a good heart. Dark-skinned and dark eyed, with a buzz cut of black hair and a goatee, he found great amusement in the detectives' nickname for him.

"You'd really be doing me a solid, Big Bar." It was a name he'd earned one Halloween when some detectives dropping by for a follow-up with Cordwell caught him wide-eyed and startled with one of the king-sized Hershey's dark chocolate bars in his mouth. Then he'd grinned at them around the chocolate, and his response had been something along the lines of "Just blew your minds, huh, detectives? A dark chocolate big bar eating a dark chocolate big bar."

Jackson gave him a sideways look and said, "Well, there are worse ways to spend the afternoon than in the company of two ladies." He gave Jilly a friendly smile and a wave, and she returned a shy little wave back.

Morris smiled, too. "Thanks, Jackson. I owe you one. Seriously."

"I take cash," Jackson called after him as Morris rushed to the elevator.

Morris pushed the down button and looked back at Ms. Harper. "Be back in a little bit. You need anything, Jackson here will take care of you."

Ms. Harper smiled and nodded. "We'll be fine. Go."

The elevator doors opened, and he slipped inside. As he pushed the button for B1, he sank against the elevator wall. In the last forty-eight hours or so, he hadn't had much time to think or feel, and he supposed that alone had kept him going. He hadn't thought about being tired or hungry or cold and so he hadn't really been aware of feeling those things. He'd just focused on fixing those feelings in others—Dan Murphy, Kathy, Jilly, and Ms. Harper.

Scared, though . . . he'd had plenty of time to be outright terrified, and although he didn't think it was throwing him too off his game, it was catching up to him. He absently rubbed at his wrist, which had swollen to an ugly, waxy red (he figured Cordwell could take a look at it and maybe bandage it or something), and thought about those creatures out there in the snow.

What he couldn't wrap his brain around was that the Hand of the Black Stars cult honestly believed they were somehow invulnerable. Okay, maybe something in the black magic they were working was actually keeping those creatures and even the Blue People, those inhuman coordinators of it all, from attacking the cultists themselves. But that Majoram woman had told him that all the horrors they'd faced, horrors which he'd bet good money had wiped out a significant portion of Colby's population in just a couple of days, were the small potatoes of the whole fiasco. They were only paving the way. So what would their masters be like? What would these greater gods do to Colby—hell, to the whole planet?

Morris wasn't a churchgoer, but he did think of himself as a spiritual, if not quite religious, person. He believed God (or whatever that force of life and creation was really called) was the ultimate force of good, and that in the system of checks and balances that kept the universe spinning and expanding, there was probably an equal but opposite force of evil. He was willing to concede that there were probably many levels of such things; people called them lesser gods, angels, demons, saints, spirits. . . . The names were countless, but the idea was the same the world over, across languages and races and religions, over time. The forces that drove the universe were very real things, pushing and pulling, fighting over humans' heads and under their noses.

But these Greater Gods were not just beings from a faraway part of the edge of this universe or entities from parallel planes, which were terrifying enough to imagine leaking into Colby. These were apparently the stuff of other worlds' nightmares, creatures from the outer edges of an alien dimension. The possibility scared him that they were devoid of any concept of compassion or respect for life, that their drives, their thoughts and feelings, were so alien to human ways of thinking as to be incomprehensible. Which meant that horrors he couldn't even begin to imagine were not only possible, but probable. And they, the human race in general and Morris and the task force in particular, seemed woefully unequipped. It made Morris wonder if the human race really was on its own. After all, where was the God of his altar boy days? Where was the God of Sunday school? Where was the God he had been taught as a boy would always be there to protect and deliver? He didn't appear to want anything to do with Colby, Connecticut, just then.

The elevator doors opened with a ding that shook him free of his thoughts. The physical weight of them, though, settled as a cold ball of nausea in the pit of his stomach and the beginnings of an ache in his head.

He walked down the long tiled hall toward the morgue, wondering for the fourth or fifth time that day who could be behind the perpetration of such monstrosity. What people could honestly believe they could control the whims of gods, once those gods got what they wanted—free passage to a new universe to devour?

The door at the end of the hall was the faded sea-foam green of most of Colby's official doors, both municipal and educational. When he knocked, Cordwell greeted him warmly, though avoided a handshake by holding up rubber-gloved hands.

Morris often eschewed visits to the morgue whenever he could. The smell of the place on the best of days was vaguely meaty overlaid with abrasive cleaners. The invasive glare from the bright round UFO lights above the stainless steel gurneys gave everything a harsh, exaggeratedly ugly cast. It was no doubt an efficient space, just one that seemed stripped of emotion and humanity. Cordwell's Cave, as the eponymous coroner called it, was a sterile room tiled in the same pale ecru of the hallway floor outside and fitted with wide white counters along two sides of the room. Above and below the counters were rows of somewhat kitchen-like cabinets in which Morris assumed supplies were kept. Trays of tools were laid out along one of the counters in between the gulfs of stainless-steel sinks, while a flat-screen monitor, a laptop, and a small printer sat on the other. There were also vents in the walls above the counters, and near one of the gurneys, on the side with the sinks, was a large scale like the kind for weighing produce, only bigger. What struck Morris as perhaps the most incongruous of all the things in the room was a stainless-steel shelf on the computer side with an assortment of mugs: #1 CORONER, I ♥ CONNECTICUT, CORONERS—A CUT ABOVE THE REST, etc. He'd had no idea that the coffee mug industry was so keyed in to the java needs of coroners. It was an idea he found both amusing and a little disturbing.

There was a filing cabinet by some cardboard boxes in the back wall's right corner and some sizable bins, each differently primary-colored and labeled as to their waste contents, in the left. Between them stood another tidy foam-green door, which Morris knew led to the re-frigerated room where bodies were literally shelved in the walls. He liked that room even less; it lacked basic human dignity, despite the ne-cessity of its existence.

Two bodies from the refrigerated room were laid out on the gur-neys. Both were naked, sliced into pretty badly, and pale gray. The open eyes of the man nearest him were clouded over in white, the blue lips slightly parted. The older man on the table next to him was little more than a head and a ravaged lump of torso. Morris swal-lowed the knot of nausea in his throat.

"So, ah, what's the word on our cult vics? Jack sent me here to pick up any info you—"

"Ahh, there's not much," Cordwell replied, the warmth in his voice cooling. He peeled off his gloves and then went to the sink to wash his hands. "Let's see. . . . No hairs and no fibers, human, ani-mal, or otherwise. No fingerprints, of course, on the bodies, and from what I could find, none on the jars, either. Victims' stomach contents vary—some ate approximately ten to twenty minutes before, some as much as two hours or more. Preliminary examination shows no signs of sexual assault on any of the victims. No drugs as far as I can tell, either, although we'll have to wait for the tox screen to confirm, and with communication to the outside world being what it is . . ." He shrugged.

Turning off the water, he grabbed some paper towels from a roll near the faucet, and as he dried his hands, he said, "Now, there are numerous contusions on most of the bodies. If I had to guess, I'd say they were overpowered and possibly restrained manually by multiple people. No unique finger marks or human bite marks, though—nothing like that." Cordwell wadded up the paper towel and pitched it into the big blue bin marked TRASH (NON-ORGANIC).

"You weren't kidding. That isn't much to go on. Do you have anything I *can* use?"

"Well, those jars . . . standard mason jars you could get at any craft store. Filled with commercial-grade formaldehyde, not hard to get. The items in the jars—the eyes, tongues, and all that . . . we identified most of those as belonging to the victims."

"Most?" Morris leaned against a gurney, but jerked and straightened as it wheeled away from him.

Cordwell looked as if he was trying to stifle a smile. "Yes. There were three fingers unaccounted for—three different people. All left ring fingers, removed from living people. Not our vics', because they have all their fingers and toes, just like the day they were born. Heh. And Brenner ran the prints on those loose fingers through AFIS but got no hits. So, I've got no idea if they belong to bodies you haven't found yet, or the cultists themselves."

"Why would they belong to the cultists?" Morris frowned.

"Well, to reap great rewards, one must be willing to make great sacrifices—isn't that an occult notion? What connects a person more strongly to one's given goal than to give a piece of himself, eh?"

Morris grimaced. "I hadn't thought of that."

"Not that those fingers are going to do you any good, without the hands they came from. These cultists you've got are ghosts."

"Yeah, you're not the first person to say that," Morris said flatly. "Anything else?"

"Hmm . . . well, the minority of lacerations, the ones we can attribute to human perpetrators, were caused by a three-inch blade. My guess would be a dagger. Flint fragments found in the wound."

"Flint?"

"Yeah. Ceremonial stone dagger, maybe."

Morris shrugged. "Probably. Seems a reasonable assumption. What about the animal attacks?"

"Animal attacks . . . yes, well, those are a little harder to identify. I've determined there are both teeth and claw marks present on two-thirds of the bodies. Teeth appear to be serrated on the inner edge, slope to a point, and run approximately an inch to an inch and a half long. I found traces of unidentified animal saliva with digestive enzymes in those wounds. The claws appear to be, oh, about three to four inches long, serrated on both sides—no flint, obviously, but tips appear to have a corrosive substance on them, something that continues eating into the flesh, after the initial wound is made."

"Jesus," Morris said.

"Like I said, they're unlike any animal-inflicted wounds I've ever seen. I'd hate to see the animal that made them."

"My guess would be the things out there made them—those things in the snow."

Cordwell gave him a baffled look. "I guess that's possible. I haven't seen them, so I couldn't tell you, although Mr. Brenner certainly offers some fascinating reports."

Morris shook his head. "Been spending a lot of time down here, huh?"

"Pretty much every waking minute since that first John Doe. What the hell, it keeps me out of trouble, right?" He winked at Morris.

"Yeah, I guess it does," Morris agreed. He found himself put off by the coroner's nonchalance about everything. He figured detachment came with the job, but Cordwell described the details of the murders with what ranged from amiable indifference to casual admiration. "Speaking of Brenner, where is he?"

Cordwell looked away. "Not sure, to be honest. Never showed up for work today, which is rather irritating, considering the amount of work I have to do here all alone. Perhaps he couldn't get his car through the snow. As they say in the cold places, *Na cnàmhach fuar ar na cnámha na naimhde an laige iontu.*" He smiled.

"I'm afraid I'm not familiar with that phrase," Morris said, smiling flatly.

Cordwell's smile grew. "It's Irish Gaelic. It means, 'The lives of others should never be of such preoccupation that it keeps you from living yours.' Roughly translated, I mean."

Morris said, "Ah. I don't know Gaelic, but I like that." It was true; he didn't know Gaelic. However, someone had read him that very phrase and others in the same language recently, someone who had told him a great deal about the kind of occultists who used it. And Morris knew Cordwell had lied. That phrase meant something very different.

Morris changed the subject. "Okay, well what about those symbols carved into all the bodies?"

"Let me show you." Cordwell led him over to the intact body. He picked up a scalpel from one of the counters and pointed out the symbol on the front of the man's left shoulder. "Okay, the invocation symbol carved into the first body, the John Doe—"

"Chris Oxer," Morris said.

"Right, the poor, unfortunate Mr. Oxer," Cordwell continued. "With him, the wound was clearly made by man, crudely, with the flint knife. It was painstakingly done, don't get me wrong, and pretty smoothly done, considering the man was alive during the entire carving of it into his skin. But still, it was done by hand. But these"—he pointed to the corpse's shoulder—"from every body retrieved at the three crime scenes last night, these were . . . branded, for lack of a better word. No variations in pressure or depth. But not branded with heat. It's actually a pretty remarkable thing; they were branded with a cold so intense that it actually caused the tissue to become necrotic and then to flake away—but with remarkable precision. I have absolutely no guesses for you regarding the tool used to make the symbols, though."

"Ah," Morris answered.

"So that's about it then. I'll call you or Jack when I have more. Hey, you be careful driving out there. Some weather, huh? Snow so late in the year?"

Cordwell hadn't really given him much to go on—not voluntarily, anyway. Morris supposed he could look at places that sold ceremonial daggers, maybe check the local stores for sales of formaldehyde or mason jars . . . that is, if any of the stores were open at this point. He didn't figure those leads would yield much. But Morris was certain Cordwell was hiding something, and that was the real thing to follow up on.

To the coroner, he said, "Oh, it's crazy, all right. You must, uh, have your hands full with more than the murders, huh?"

"Well, these killings are first priority, but yes," Cordwell replied, somewhat less jovially. But his eyes sparkled when he added, "And of course, there are all these hypothermia deaths. It's fascinating, how the body undergoes such incredible changes when it freezes to death. I have to admit, I admire snow as a force of nature."

"You sound like a winter person if ever I met one."

"Oh, I am," Cordwell said, turning back to the body.

"You ski, do you?" Morris asked, aware of how stupid the words sounded even as he was saying them. "I mean, everyone I know who loves the snow is into winter sports, skiing and snowboarding and whatnot."

"No, not really. Just love the snow. I always thought it was so beautiful. That first snowfall of the season. All glittery, you know? It reminds me of diamonds and stars, hard and cold and pure, just . . . clean. Like a new soul. Its pristine white, its unbroken smoothness. Then people come along with their cars and dirt and traffic and slush it up, like . . . like mashed potatoes, but dirty. And it loses that perfect whiteness, that purity. It becomes something ugly, because we touched it. Just like this planet. And like children. Children are pure. Even the devil loves children." He laughed in a way that made Morris uncomfortable. More to himself than out loud, he continued, "But it's still a hell of a force of nature—brutal. Oh, sheets of it are hard enough to hurt, and ice edges sharp enough to cut, and the cold—that's enough to burn right into the skin. That's where the metaphorical comparison to children diverges. Because the snow, the ice and cold—it has power. Maybe we change it by touching it, but it changes us by touching us, too. In a way, it gives us a gift. It tries to preserve us, stripping out our softness and warmth because those things make us weak and rotting. The cold, it keeps us as we were in life, in childhood, a snapshot of our most tangible assets. It makes the water in us freeze . . . and there we are: cool and beautiful and pure."

"I . . . suppose," Morris said. The tone of the conversation, particularly given what he'd seen the last few days, had taken an uncomfortably weird turn.

"You know," Cordwell said, turning to him, "most of our universe is cold. Do you know what the percentage of outer space is that is not near a star? How much of it is just cold, empty space? Well, empty to us, maybe, but who knows? Who knows? There's something to be said, I think, about how the most powerful, impossibly large, and wonderfully majestic locations in our existence are pure cold." Lost in the reverie of his own words, Cordwell didn't notice the look Morris gave him behind his back.

"I hadn't really thought about it." Morris frowned.

"Oh, I think about it. I think about it a lot." Cordwell smiled, turning back to the detective. "But, I'm keeping you. Please, give my best to Kathy and Reece, and tell Jack I'm sorry there isn't much to go on from the preliminaries, but I'll get him the final reports as soon as I can. I know you all are under a lot of pressure to find these people."

"We are. Thanks, Dr. Cordwell." Morris turned to go.

"You will never find them," Cordwell's voice came from behind him.

Morris paused. "Excuse me?" He turned to see Cordwell staring at him with a small, unpleasantly smug smile on his face.

"I said, 'I hope you find them,' Detective Morris."

"Uh, thanks," Morris replied. He was suddenly very eager to get out of there, away from Cordwell and his talk of snow and space and his nonchalance with the mutilated dead.

Before he had even made it to the elevator, he'd written most of the text to Jack, Teagan, and Kathy. He hit send, praying it would go through, then pressed the elevator button and waited. As he did so, he absently touched the handle of his gun, wishing that some other member of the team was with him. He'd texted a hunch, but it was a strong one—so strong, in fact, that it had actually made Morris feel a little sick.

Cordwell's preoccupation with the snow and its ability to kill was unnerving, to say the least; it wasn't just idle philosophy, but a kind of gloating. But that was not what set off the alarm bells in Morris's head.

He suspected that Cordwell had let more slip than usual because he thought Morris was either too stupid or too green to catch on, too uninitiated. But Morris had eaten, slept, and breathed this case for two days, and while he found aspects of it almost too terrible to think about, a lot of little things had stuck with him. And those things, more than anything, had formed the basis of the hunch, had nudged it in the right direction.

For one thing, he knew he'd heard Cordwell right the first time, about finding the cultists. And the more he thought about it, the more he thought he'd heard something else in Cordwell's voice, something hostile, even hateful. What had Jack said that morning in his office, during his debriefing about the crime scene from the night before? Something about how the cultists didn't much care who knew what now, because they believed they were so close to their goal? It was like Cordwell had given up the pretense of caring what Morris and the others thought—about him, the case, everything.

What really bothered him, though, was the phrase in Gaelic. It didn't mean anything as live-and-let-live as Cordwell had made it out to be. Professor Majoram had translated it for him from an old, obscure book as an actual part of the summoning of the Blue People. He remembered, because he'd written it down phonetically in case it might be important later. It meant, "The cold chews on the bones of the enemies of the unfaithful." And was a reference to the cold between the stars, like Cordwell mentioned. It was part of their belief system that the space between the stars was cold but not empty. Not empty. Because that's where those Old God things—

A sunburst of pain in his head made him stagger forward just as the elevator doors opened. He slapped a hand clumsily on the open door frame but was yanked backward into the hall. His vision swam, and for just a moment before everything went black, he saw Cordwell standing in his doorway, behind three figures in blue-white robes.

The text from Morris came through to Jack's cell with a little ding as he was driving back from Katie's house. When Jack read it, his heart sank.

Cordwell involved in cult. May know I know. Please advise.

Cordwell? Fucking Terrence Cordwell, a cultist? It made him sick to think that the very man who had examined and handled the bodies of the deceased—Oxer, Casper, poor little Gracie Anderson—was the same man who had had a hand in cutting and gouging and slicing them, and who had participated in unleashing this terrible never-ending winter and its horrors out there in the drifts. A sick welt of betrayal swelled inside him, enmeshed with anger.

It made sense. Cordwell would know exactly how much information to keep from him and his task force to keep them a step behind the HBS. He could lie about forensic evidence, could hide or destroy it if any were present. He could report back to the cult about who was involved in the case and how far the task force had gotten in the investigation. He could—

A terrible realization occurred to him, and that sick feeling intensified all through him. The handwriting on the note—he had recognized it, but hadn't been able to place it. He knew it now, though. He remembered seeing it in reports, mostly in the signature at the bottom.

Cordwell had written the note. Which meant Cordwell either had his family, or knew who did.

"I'm going to kill him," Jack said to himself, and pressed harder on the gas.

The faces in the snow raced alongside his car, twisted into savage snarls and distorted screams.

"I'm going to kill him," he repeated, as much to those faces as himself.

The wind howled at him in reply.

Chapter Ten

"Well, no word from Morris or Jack yet," Teagan said, returning from the kitchen with two fresh glasses of vodka. "Just checked my phone." It was possible the other detectives were out of range. It was equally possible, he supposed, that whatever forces were at work in Colby were deliberately blocking messages, particularly calls for help. It was an idea he didn't especially want to dwell on. He set Kathy's glass on the desk and moved to the couch, sipping his own. Like Kathy, he was on his third. He was starting to feel the soft, warm haze of a mild buzz. That they were technically still on duty hardly seemed relevant anymore. Both of them functioned just fine on the stuff. In fact, Teagan always thought he worked better that way, with distractions and old ghosts dampened down and his spirits lifted up. It came back to the job, both here and across the pond. It wasn't just the brutality, the blood, the butchery of it. It wasn't the body parts and the body fluids. It was the crying of the family members, the sad, lost look of orphaned kids. It was knowing secrets that kept a man and the ghosts of his sins up at night. It was sometimes not knowing and not caring where exactly the line between cop and criminal really lay. And it was the waiting, the not knowing, like his current position with Jack and Morris.

"That doesn't surprise me, coming from Jack, but Morris? He's usually like clockwork. Did you try calling either of them?"

"Aye. Both are going straight to voicemail."

Kathy frowned, then turned back to the computer. She took a gulp of vodka and said, "Well, the sooner we can reverse the summoning spell, the sooner we can confirm they're okay." Her voice dropped to an excited almost-whisper. "I found it, Reece. I found the spell."

"Oh, damn. Okay, so what do we have to do?"

"I'll show you." She got out of the chair, a little unsteadily, and motioned for Teagan to sit.

Teagan stared at the screen. The file name for the PDF he was looking at was simple enough—*Book9Worlds*—but the contents laid out in lines of black print made no sense to him whatsoever. It looked like a language, given the frequency of certain characters and breaks in the lines, but the characters themselves were odd arabesque curves and squiggles, occasionally speared with a straight line, dotted, or swept with a tilde. Each character had a certain beveled, three-dimensional quality that Teagan couldn't help feeling gave them a kind of sinister import, a life and power of their own separate from their meaning.

"What is this? The secret code?"

"No," Kathy said, and her voice trembled with barely controlled excitement. "This particular language isn't coded, because it is, itself, almost impossible to use. The percentage of people who even recognize this as a language is so small that for all intents and purposes, it's a legend and nothing more. Even most occult experts don't know about it. This is the original language of the spell the cultists used to open the door—and the same language of the spell that we can use to close it."

He looked at her. Her excitement shone in her eyes.

"Anyway," she continued, "I didn't know what it was at first, either. I suspected, but I didn't know for sure. So I ran it through the usual decoding software I mentioned, and it gave me nothing. Knowing what I know now, I can see why. We're a small, watchful group, but we can't vet everybody in as timely a fashion as we would like, and the possibility for absolute chaos should translations fall into the wrong hands is too great. So my guess is that the Decoders, the creators of the software, whoever they are out there, deliberately let the means of translating this language fall into obscurity."

"Why would they do that? What's so different about this language?"

She grinned at him. "Well, because supposedly, Reece, this here is the language of creation and destruction itself, the language that echoes the sound of the Convergence, the substance between dimensions and the space between the stars."

"Jaysus Christ," he said. "You're kidding."

"I'm not. So I ran it through an NSA-pirated translator program I obtained through the usual means—"

"Of course." Teagan winked at her.

"Of course," she repeated with a smile. "And I have to say, I'm surprised the NSA didn't include an anti-pirating failsafe for this particular language. I mean, would you put it past the American government—or the small group of corporations and individuals who run it—to have discovered the language of creation and not do everything in their power to guard the translation of it?"

"I wouldn't put anything past your government, love. Or any government, at that."

"Me neither. Anyway, I guess it's a moot point, because the NSA program returned all kinds of errors, giving me words from various Native American tribes, Aramaic, Latin, Sumerian, Egyptian. So then I got the two programs to run it together—a little trick of the trade—and all of a sudden, it just kind of came together. The programs started translating it all into one language—the only language, aside from the original language of the stars, so to speak, that the human tongue can evoke the same power with. It's the only language, evidently, that the portal-closing spells can be performed in. Want to take a guess what language that is?"

"Astound me, love."

"It's Gaelic. Irish Gaelic, to be specific. Please tell me you know it."

Teagan whistled. Finally, a language he understood, and a part of this whole process that he felt he could contribute to. "You're serious? Gaelic."

She nodded. Her expression was hopeful, excited. "We've nailed this, Reece, but it comes down to one thing—you pronouncing and understanding Gaelic. It has to be exact, and not parroted. You have to truly understand what you're saying and how to say it."

"Well, then consider it nailed. I grew up with the language. Me grandparents made sure I could speak it as fluently as English."

She smiled, the warmth of her relief almost palpable. It made him happy to please her.

"Great! Okay, we'll have to make some preparations. . . . It'll take a little time, but . . ." She was already pacing with her cell phone, ostensibly texting the good news to Jack and Morris. "But then we can close the door and end this."

"Close it forever?"

Kathy gave him a pained quarter-smile. "Well, probably not...
Nothing's forever, is it?"

Reece looked into her eyes and in that moment, when they were
held by each other's gaze, he saw that she both believed that and
hated that she believed it.

"Some few things are," he said, and he meant it.

"Maybe that's true," she said softly, then turned back to the computer. She minimized the document she'd shown him and waiting in
its place was another document, this time in Gaelic:

Coimeádaí na geataí, Máistir na Doirse agus Eochracha
Iarraimid ort a dhúnadh ar a bhfuil d'oscail
Sliocht a barra agus faoi ghlas suas ar an mbealach rúnda...

Teagan understood it, all right, if not the references made. Roughly
translated, it meant:

Keeper of gates, Master of Doors and Keys
We implore you to close what has been opened
To bar passage and lock up the secret way....

"First, we should sleep. We have to wait for the day–experiences,
thoughts, alcohol, food, everything—to work its way out of our systems. You know, clear minds and bodies and all that. Then there are
a few things we'll need to gather, a few things to set up.... I'll set
the alarm for, say"—she checked the clock in the bottom corner of
her computer—"eleven p.m.? That'll give us six hours. Then we can
get to work."

"Sounds good to me. I'm beat."

"Okay. I'm going to use the bathroom. Be right back." She padded
off with a little wobble toward the bathroom. Teagan made his way to
the bedroom but hesitated by the bed, hovering over his coat. Should
he leave? Drive back home for those six hours and meet up with her
again? He looked out her bedroom window. He'd been drinking, too,
and the snow had blown up in a thick drift against the doors of his
car. He turned his gaze to her front door, thinking about the break-in,
thinking about little Gracie carved up and bagged on a picnic table in
a nightmare snowfall of early June. Maybe Kathy wasn't afraid and
maybe she didn't need him there, but the kind of man he wanted her

to see, the kind of man he wanted to be, wouldn't leave her alone in that apartment on a night like that.

"Stay," she said from behind him as if in answer to his thoughts. He turned and let out a low whistle of appreciation. She had stripped down to a white tank top and panties and made her way across the room to sit next to his coat on the bed. Her eyes shone, and he could tell by her expression that she knew he wanted her. She smelled lightly like flowers and summer breezes and vodka. She was so beautiful.

He smiled, just taking her in for a moment, then sat down beside her. "Kathy, I—"

"In fact, stay here, in bed. With me. Sex, sleep, the whole deal." Her voice was soft with booze and a tenuous, vulnerable honesty that made Teagan's love for her well up inside him. It also made him noticeably hard, and he shifted uncomfortably next to her on the bed.

"There is nothing I would rather do more, love," he said huskily, touching her cheek, "than spend the next six hours making love to you. Believe that. But . . . you're a bit in the numbs, love, and you don't need some horny, lovesick Brit, also scuttered himself, giving you any reason not to trust him. I'd like your respect, if nothing else."

"Lovesick?" It was almost a whisper.

"Aye," he replied, just as softly. "Good night, Katherine. I'll lock up the flat." He kissed the top of her head before getting up, then turned out the light on her night table, which left her in the soft glow of moonlight from the window. She snuggled under the covers, her eyelids already closing. A small, uncharacteristically content smile hung on her lips.

At the door to her bedroom, he paused, looking back at her. She was watching him sleepily, that smile still there.

He smiled back. "I'll take you up on that acid death swill you try to pass off as coffee later tonight, though, if you're keen. I'll see you at eleven, will I?"

"I'll see you then," she murmured.

Teagan turned to go when he heard his name. He looked back, and when he met her gaze, there was a surprisingly serious and sober look in her eyes, as if in that moment, her will had sublimated the vodka inside her. She might have been drunk, but a part of her was all there, meaning everything she'd said, remembering it all, taking in everything between them.

"Thank you."

He winked at her. "Any time, love. Any time."

Teagan made his way to the front door, which he promptly locked, before looking back at the bedroom. She was in there, beyond the small, dark door. So much of his body wanted to be back in that room with her, lying next to her in the cool darkness. Any other bird in his past he would have shagged without thinking too heavily about it, but none of them had ever come close to stirring him like Kathy. The thing was, it wasn't just the sex with her that he wanted in that bedroom, even though that was a part of it. That was a big part of it, the ache in his crotch reminded him. It was also the intimacy with her, a kindred soul. *Lovesick? Oh fuck yes, Kathy m'girl.* That had been the truest thing he'd said to anyone in a long time; he loved her.

He really loved her.

There were so many inexplicably cruel, dirty, ugly things about the world, and a part of his mind argued that he had nothing to feel bad about in enjoying beauty and solace when it was offered to him.

What happened between them was the right thing, all the right words, but the wrong time. He wasn't worried about awkwardness or regret, and didn't believe this one chance to be close to her would be the only one. They had been honest with each other with no avoidance and no walls, and neither of them were the types to deny the significance of that. Kathy had her demons, but dishonesty, to herself or anyone else, was not a part of her survival mode. And, Teagan flattered himself to think, neither was it a part of his.

He supposed he'd left that bedroom because it meant something to him that she continue to think him a decent, honorable man, a man who took his moments with her seriously. There weren't many women he'd known, his own mum included, who held the simple, frank, unconditional belief that Teagan was a good man, not the way Kathy did. It was one of the reasons he loved her, and it was one of those things he wasn't willing to risk damaging or losing altogether. He needed that from her as much as he wanted sex with her. Kathy didn't trust people in general, and men in particular. Whatever had happened to her in the past, it had hollowed out a part of her that had never quite grown back. Until he knew what that missing part was, he didn't want to take the chance of ripping it open further. He didn't think he could abide her disappointment in him.

When he checked in on her, she was asleep, her hair streaming across the pillow, her fists clenched as she dreamed. She mumbled something about finger bones and turned over, fists still clenched. He went back out into the den, made sure he'd relocked the front door, tucked his gun under one of the couch's throw pillows, picked up a blanket from a folded pile in a basket by an armchair, and lay down on the couch. Teagan wanted to get to sleep before his resolve crumbled altogether. And for the first time in a long time, he fell peacefully asleep. His dreams, though, took a decidedly sharp downturn pretty quickly after.

It started with the snow.

In the dream, Teagan was standing in the center of a familiar pub in Cork. He was looking up at the raftered ceiling, watching with vague interest as snowflakes materialized and fell on him from above. He was aware that the well-worn, wooden bar, well-loved by its patrons, had a row of full shot glasses along its length, but the stools in front of each were empty. Likewise, the booths that lined the other walls of the pub were unoccupied as well. The door blowing open drew his attention to it. The dark opening let in cold air, but no one stood in the doorway. When the door closed, the howl of the wind sounded as if it were trapped inside with him.

As dream-knowledge goes, Teagan knew something had come through the door, but he couldn't see it. It was the throat that voiced the banshee wail of the wind; its fingers drew almost painfully cold lines across the backs of his shoulders and his neck, setting his hairs on end and making him shiver. He looked to the bar and noticed with horror that the shot glasses, in which he had presumed the dark liquid was whiskey, now contained a much darker, thicker substance.

The light from the electric wall sconces dimmed and the temperature dropped noticeably. The light above the bar, though, grew brighter.

Suddenly, a shot glass flew off the bar and shattered against the wall above the booth behind him. He flinched, turning to see the dark thick liquid splattered in a deep crimson starburst over an old-fashioned map of the county. There were little hard-looking white bits sprinkled in with the red, but Teagan had no desire to get close enough to identify them.

Immediately another shot glass flew off the bar, smashing into the divider between two booths. A spray of glass and liquid (*blood, oh Lord in Heaven, it's blood*) pelted his shirt. That close, a reek reminiscent of something gone bad in the frozen foods aisle at the grocer's flooded his nose and throat and turned his stomach.

Three more glasses sailed off the bar in quick succession. He flinched again as one grazed his ear and another crashed near his foot. The splashes of blood were everywhere.

He chanced looking up at the bar to see the silvery flicker of an inhuman outline. It was making its way down the bar, kicking at the remaining shot glasses. One broke against the bar itself and the back splash of blood painted a more definitive form.

Teagan couldn't move. He looked down and saw that a sheet of ice on the pub floor had formed jagged twists up his legs that held him in place. He struggled to free himself, but the ice was too thick. The cold of it seeped unpleasantly through his pants and onto his skin.

The thing on the counter flickered and materialized. Teagan could only stare at it, an appalled, sick feeling feeding into the limbs of his body along with the cold. The thing had many faces melded together, frozen in their expressions of shock and horror, or in the distorted shrieking of some last few terrified moments. In each of these faces, the eyes moved independently, seeking him out, following his limited movements.

Beneath the bulk of varied countenances was a stumpy trunk, but the two pairs of legs beneath rippled with muscle beneath colorless, scaly skin. The legs ended in wide, flat feet whose shiny black claws arced out and up. Above the hip sockets of those legs were two human-looking arms and hands, though the skin held the pallor of a corpse. These arms were raised so that the palms were facing up and forward, and embedded in the center of each was a thin-lipped mouth. The mouths opened, and a strong winter wind howled around him.

Teagan crouched slowly, as well as he was able, to try to chip at the ice, but dream-gravity prevented him. The thing hopped off the bar and began creeping toward him. He began to struggle in earnest, but the cold from the ice bands around his legs had reached his thighs. Below his waist, everything felt fragile, pins-and-needles sensitive. He thought he probably wouldn't have been able to run even if his legs were free.

Still, he kept struggling, and when the thing lunged at his face, he screamed.

Teagan jerked awake on Kathy's couch. It took a few seconds to bring the waking world into focus, but as he became more aware of his surroundings, a bad feeling knocked painfully around his head.

There was frost on the coffee table in front of him. He ran a finger along it, collecting the tiny ice crystals. He looked around, his breath puffing ahead of him in little white clouds. The couch had a layer of frost as well, and his blanket had grown stiff with infused ice. He shoved it aside and sat up. All around Kathy's apartment, the winter outside had found its way in. Icicles hung from the shades of her lamps and the blades of the ceiling fan above him. The windows were opaque with cataracts of ice. The laptop on the desk lay encased in ice. The hardwood floors were glittering sheets of black ice.

Teagan slipped on his shoes, ran a hand through his hair, and stood up. The hallway was slippery, but he managed to get to Kathy's door without falling on his ass. When he tried turning the knob, though, it wouldn't budge. He leaned down and peered through the keyhole, but could see nothing. From the tinkling of ice when he jiggled the handle, he figured the ice had frozen it shut.

Not wanting to alarm Kathy before he needed to, he slipped and slid back down the hallway to the kitchen. He was pretty sure Kathy had a stove pilot lighter in one of the drawers, and he thought he might be able to use it to melt some of the ice. In the kitchen, the ice covered most of the counters and hung stiffly from the cabinets in long-toothed icicles. Most of the drawers were frozen shut, but he managed, between pours of vodka and some chipping away with a pocket knife, to unstick the drawer he thought contained the lighter. He forced it open and rifled through the kitchen utensils until he found what he needed, then went back to Kathy's door. The ice in the lock had formed a tiny cascade down the front of the door. Teagan clicked on the lighter and held it cautiously to the lock for a few seconds, then tried picking away at the ice with his pocket knife. He repeated the process, lighter then knife, a few times before trying the knob again. On the third attempt, the doorknob moved in his hand, and with a small victory sound, he opened the door.

Inside her bedroom, it was snowing.

He was relieved to find Kathy in her bed, sleeping peacefully; as he'd worked the lock, he'd been gnawed at by the idea, possibly left over from his nightmare, that she would somehow be gone, or that, if present, she'd be hurt or worse. She appeared to be okay, although her bed had grown a sizable crust of ice around it that reached up with icy tendrils to grip her blanket. She stirred, seemingly aware someone else was in the room and, in the next moment, was awake and aware and trying to sit up. The blanket held her down.

"Reece?" She looked confused. "What the hell is going on?"

"It's like this all over your flat, love. Come, let me get you out of there." He skated to the side of her bed and the two of them worked at pulling the fibers of the blanket free of the ice. Teagan used the knife to cut away strips of cloth, and they had nearly gotten her free when they heard a growl from the den.

Both paused and held their breaths a moment.

"What the hell was that?" Kathy whispered.

"I don't know," he whispered back. He helped her out of bed and, glancing down at her underwear, handed her the pocket knife. She nodded her thanks and took little leaps over the accumulated snow on the floor to get to her closet. Her feet were bare, and she hopped painfully from one foot to the other as she chipped away at the ice that sealed her closet door shut. He followed her over there, picking at the chunks of ice with his fingers. They were cold enough to stick to his skin, but with some effort, the two of them finally managed to pry the door open.

As she slipped on a pair of jeans and winter boots from the closet, Teagan drew his gun and went to stand guard by the bedroom door. He peered out into the hallway, listening. In the room beyond, he heard something bang into the coffee table, grunt, and move across the floorboards toward the hall kitchen.

She joined him by the door, her own gun drawn, and together, they crept to the end of the hall and peered around the corner.

In the den, a thing that looked like a cross between an albino monkey and an anglerfish was limping around the coffee table. It flickered like an old 8mm bit of film, sometimes there and sometimes only partially there. Teagan was no expert, but from the way the thing was moving and the spiky, rough-looking blue patches along the left side of its head and body, he assumed the thing was injured. How it had gotten into Kathy's apartment, Teagan hadn't a clue. But there it was, a caged and injured animal, in pain and probably very pissed off.

Which made it very dangerous.

Without a sound, he aimed at the thing's head, but felt Kathy's hand on his arm. She shook her head and motioned at the kitchen lighter he'd shoved in his back pocket, the one he'd used to melt the ice in the lock on her bedroom door. Then she mouthed out, *Paint thinner under the sink in the kitchen. Accelerant.*

He nodded that he understood. Getting to the kitchen without the thing seeing them, however, would be tricky. From the right angle, the thing would have a clear view of the kitchen entrance. He watched the thing in the den as it swung its massive head, bellowed in irritation, and turned to limp back toward Kathy's desk. Teagan signaled to Kathy and crouched down, sneaking as quickly and quietly as he could toward the kitchen. Kathy followed behind him.

In the room beyond, the thing bellowed again. Teagan kept moving, hoping the thing hadn't spotted them.

When they reached the kitchen sink, Kathy eased open the door of the cabinet beneath. Bottles of cleaning supplies and a small toolbox crowded beneath the sink pipes. Her hand closed around a flat, metallic, rectangular container and she eased it away from the others. It knocked against the lip of the cabinet with a small thump and the two froze, listening.

For several seconds, the silence reigned, and it was terrifying.

Then they heard the irregular thump and grumble of the thing still wobbling around in the den, and they let out twin breaths of relief. Kathy handed Teagan the paint thinner and quietly closed the cabinet door. The two turned to the door and jumped, Kathy making a tiny noise of surprise in her throat.

The damaged monster stood in the doorway, glaring up at them from its one good eye. It winked out for a second or two before reappearing in the doorway and growled low, but it made no move to advance on them. Teagan carefully unscrewed the cap on the paint thinner, his gaze all the while on the thing in the doorway. He was pretty sure that if he made any sudden moves, the creature would attack him, injured or not, and he wasn't all that sure a bullet would stop it.

Behind him, he felt Kathy take the lighter out of his back pocket.

He considered saying something—anything—to Kathy in case something went wrong, but couldn't really think of what to say. Instead, she whispered, "Do it," and she gave his arm an encouraging squeeze.

Before he could overthink it and back out, he splashed the creature with the paint thinner once, twice, and Kathy lit the lighter beside him. The thing shook the paint thinner out of its eyes, growling in what Teagan thought to be surprise and rage.

Teagan backed away around the kitchen table to give Kathy space to light the creature up. There wasn't much room; if the thing charged them, its body engulfed in flames, there would be nowhere to run and no way to stop it.

The creature staggered forward toward Kathy, and she sidestepped it, inching around toward the door. It limped around to face her, and she gestured for Teagan to go. He said a quick prayer to the God of his youth and leaped onto and over the kitchen table while Kathy torched the creature. Its roar shook the little kitchen as Teagan skidded toward the door. Kathy yanked her hand back quickly as the fire spilled in rivers down its body, then swung out of the kitchen doorway behind him.

From the kitchen, they could hear the crackle of flame and the crashing of the burning creature into walls as it ostensibly tried to put out the fire all over it. Then it came charging into the den. The frost covering everything seemed to keep the place from going up in its peripheral flames, and for that, Teagan was glad. But if that thing decided to pounce on them . . .

It roared at Kathy and leaped at her. As she attempted to dive out of the way, Teagan emptied his gun into the creature's head and dropped it mid-air. It landed on the coffee table with a wood-splintering thud and lay there, smoldering and motionless.

"Nice shooting," Kathy said breathlessly, joining him by the remains of the creature.

"Thanks," Teagan replied. "Now, might we get on with that door-closing spell?"

Jack arrived at the coroner's office a little after dark. The snow had piled up against the front door, and all the lights were off. Neither were good signs—the former, because Jack was convinced the snow was doing what it could to keep him from Cordwell, and the latter because there should have been people still there. Cordwell, Morris—they both should have still been there. Their cars were in the lot, he noticed. He got out of the car with his gun, his keys, and the snow brush he used to clear his windshield. Brandishing the brush like a weapon, he strode purposefully up to the front door and began knocking away the snow. It was not a great tool for the job, but it was better than nothing. He worked himself into a sweat beneath his coat and gloves trying to clear the snow away, but it seemed like every time he made progress, a gust of wind blew more snow onto the spot he'd just cleared. Eventually, he collapsed to his knees and started throwing fistfuls of snow out of his way. That seemed to help. He'd cleared just enough to begin wedging the door open when he heard a shout. He doubled his efforts, and soon had dug enough snow away from the door to slide it open about ten inches. He sucked in his gut and squeezed through.

Inside, the lobby was cold and dark. Jack noticed right away that Big Bar was not at his usual place at the guard station—another bad sign. What he did see there was a light frost that covered the surface of the desk. The sign-in book, like the telephone, was firmly rooted to it in a small sheath of ice. In fact, as he looked around, he saw the entire lobby was defined by a surreal, hoary halo of ice crystals. A cocoon of ice encased the light bulb in the overhead light. Patches of black ice covered random parts of the floor all the way to the elevator. At least, it looked like black ice until he looked closer. A wide drag mark of blood had been covered over with layers of ice. Jack also noticed what looked like two sets of bloody footprints, a child's and an adult's, scattered around the room and ending near the front door. He hoped whoever the footprints belonged to had made it out and to somewhere safe.

The lobby silence hung over everything like a low fog, a haunting kind of silence that held on to soundless echoes of things that had happened but not the voices that perpetrated them. He skidded a little as he made his way to the elevator, his heart leaping into his chest. His breath clouded in front of him as he huffed at the control panel— ice hung over the down arrow button. He cracked it with the ice-chipping end of his snow brush and dusted away the shards, then pushed the button, watching with a wary eye the precariously hanging icicles just above his head. He had an ugly mental image of one of them cracking and spearing him straight through the skull, and it made him shiver.

After a moment, the elevator *ding*ed and the silvery doors opened.

Stepping inside was like walking into a refrigerator. He pushed the button for the basement morgue as the doors slid closed and after a moment, the elevator lurched into movement. He half-believed that by the time he reached his floor, the elevator doors would be frozen shut and he'd be trapped in there like a steak in a freezer.

To his relief, though, the elevator chimed again and the doors opened onto the hallway to the morgue. As Jack stepped out, that relief crumbled away. There was blood on the floor, frozen in a small pool and in a splatter pattern against the outside of the elevator doors. He drew his gun and clicked off the safety.

He hoped Morris was okay. He was still a little wet behind the ears, but he was a decent, hardworking man whom Jack had come to very much admire.

His boots crunched against the ice on the floor, and to Jack, it sounded unnaturally loud. When he reached the morgue, he turned the knob slowly and quietly and opened the door.

Two gurneys were set up in the center of the room, but otherwise, the place was empty—no sign of Cordwell or Morris.

"Fuck," Jack muttered to himself, glancing helplessly around. Where could they have gone?

The door to the refrigerated room was ajar. Both hope and fear interlocked in Jack's chest.

He pointed the gun at the door as he advanced, acutely aware of every tick and hum around him. The steel of the door was almost painfully cold to the touch, even through his gloves. He eased it open and looked into the darkness.

From what he could make out in the gloom, all the drawers for the corpses were closed. He didn't relish the idea of opening any of them, but if Morris was in there. . . .

The first drawer was either locked or jammed shut. He gave it several good tugs, but it wouldn't budge. Frustrated, he moved onto the next one. This one slid out so easily it startled him, and he flinched at the smack of both the smell of decaying flesh and the numerous cuts crisscrossing the eyeless young man on the slab. The face belonged to Morris—but only for a second. Similar age, hair color, build, but the dead man was most definitely not his detective. Jack breathed a sigh of relief.

The next drawer contained a young blond woman—also definitely not Morris—and the next, a young boy of about twelve or thirteen. What he did find in those drawers was that damned symbol carved on the woman's forehead and the boy's empty eye sockets (Jack turned away from that one, sick in his heart with disgust for the people who had done that to the boy). What he didn't find was Oliver Morris.

He had reached the end of the row of drawers when he noticed the small door. He had never seen it before, but then, he had seldom been in this particular part of the morgue. It was a narrow metal door with a lever handle, sandwiched between the wall and the leftmost column of drawers in the back corner of the room, and only visible if one moved far enough to the left to see past the drawers. Gut instinct told him if Morris was anywhere, he was through that door. Jack thought if he turned sideways, he might be able to fit through it. With some trepidation, he pushed down on the handle and pulled open the little door.

The gloom inside the refrigerated room was nothing compared to the lightless void before him. He could see a single step, and assumed others followed, leading away into the pitch. He took a deep breath and squeezed through the door. Feeling for each step with his foot, he moved forward and let the darkness surround him.

Chapter Eleven

Kathy figured they had one shot at getting the door-closing ritual right. What they did have on their side was the delicacy of the opening ritual, and its tendency to collapse if anything deviated from the very precise order of things. However, it had been noted in all the books that made reference to this particular ritual that the side effects of simply disrupting the opening ritual varied from the tragic to the outright ghastly. To achieve low-risk results in their favor, she and Teagan would have to perform their ritual with a minimum of error, and even then, with her unfamiliarity and inexperience being what it was, things could still go terribly wrong.

No pressure, she told herself, and added, *Yeah, right. Your life* is *pressure.*

She gathered some pure beeswax candles—silver, in this case, to channel astral energy, and magenta for its intense energizing properties in difficult rites such as the one she was attempting. She gathered the printed-out copy of the words Teagan needed to read, the miniature dollhouse door, and a straight pin, as well as the lighter she had used to torch the monster whose remains were melting in her den. She rummaged through a small trunk she kept in the secret compartment behind her headboard in her bedroom for a bottle of dark, iridescent liquid, and some sticks of yerba santa leaf and desert sage incense and their holders, plus some more salt and chalk. All these things she piled on the hallway floor, since the coffee table in the den was now in charred splinters.

All the while, Teagan watched her, hovering nearby in case she instructed him to do something. She felt a little sorry for him in a way. His helpless pacing and the occasional quizzical expression told her he was clearly out of his element, and the way he puffed on his unlit cigarette and ran a hand through his hair told her he was nervous.

"You'll be fine," she said to him over her shoulder as she went into the little foyer area of the apartment. She'd decided that space between the kitchen, den, and hallway to the bed- and bathrooms was the only area large enough for their purposes.

She crouched on her haunches and began drawing a very large circle, about six and a half feet across, on the hardwood floor with the chalk. She left a small opening, then drew an inner ring about three inches smaller around than the first, leaving an opening in the same place. Next, she began copying with great care the symbols from one of the printed-out pages in the space between the inner ring and the outer ring.

Teagan had followed her out of the kitchen, and stood with his lips clamped around his cigarette and his hands in his jeans pockets as he watched her. "I hope you're right, love," he muttered. "All of this is . . ." He gestured around him, dropping the smoke back in his front pocket. The frost around the apartment was starting to melt, dampening the couch cushions in uneven patches and making slippery wet spots on the floor. From time to time, though, a sourceless gust of cold wind would blow across their skin, making them shiver. The winter had relinquished its grip on the apartment for now, but it was never too far away.

"I know. It's a lot to digest. But we're going to be okay." Referring to the printed pages again, she drew the appropriate greater sigils in the four directional corners surrounding the circle, and some lesser sigils in between those. On the greater sigils, she placed the magenta candles, and on the lesser sigils, the silver ones. She poured one of the dark-colored oils just outside the outer chalk border, and another of the oils just inside the inner one, leaving the same small opening. The heavy, musky scents of them mingled in her nose. It reminded her, for reasons she couldn't quite place, of her brother's old room.

She stuck the straight pin horizontally through the soft wood of the dollhouse door frame and into the center of the wood of the little door, effectively jamming it closed. Then she poured a little of the oils onto her fingertips and rubbed them around the outline of the door where it met the frame, as well as underneath it.

"What's that for, the opening there?" Teagan asked, pointing.

"For us to enter. If I seal the circle up now and then we step inside, we're not really inside it, so we're not protected by it. We have to finish the circle once we're both in the center of it."

"Ahh. Okay. And the oils?"

"Like the chalk, they strengthen the wall around the safety zone we're creating."

Teagan clapped his hands together. "Aye, okay. Now what?"

Kathy let out a long breath as she stood. It had been getting colder since they'd been talking, and her exhalation condensed in wispy plumes of white. "Well, first, I need you to come into the circle through that opening, with those papers you're going to read." Teagan did so, joining her in the center. With the chalk and the oils, she sealed the circle. "Now we light each of the candles." She lit the magenta ones in order of the directions where they were placed—north, south, west, and then east—and then lit the silver ones in a counterclockwise direction from the one to the right of the northern candle. The little flames danced in unfelt breezes.

Teagan gave her a nervous look, the papers with the closing ritual fluttering in his hand as he shifted his weight from one leg to the other. "Do I . . . ?"

"Not yet," she told him. She set eight incense holders out, one between each of the candles, and alternated types of incense sticks. She lit them with the kitchen lighter and once the sweet smoke began floating through the circle, she rose.

"Okay," she said, taking a deep breath. "Now you read. Go slow—read each word correctly, and with as much belief in the words as you are capable of feeling. When you get to the end, start over and read it again. I'll tell you when to stop. You can do this, Reece." She gave him a quick, reassuring squeeze on his forearm. "I'm right here with you."

Teagan regarded her with a tender look that warmed every part of her. Then his gaze dropped to the pages as he scanned the words in his head. Finally he nodded, ran a hand through his hair, popped the unlit cigarette in his mouth, considered that, then took it out and dropped it back in his pocket. He looked up at her. "I'm ready."

She nodded. In a soft voice, she said, "Let's do this."

Teagan began to read:

Coimeádaí na geataí, Máistir na Doirse agus Eochracha
Iarraimid ort a dhúnadh ar a bhfuil d'oscail
Sliocht a barra agus faoi ghlas suas ar an mbealach rúnda
Le do thoil a chosaint i ár gcuid ama an ghátair . . .

As Teagan spoke the words—which, he'd told her, were mostly pleas to the Master of Doors and Keys to banish these creatures and close the door behind them—Kathy felt the room get both darker and colder. A thin sheen of ice began knitting a fractal pattern of tiny sparkling crystals from the far corners of the room right up to the chalk-and-oil boundary of the circle.

Kathy thought the physical evidence around her, despite its eeriness, was probably a good sign. They were getting the attention of the winter creatures, which were recognizing their limits, the boundaries to their power in the presence of whoever or whatever the being known as the Master of Doors and Keys actually was. Personally, Kathy found the concept of any entity that could bend the wills of lesser gods to its demands to be just beyond the outer edge of a sane and comfortable zone of beliefs, but she did her best to squash such thoughts. Evidently, the oldest elements from multiple universes believed this Master was a just and reasonable creature who could be called upon to assist in ridding a world of chaotic, hostile, negative forces, and that had to be of some comfort.

Teagan continued reciting the spell.

The dimness in the room had begun to take on a faint, blue-tinted glow, and the temperature dropped enough that Kathy could see her breath again. If Teagan noticed any of it, he didn't let on. He was focused on the words, on the power behind the words, and on the unspoken notion hanging as heavy as the cold in the air that the unimaginable could happen if he screwed up.

He started the invocation over as Kathy had instructed. She had told him that it gained power, a kind of magical momentum, each time he recited it, and he figured they needed all the momentum they could get.

It was then that part of the gloom resolved itself into shapes suggestive of humanoid entities. Kathy's eyes grew wide, and speech failed her. They gave off a bluish light that filled the room, pushing the darkness toward the outermost corners. The cold, though, became an almost living, breathing thing, pacing and panting all around them. As the details of those humanoid entities became more defined, Kathy touched Teagan's arm and he looked up, the rest of his words trailing off.

Kathy couldn't say for sure, but she thought the five beings standing before them just outside their circle of protection were the Blue People.

Chapter Twelve

It felt to Jack like he was going down a long, long way. The wall was rough beneath his hand, and cool, though not as cold as it had been upstairs in the morgue. The air smelled vaguely musty, like a damp basement. He felt very vulnerable in that limitless darkness, like he was adrift at sea and sinking farther and farther, and the sharks had come circling around him.

As he made his way down, he thought about his kids. Jack Jr. was still scared of the dark. He had a night-light in his room that he asked Jack to make sure was on every time he stayed over. He also had asthma. Jack could only wonder what the cold and the dampness of some underground prison was doing to the poor kid's lungs.

He thought about Carly, too. So often, she reminded him of a tiny grown-up in a little girl's body. Jack imagined her trying to soothe her brother and probably even her mother. She wouldn't let her terror show, not too much. But she had to be scared. They all had to be scared, and it made Jack's chest ache that they had been put in that position.

It made Jack roil with anger toward Cordwell.

Just when he thought he'd be descending into that pit of the earth forever, his foot stumbled on a hard floor. He left the security of the wall beneath his fingers and moved forward. Ahead, down what he thought was a long tunnel, he thought he saw a faint, flickering light. He headed toward it, listening. He thought he heard voices far off in rhythmic chant—another bad sign. It suggested maybe he'd found the cultists' meeting place, and worse, it suggested that those present were actively participating in something. For the first time in a long while, he wished Kathy were there to guide him through how to handle these people.

As he got closer, the small patch of light resolved itself into a cave opening, and beyond it, Jack caught glimpses of a round, rough-hewn room with a cavernously high ceiling. Within, he could see several figures—Jack counted nine—in icy blue robes surrounding what looked to Jack like an immense circular altar made of ice. Torches lined the circumference of the cavern, and between them were several irregular, large stone statues, with a few feet between each and the rough cavern walls. The latter were terribly detailed in their carving, not only suggestive of horrific alien forms but of the movement of those forms. The statues continued up along the diameter like sentinels, flanking a pathway right to the altar itself. Suspended in a large wire cage above it was Morris—and the kids and Katie! Jack's heart leaped in his chest. They looked a little bruised and bloody and absolutely terrified, but otherwise, they were okay. He checked the bullets in his .45. He had a full magazine and one in the chamber. It would have to be enough.

Jack considered his options. There would be no backup; even if there were any other police officers around town at this point, his cell wasn't sending texts or making calls anymore. He could charge in there, gun drawn, but it didn't seem wise to leap before he looked, in a sense. In a best-case scenario, Jack imagined the folds of those robes would be hiding guns or knives. Likely, they had weapons on them of a less tangible source that he couldn't even imagine. It wasn't his life so much that he was worried about. His family was in there, along with one of his best detectives, and he didn't want to engage in any impulsive behavior that might put their lives in danger.

Eight of the cultists were gathered in a semi-circle around the altar. They wore hoods, so Jack couldn't make out the faces of any of them except the ninth, who was facing him from the other side of the altar, his arms raised.

It was Terence Cordwell.

He was speaking in a language unfamiliar to Jack, though, if he had to guess, he would have thought it some old version of Irish or Welsh, maybe.

Unlike most of the other things he had seen out in the snow—the echoes, the ghosts, the hallucinations—there was a kind of substantial horror to seeing him there, the perpetrator of such cruelty and madness, a liar as close to some of his department as clothes were to skin.

Jack wanted to kill him. His hand closed around the butt of his gun. One shot, straight to the head. He saw his kids, little Jack Jr. and Carly, dangling within that cage, tears streaking their faces, and he began to withdraw his weapon. But then he saw Morris, doing his best to keep Katie and the kids calm, no doubt reassuring them with his special Morris brand of almost naive charm, and he let the gun rest. Soon, maybe, but not now. Now, he had to get in there and get closer.

Jack listened for another moment to the words the cultists were saying, the syllables that meant absolutely nothing to him, and saw his chance to move in when, as a group, the cultists closed their eyes. He crept in and hid behind the nearest statue. There were two between him and the one nearest Cordwell, and he hoped there would be another instance of their being distracted enough for him to get closer.

Luck, for once, was with him; again they closed their eyes, their chanting loud and long, and he crept on a swift diagonal to the statue right behind Cordwell. He was so close, he could smell the man, a mix of his expensive cologne and bleach and some odd incense burning on the edge of the altar whose smoke wafted back over him to Jack.

From here, he could see the altar and his stomach tightened; he was glad he'd been cautious. The entire center fell away to a black pit. Whether it had a bottom or not, Jack couldn't tell, but he suspected it was very deep. Which meant, he realized, that if his family and Morris should fall . . .

He didn't want to think about that. Jack was a thinker, had always been a thinker. Now was the time to be a doer. For his kids, he needed to do something.

Jack stepped out from behind the statue and pointed the gun at Cordwell's head. The trailing off of the cultists' chanting as they became aware of him arrested Cordwell's chanting. He turned his head to see Jack's gun level with the bridge of his nose and nodded as if he'd been expecting him. In his other hand, Jack still clutched the snow brush.

"Jack, you made it. I'm afraid we've had to start without you, but I'm certainly glad you'll be here to witness the final stage of our preparations."

"Daddy!" Jack Jr.'s and Carly's little faces pressed eagerly against the bars.

"Jack! Oh, thank God." Even Katie looked relieved to see him.

"Let my family and my detective go," Jack growled, "or I'll kill you."

"Kill me?"

"You and every one of these murdering bastards along with you." Jack chanced a quick look at the faces, now unhooded, that stared at him with vague unease. They lacked the evident confidence their leader had in the face of Jack's intrusion.

"I'm afraid it's a little too late for that, Jack. See, my friends and I have been industriously working toward opening the way to Xíonathymia, the Great Far Place beyond the realms of starless space. And now, the way is opened." Cordwell turned back to the altar. "One last collective show of wills, my brothers and sisters, and we will welcome a new age, a multiverse of limitless possibility. We welcome Iaroki the Swallower of Suns, Imnamoun the She-Beast Mother of the Spheres, Xixiath-Ahk the Blood-Washed, Okatik'Nehr the Watcher, and Thniaxom the Traveler to the very nexus of a new co-mingling of universes! Now, my brothers and sisters! Now! Now!"

The hands of the cultists began to glow with silvery light. Their mouths moved, but Jack couldn't make out what they were saying.

"Jack!"

He looked up to see Morris leaning against the bars. "Jack, you have to stop them. This is beyond the law now. They're opening the door. You need to stop them."

Jack looked at his kids.

"Your family is here as a sacrifice. We're all here as a sacrifice—a man, a woman, a boy child, a girl child. And Cordwell—he wanted you to see it. Apparently despair strengthens these Old Gods."

The chanting around them got louder. They no longer seemed to care or even be aware of Jack. They were supremely confident that they were beyond his reckoning now.

"Stop them, Jack. It's the only way now. Stop them from opening the door."

"But you and the kids and—"

"Don't worry about us. Toss me that snow brush and I've got this. Just stop them, before we become creepy creature corn chips, eh?" He tried to smile as he reached through the bars for the snow brush from Jack. Jack handed it to him and he pulled it back through the bars, and his expression grew serious. Morris looked him in the eye. "Kill them. Nothing standing, boss."

With a grim nod of determination, Jack began to fire.

Each of the Blue People seemed to be made of a translucent blue, somewhat crystalline substance that molded itself, at will, into the semblance of a tall, gaunt person-shape. This shape, with its long, rather sharp features, was swathed in an assortment of sapphire folds of plush cloth embroidered, or so it looked, with silvery-white threads, so that only the skeletal head and hands could be seen. In the cavernous sockets of their eyes was a deep blackness that seemed almost a tangible thing, twin subzero caverns of disdain and impenetrable contempt.

The being in front opened its mouth, and the others followed suit. A bright light issued from their throats and carried their voices in unison to her. "You are in our way."

Kathy and Teagan glanced at each other, then squinted at the figures.

The voices continued. "We were summoned. The Sixth Door of Nine was opened."

Kathy raised a hand to shield her eyes from the brunt of their light. "We didn't summon you. We—"

The one closest to her held its hand out to her, palm up. The long, clear nails of its last two fingers reached sharply into icicle points, while those of the thumbs and first two fingers curved slightly over the tips. Again, without moving or closing their mouths, unified voices of the group came from within the depths of light pouring out of their throats. "Not you. Others. But you are attempting to close the Sixth Door of Nine. You must not."

"Yes, we must. We can't allow you to cleanse this world."

"You cannot stop that."

"We intend to."

The blazing light in their throats flickered as if they were considering that, and then the beacons resumed as the voices said, "Then you will have to die." The light in their throats faded as the Blue People spread out around the circle. She noticed that although they came close to the outermost ring of oil, not so much as a hem of their robes crossed it.

"Teagan," she said without taking her eyes off the figures, "start the invocation again." When he didn't move or speak, Kathy nudged him. "Teagan!"

Beside her, he began to read the invocation. Kathy wished she could read it, too, to take comfort in the flow of the language and the power behind the words, but she didn't want to risk messing them up.

The Blue People raised their arms in unison as if pleading with the ceiling, and a wind blew up around them, whipping through the circle, yanking at their hair and clothes and the papers Teagan held tightly in his hand. He kept reading.

The corners of the room grew very dark with amorphous shadows. Those shape-shadows crowded closer, pulsing and twisting, forming and reforming. Frost outlined them, and as they moved, it cracked, chipped off, and recovered them immediately, giving their definition a kind of jerking movement. There was something abjectly horrific to Kathy about these things, more than the scorpion things or even the Blue People themselves, perhaps because they were simply darkness beneath the cold, a darkness more alien than anything in her universe. Perhaps they were the very substance of the dark of starless space. These were the things that drove the odd behavior of the snow, and wore it like a disguise. They were the *real* cleaners; she was sure of that. They were the faces, the voices, the hands of that unnatural winter that had Colby in its grip.

Kathy shivered. She looked down at the symbols she had drawn within the circle and hoped they would hold.

The Blue People stepped back as the shadows, the cleaners, surged and billowed right up to the circle. The temperature dropped immediately to a painful low. The air felt raw and uncomfortable, almost like sandpaper against her skin and inside her nose and throat. She felt the light pelting of snowflakes on her arms and face, and looked up to see a swirling cloud of blue-black blotting out the ceiling. Snow appeared to be materializing from it and falling lightly all around. Kathy didn't think the snow covering up the circle would have any bearing on its effectiveness, but wondered if it was possible for melting flakes to wash the chalk or even the oil away. That would be bad. That would be very bad.

More pressing in her thoughts was the worry that these cleaners might have a way around or through the circle. She had created these circles of protection before in her line of work, and had done so with confidence in their strength. But these creatures . . . they weren't demons, even Duke or King demons. These weren't ghosts. These weren't even Hollowers, Hinshing, or Scions, creatures she understood to be hardly, if at all, affected by most protection circles and protection spells. Kathy tried to tell herself that this particular circle and its symbols were specific to the Blue People and those that were bound to serve them, but still . . . that tendril of frosted darkness was coming awfully close to the outer oil ring. . . .

From the black center of one of the cleaners' masses, a bass growl actually vibrated the floor beneath their feet.

Teagan, to his credit, kept reading. He didn't look up, and his voice didn't waver. Kathy suspected it was what was keeping him together.

From their semi-circle behind the cleaners, the mouths of the Blue People opened again. The light and the voices surrounded them.

"Now you will die," the voices said. The mouths shut and the light snapped off. A cool blue puff of her breath was the last thing Kathy could make out clearly before she and Teagan were engulfed by the alien darkness.

Chapter Thirteen

Jack had managed to get off head shots to one older man, a woman, and another twenty-something young guy, dropping them where they stood, before Cordwell turned on him. Jack had just enough time to see the glow fade from their hands before Cordwell's fingers were clawing Jack's throat with one hand while a stone dagger had been raised above his head with the other. Jack caught the descent of the knife with his free hand, but not before the blade bit into his palm. He winced from the pain, but wrestled the gun around Cordwell's arm and aimed it at his face.

Cordwell tossed him with amazing strength against the altar, and for one dizzying moment, Jack thought he was going to go right over the edge, into what he now confirmed was a deep black, a black that seemed to go all the way to the center of the earth—or more likely, all the way through this universe and into another one.

Jack turned to take another go at Cordwell, but a moose of a man was standing there between them, his eyes flashing with lunatic purpose. He swung a meaty fist like a sledgehammer against the side of Jack's head, and Jack reeled a moment, seeing bright fireworks of light. The man hit him again, this time in the mouth, and Jack tasted blood as it flowed over his teeth and tongue. The side of his eye was already beginning to swell and tear, making it hard to see, but Jack knew immediately what the man intended when he wrapped his steel cable arms around Jack's midsection.

He hoisted Jack off his feet, and a flash of fear lit Jack up inside. He felt himself pushed backward toward the opening in the altar and his feet kicked out, trying to connect with the big man. His arms were pinned, but Jack managed to raise his gun enough to fire a gut shot.

The big man staggered backward, dropping Jack, whose elbow

connected hard with the side of the altar. Jack saw stars. It was nothing, though, compared to the look of shock on the other man's face as he pressed a hand to his wound and studied the blood flowing between his fingers. Jack felt no sympathy. He dispatched the man with a shot to the head.

Three of the remaining cult members' hands still glowed, but their faces looked worried as they mouthed the words of their spell. Jack shot a woman in the shoulder, but she took the hit and kept conjuring. That resolved Jack's last remaining shred of hesitation regarding killing them, and he shot her in the head.

He looked up to check on Morris's progress with his family. He could see Morris working on smashing the cage's lock with the snow brush. Jack suspected he was doing more damage to the snow brush than the lock, but he gave Morris credit for trying.

Then he felt a bright explosion of pain in his right shoulder. It was gigantic, the kind of pain that made him nauseous, and he felt his grip on the gun weaken. He turned to see Cordwell stepping back with a smug smirk, and with his left hand, he felt for the source of the pain. His hand closed around the hilt of the ceremonial dagger, but his awkward grasp kept slipping. He tried to raise the gun, but the fireworks went off again.

"Sonofa . . ." he muttered, and tried to raise his arm again. His whole arm felt like it had been lit on fire, but Jack squeezed the trigger anyway. He hit Cordwell in the leg, and the coroner dropped with a howl.

Jack turned to the other two cultists, but they were running away. Jack allowed himself a small smile of victory—until he heard the echoing animal call coming up out of the well in front of him. Behind him, he heard Cordwell crying and laughing. Both were terrible sounds.

In the dark, Kathy could hear the cleaners hovering around the circle. Teagan had stopped reading; it was too dark to see. But just before the light had gone out, he had grabbed her hand, and she could smell his cologne, and it was reassuring that he was still there with her.

"Now what, love?" he asked in a voice barely above a whisper.

Before she could answer, a sudden spotlight appeared to the left of Kathy. In it, her brother was sitting on a folding chair like they had at the hospital.

She felt her stomach bottom out and was only vaguely aware of squeezing Teagan's hand even harder. It couldn't possibly be her brother sitting in that chair—part of her knew that, not just in her mind but in her bones. But a thousand thoughts cascaded over each other at once. Toby did have ties to the Hand of the Black Stars cult, after all. That he might have lied about the extent of his knowledge and/or involvement in this whole mess would not have surprised her. But Toby was under surveillance, and the monitoring system at that hospital—she had looked into it herself—was maximum security. So how had he gotten there? Had the Blue People or even the cleaners whisked him away with their dark magic? Or was this a trick, a thing masquerading as Toby to somehow get her to leave the circle? It sure looked like her brother, down to birthmarks and tiny scars. He wore the same bland hospital-issued clothes she had last seen him in. He looked pale. The bags under his eyes were dark and his eyes themselves flashed in the dim light, but otherwise . . .

"Hello, little sister," he said with a sly grin, and for a moment, the world wavered. She willed it to steady itself again.

"You are not my brother," she said.

He looked amused as he leaned forward toward her. "Aren't I? A monster's a monster, right?" Before she could answer, he added, "Oh, I know you like to think you see them as people, all those creatures who can kill their own, can rape women and molest children, can beat old people to a pulp, all to feed the darkness inside them. You like to think you believe that darkness doesn't make them less human, but that's only because you need to see *me* as human . . . and yourself, as well. Isn't that right?"

Teagan didn't try to get in the way of the conversation, but Kathy felt him squeeze her hand.

"Does your ex-pat here know about me? About any of your family? Your dead mother, your dead drunk father, your serial killer brother . . . I mean, wow, Kathy. If only he could have come to Thanksgiving or Christmas sometime. You know, back when all those little squares in your bedroom picture frame actually had pictures in them of people who at least pretended to still care whether you lived or died."

Kathy clamped down on her embarrassment until it turned to rage, and then she clamped down on it even harder. To let it go would have been exactly what the Toby-thing wanted. For her to lose control and lunge at him, leave the circle . . . or make Teagan so horrified by or disgusted with her that he would leave it to get away from her. . . . That was exactly what it wanted.

Neither was happening.

"What, Kathy? What are you thinking right now? Are you thinking about the night I gave you that scar?"

Kathy breathed slowly, counting her breaths, just like her college therapist had taught her years ago. Teagan squeezed her hand again in the dark.

"Oh, Kaaathyyy, I know you can hear me. It's very hard to have a rapport when the conversation is so one-sided."

"I was thinking about how good it is going to feel to send you back to the hell you came from."

The Toby-thing gave her a sly grin. "Oh, you think you can do that? You and the IRA sympathizer, with your broken minds and your broken hearts and your silly optimism? You both have faith in nothing. You think either of you is strong enough to close the Sixth of Nine?"

Kathy locked her gaze with those eyes that looked so much like Toby's, those dead eyes, but dropped Teagan's hand and slid down to pick up the kitchen lighter from the floor inside the circle. Then she rose and clicked it on so Teagan could see the papers with the invocation.

"Keep going," she told him, and Teagan began to read again.

The Toby-thing frowned, then wavered like a picture on a scrambled TV channel. The face that looked like her brother's, the voice that sounded so much like his, distorted as it cried out in frustration, and the ice-crusted shadow beneath it retreated into the dark.

For a while, the only light in the room came from the lighter's tiny flame. Kathy shivered with the cold, but held the lighter as still as she could. She could feel the things all around them, seething, looking for a way in.

Then another patch of light appeared, this time near Teagan, and at first, he only glanced at it, but then recognition crossed his face and he stopped reading.

"Reece?" Kathy's voice was small.

Something broken flitted behind Teagan's eyes, something old and never quite forgotten. "It's me grandmother," he told her, and his voice sounded even smaller.

An ancient woman sat rocking in an old-fashioned rocking chair. She wore a wool shawl over a pale and shapeless dress, with heavy black shoes. Her face was deeply lined, so much so that it reminded Kathy of the striations of rock. Her skin was pale and paper-thin, veined with thin lines of blue-black. She regarded Teagan with one rheumy blue eye; the other was fogged over with a thick cataract.

"You're wrong to be in it, lad," the woman said in a thick, watery voice. "To be caught up in all this. 'Tis the divil's work, it is."

Teagan seemed to be remembering a night prior to this; his eyes, his stance, were someplace else. "I'm not," he told her. "I'm where I'm meant to be, *máthair mhór*."

"You say so," the old woman replied, pointing a long, crooked finger at him. "But what good've ye done, eh? Have you changed any minds? Saved any lives? It's a war you can't win, against an enemy that has been stronger, more powerful, and more numerous than ye for centuries."

"That don't mean it's not a war worth fighting," he told her.

"Not so worth fighting that you can't walk away, as you did before, under similar circumstances. You remember, she nearly got you killed, that lass, because you wanted to get in her knickers. Blowed her own damn self up, she and her terrorist brother, and how many others? How many children? And you would have been a part of it, a murderer, but for your own lack of loyalty to anyone or anything. Even your own mum knew you were nothing, just bullheaded anger and faithlessness."

"I was a child. And I didn't walk away. I grew up. Became a police officer. I found a side to fight on in a war I could join with a clean conscience, if not a heavy heart."

Kathy could see that despite the evenness of his tone, the woman was getting to him, agitating him, cutting him open with the sharpness of his own memories, just as she (it) had done to her. The difference was, Kathy had been cut deeply before, and thought she knew something about the way to block out the pain.

She took his hand and squeezed it. "She's not your grandmother," she said.

Teagan looked at her, his eyes coming back to that night and that place, but when he and Kathy both glanced back, a little girl stood where the old woman had been. She had one blue eye as well, a doll's eye; the other was lost to the mess of charred black which had eaten that half of her face. She stood perfectly still on a single leg; the other was missing.

"I hope you haven't forgotten me, Reece Teagan," the little voice rasped. "I haven't forgotten you."

"Bloody hell," Teagan whispered.

"Remind you of little Gracie Anderson, do I? Oh, I know her. Dead girls whisper to each other on these winter breezes."

"You're not my fault," he said in a voice thick with emotion. "I tried to get there in time, but—"

"You could have stopped it and you didn't," the girl-thing told him.

"I tried!" he shouted.

"Read," Kathy prodded. "Forget that thing over there. It's not a little girl. It's nothing but ice dust and shadows."

"I. Am NOT. NOTHING!" the little girl screamed, seeming to grow, to bloom in Teagan's direction. He flinched, dropping the papers. Immediately, a gust of wind blew the papers up into a little dervish. Teagan and Kathy tried to grab them, but the wind whisked them out of the circle, out of reach.

"Damn it!" Teagan shouted, turning to Kathy. "I'm so sorry—"

She shook her head. "Don't worry about it. We can still finish this."

The girl and the light surrounding her winked out. When the sourceless spotlight blazed on again, it was across the room, where the papers were, and Jack Glazier stood in the center of it.

"No bloody way," Teagan said.

Behind Jack was one of the cleaners. Jack tried to speak to them, but as soon as he parted his lips, his mouth filled with ice. The pain in his eyes made Kathy wince.

One of the tendrils of the cleaner behind him whispered over his clothes to his throat. It wrapped itself around his neck and began squeezing. Jack—or the thing that was pretending to be Jack—began flailing, his hands slapping uselessly at the tendril. It took all of Kathy's will not to step out of the circle, to help him. Sensing Teagan was feeling the same, she placed a hand on his arm to keep him there. She fought back tears. It was hurting her heart to watch.

Blood began to pour from the place where the tendril touched Jack (*not* Jack, *not* Jack, she kept telling herself), and his eyes grew wide. His skin grew pale and began to turn blue, and slivers of ice fell from his mouth.

Teagan fired at the Jack-thing before Kathy even knew he'd taken out his gun. Both it and the cleaner behind it splattered like an ink spot, froze, then pulled back together.

Now they were angry; Kathy could feel it pulsing off the cleaners. The Blue People, in the unlit corners of the room, were angry, too. She and Teagan had proved more formidable opposition than they had expected.

The light came on again, and Kathy could see the papers fluttering in the wind. They were held down by a man's bare foot. Kathy followed that foot to the hem of a silvery robe, and up the folds of the robe to a face—a human face. She didn't recognize the face, but she recognized the tattooed symbol on the muscular forearm. This man was one of the cultists.

He looked disoriented for a minute, and then, taking in the cleaners and the Blue People, he bowed his head in awed reverence, and turned to Kathy and Teagan.

Kathy realized what the Blue People had done. Neither they nor the cleaners could access Kathy or Teagan as long as they were in the circle. The monsters had tried to lure them out, to make them angry or scared, to play on their senses of loyalty, guilt, and sympathy, and none of that had worked. If they couldn't draw Kathy or Teagan out, then they would have to send someone in.

The cultist strode purposefully over to them and reached into the circle. Teagan pointed his gun at the man's head. The man regarded the gun with a patient look before suddenly yanking Kathy over the border. She cried out as her toes skidded over the circle, smearing the chalk and oil. Her heart sank. Nothing would protect them now.

"Stop right fucking there," Teagan said. "I swear to God, I will shoot you dead where you stand. Get your hands off her."

The man let Kathy go, holding up his hands palms up in a gesture of acquiescence. But he was smiling. The damage had already been done.

Teagan hadn't fully understood what the man had done until he looked down at Kathy's feet. Then the light dawned in his eyes. With a kind of resignation, he took a step voluntarily out of the circle.

"No, don't!" She cried out, but it was too late.

"I'm not leaving you out here alone," he told her.

Then the cultist punched him. Teagan shook it off, touching the corner of his mouth. His fingers came away with blood on them. He chuckled sardonically and said to the man, "Bring it, arsehole."

The man swung again, and this time Teagan dodged out of the way. His return swing hit the cultist squarely on the jaw and sent him stumbling backward. The cleaners caught him in their tendrils. He looked triumphant for a moment, and then scared, and then in pain as the tendrils yanked off first one arm, then the other, then his head and legs. The tendrils didn't stop there, though. They tossed the body parts in the air, and the ice sheaths covering them grew stiff and sharp. The tendrils lashed wildly, slicing the icy body parts to shreds before they hit the floor with a messy, pulpy *plop*. Kathy felt her gorge rise and fought to keep down the bile.

Having served his purpose to them, the creatures no longer needed the cultist.

One of the tendrils snaked its way over to Teagan. She cried out to warn him, but it was around his ankle, yanking him off his feet. He fell with a thud, and the tendril lashed him across the face, drawing blood on his cheek.

Kathy lit the kitchen lighter and rushed the thing, thrusting the fire under the nearest tendril. It jerked back in pain, forming first a face twisted in anger and then a hand that it clamped down on her bad wrist. A liquid cold formed a band of pain over her injury so intense that she dropped the lighter. The tendril let go and immediately smacked her in the face, knocking her off her feet.

The cleaner surged forward over her, forming a montage of angry faces in bas-relief. She reached blindly for the lighter; she thought it was somewhere nearby. Another tendril dropped like a sewing needle, spearing her in the side, filling her with that crippling, acid-etching cold, and Kathy groaned, feeling more frantically for the lighter. Her fingers closed around it and she gratefully pulled it toward her as another tendril injected its frozen agony into her shoulder. She could feel the cold slowly spreading outward from each of the wounds, and felt sure that it would begin killing tissue and then organs if she couldn't banish these creatures quickly.

Nearby, Teagan was struggling with tentacles looking to spear him in the chest. He was holding his own, but his grip on the whips of darkness was awkward and weakening.

She had to stop this. With effort, she crab-crawled backward toward the circle, and the amorphous shadow above her kept pace, readying for another attack. Kathy felt around the circle again, and gave a little victory cry when she found what she was looking for.

With the lighter, she set fire to the little door.

From the corners of the room where the Blue People had been directing the cleaners, their mouths opened as one and the light in those cavernous throats became so bright it hurt her head and chest as well as her eyes. A thunderous roar issued forth like a storm wind through a cave, and as the light got brighter, the sound rose in pitch until it was a wail, then a scream, then a shriek as bright and painful as the light.

The cleaners flickered and roared, their tendrils waving wildly, snapping at the air above and around them with tiny blue electric sparks.

She heard Teagan's voice. He had left behind the cleaner that had been attacking him, its own tendrils speared through a solid part of its otherwise amorphous mass. Teagan had made it over to the papers while she had been fighting off her own cleaner, and he had begun reading the incantation again, his voice steady and clear, all his sanity and sense of self control hanging from that single thread of focus.

They were close. The hold the winter had over Colby was finally weakening.

The Blue People advanced on her as one, and she lit another part of the door to make it burn faster. From the reaction of the creatures, it was as if she had set fire to them . . . which, she decided, wasn't a bad idea.

She touched the lighter to the hem of the robe closest to her and was delighted to see it blaze up. The creatures screamed as if she had set fire to the lot of them, and the light from their throats was blinding. She shielded her eyes but it did little good, so she started swiping blindly in wide arcs with the lighter. The light surrounded her, swallowed her whole. For several long seconds, the light and their screams were all that existed. They filled her body and soul, inside and out.

There was a flash of light so bright she could practically see it through her eyelids.

Then it was gone. The screams, the light, the cold—all of it was gone.

She opened her eyes. The cold in her wounds was receding slowly, and although she was bleeding, she saw the wounds weren't too deep. She looked up. Teagan was in the same place on the floor, breathing heavily and clutching the papers, looking visibly relieved. He smiled broadly at her when he caught her eye. She smiled back, then slowly surveyed the room. The ice and snow were mostly gone, and the temperature, though still cold, was rising. The creature they had killed was gone, the cleaners were gone . . . and the Blue People were gone, too. The little door she had burned had been reduced to a tiny splinter and a pile of ash.

"Did we get them, love? Is it over?"

"I think it is," she told him, still amazed. "I think we did it."

She stood on shaky legs, helped Teagan up, then made her way over to the window. It was still the blue of early morning, but she could see well enough to notice that, outside, the snow was already melting. She could see the icicles dripping from the eaves of the roofs across the street, and the snow drifts looked, at least to her, significantly smaller than they had the night before. Teagan's car tires were visible now, as were the tops of some of the mailboxes.

The snow was melting. Winter was finally leaving Colby.

While Kathy and Teagan were fighting cleaners outside the circle of protection, Jack was watching the pit at the center of the cultist's ice altar and hoping to his own God that wherever Kathy and Teagan were, they could stop anything from coming up through it.

It was no longer completely dark down there; there was a faint greenish light now, and although it didn't even begin to illuminate the bottom, Jack could see gray tentacles climbing upward. They were hideous things that made Jack's stomach turn—hell, they made his *soul* turn. He could see black orbs full of intelligence and malicious intent swimming in the substance of what passed for flesh. Mouths with rows of shark-like teeth moved freely, too, gaping to reveal impossibly deep throats, deep as the pit from which they were rising.

Within minutes, they were close enough for the tips of the tentacles to snap at the stones within feet of him, and he could finally see with some clarity what those tentacles were attached to.

"Oh my God," he breathed.

The Old Gods were coming.

He didn't have to look up to know that Morris had seen them, too;

he was firm in directing Katie to shield the children's eyes, and his efforts at breaking the lock were renewed with vigor.

Cordwell continued to laugh, the frenzy of a madman's soul. The children were frantic. Katie was crying. Jack turned to Morris.

"Get out of the way," he said, and Morris did. Jack aimed, focusing all of himself into making this one shot count, and fired at the lock. It broke, and the door fell open, throwing off their balance, and the cage swung. Katie cried out and the children clung to the sides, but Morris threw himself into the momentum of it.

"Okay, when I tell you, jump, okay?"

"We can't!" Carly said.

"You have to!" Morris told them. "You'll be fine. Your daddy'll be there when you land, okay? I need you to be brave."

"Come one, baby, do this for me," Katie sniffled through her tears.

"I'm right here," Jack called up to them. "You can do this. I'm right here."

"They're going to die," Cordwell said. He had pulled himself up to a standing position using cracks in the altar, and now he peered over the side. "It's too late for them, and for you. They're here. They're here!" He raised his arms in triumph, and in that moment, all the fatigue and anger Jack felt overwhelmed him. He lunged at Cordwell and pushed him over the side.

Seeming unsurprised, the coroner laughed madly as he fell. That is, until the tentacles found him. They greedily grabbed at his body, simultaneously tearing it apart and sucking out the warmth and life of each part. He stopped laughing then and started screeching, until there was nothing left of him to make noise. The creatures, though, had raised an incredible din. It sounded to Jack like wind and thunder, and it was growing louder.

Morris, meanwhile, distracted the children by swinging the cage and counting.

"One!" he shouted, and the cage swung back. Then it swung over and past the pit again.

"Two!" The cage returned like a pendulum, then swung out again. Beneath them, the storm sounds raged on.

"Three!" Morris shouted, and as it swung back, he instructed them to jump on the next outswing.

"Jump!"

Jack Jr. jumped. Jack's heart clenched in his chest while his boy was in the air and didn't relax until Jack Jr. had safely cleared the pit and landed on the stone floor on the other side.

On the next swing, Morris yelled for Carly to jump, and she did. Jack's heart leaped with her, and he breathed a sigh of relief when she landed safely next to her brother.

When Katie jumped, a tentacle reached up and grabbed her ankle. It snatched her from the air and yanked her down. He could hear her screaming over the cacophony from the pit. It cut right through Jack, and the terrified cries of the children broke his heart. They knew, even without having seen, that those things were killing their mother. Jack ran to them and held them, burying their faces in his chest, hoping to shield them from as much of the scene as possible.

When her screams died down, Jack looked up at Morris, who was still swinging, somewhat uncertainly, over the pit. A spatter of Katie's blood dripped off the underside of the cage. Beneath Morris, the pit roared. His gaze was fixed on the waving tips of tendrils that were just starting to grasp the rim of the altar. He increased the momentum of the swinging cage again, took a deep breath, and when the cage had cleared the pit, he jumped, too.

Jack held his breath and prayed.

Morris landed in a less-than-graceful, jumbled heap by Jack and the kids, rolled over with a groan, and sat up. Jack beamed at him, and he grinned back. He looked touched by Jack's relief.

The relief was short-lived, though. The tentacles were reaching wide now, and one of them was hauling something over the edge of the altar. The sounds the creatures made were deafening.

Jack told his kids to run, but they remained frozen in shock and fear. He reloaded and aimed at the thing coming out of the pit, both he and Morris firing all the bullets in their guns. Some passed through the flesh of the thing, and others simply bounced off. The children screamed, and Jack pulled them close in a quick hug before commanding them to run. This time, they moved, spurred by the authority of his voice, but paused in the doorway.

"This is it," Morris told Jack. His voice was calm, his face serene. Morris knew none of them would get far. They probably wouldn't even make it out of that subterranean cavern. But Jack was determined to get his kids as far from there as he could before the inevitable caught up to them. Those things would have to work at killing them.

"Don't look," he shouted to the children, clutching his empty gun tighter as he and Morris backed toward the door. "Don't look! Just run, for God's sake! Run now!"

He watched the terrible bulk of the first of the Old Gods in this world emerge from the center of the altar. Then he turned away. He had spent so much of his professional life facing the ugly things, staring them down. He thought he'd earned the right to turn away. He looked at his kids instead. He and Morris, they could stay and fight, slow it down, maybe give the kids a head start. . . .

There was a single breath of cold on his cheek and a lingering reek of dead fishy things, and then . . . silence. From the doorway, the kids' eyes were wide as they stared beyond him.

Jack turned back to the altar.

The tentacles, and the hideous bulks from which they sprouted, were gone. Jack looked around. There was no sign of them—no sound, no smell, no evidence whatsoever that they had even been there.

Morris laughed through his ragged breathing and clapped Jack on the shoulder.

"Kathy," he said. "Kathy and Teagan. They did it."

"Yeah," Jack said, shaking his head in disbelief. "Yeah, it looks like they did." The kids ran to him and he hugged them tightly. They were okay. He felt tears in his eyes that he blinked away. They were okay.

There was a sharp crack, and then pieces of the altar began falling inward until, inexplicably, the rubble of the altar covered the opening completely. The four of them still in shock, watched it happen with exhaustion and satisfaction.

"Daddy?" Jack looked down at the tear-streaked face of his son. "Can we go home now?"

Chapter Fourteen

The following morning found the task force assembled in Jack's office, bruised and cut but otherwise alive and kicking. All around Colby, the snow was melting. The temperature had risen to sixty-five, and in the days that followed, it was expected to hit the high seventies. There would be clean-up and inquiries, paperwork and follow-ups, none of which interested Kathy. Usually, after a case, she tried to get as far away from the location as possible—leave the bad juju behind and all that. She intended to hang around long enough to debrief Jack for the final reports and collect her check. But she had plans with Teagan, as well, which was far more incentive to take that time off in earnest and stick around town. In fact, all of them were planning some time off to relax.

It was, after all, the beginning of the summer.

In a hospital just outside of town, Toby Ryan sat in his cell. He hadn't eaten in a day and a half nor slept in twice as long. He was given to fits of moodiness which he found, at times, absolutely crippling since they'd stripped away his freedom and his means of . . . expression. He missed killing. God, he missed it. It gave him purpose. It gave him power. It satisfied him in a way that even the Hand of the Black Stars never had. But this wasn't about that.

It was about the dreams.

He would have given anything to have been a part of bringing about the ritual. Well, almost anything. If he had been in charge instead of that blithering idiot, Cordwell, it just might have worked. Then again, maybe not. He thought of his beloved Kathy, and her pretty little scar. . . .

And he thought of the ritual gone awry, thanks to her, and it made him morose. The Hand had failed . . . again. The only Hand survivor had reported to him what had happened. The failure had been spectacularly complete. Little sister had done well, for an outsider.

Still, there was hope for a new world, one in which the limits of this one would be wiped away. The door had been opened, and the Old Gods had had a taste of this universe. That would make any repeat attempts a little easier. He smiled to himself. Sometimes, it really was the little things that kept one going.

In the dreams, the Blue People spoke to him, offering him ways to improve on what Cordwell had started. Offering ways to get around this delicate issue of Kathy. He could have her, they promised, if he could make good on what his brothers and sisters had failed to do.

When he was awake, he was surrounded by constant reminders of everything he was denied. But in the dreams, there was hope.

Kathy had closed the door, but she hadn't locked it. And it was an old door, with rusty hinges, so to speak.

In the dreams, there was the promise of release.

And in his cell, under his bed, was a shiv carved with a certain symbol he'd been given in those dreams. It was just a matter of time and opportunity. The Blue People would guide him, through dreams.

Toby settled into bed and closed his eyes and welcomed the darkness.

In the dreams, the endless winter was only the beginning.

Mary SanGiovanni is the author of the Hollower trilogy (the first of which was nominated for the Bram Stoker Award), *Thrall*, *Chaos*, and *Chills* (aka *The Blue People*), and the novellas *For Emmy*, *Possessing Amy*, *The Fading Place*, and *No Songs for the Stars*, as well as the collections *Under Cover Of Night* and *A Darkling Plain*, and numerous short stories. She has been writing fiction for over a decade, has a Masters in writing popular fiction from Seton Hill University, and is a member of The Authors Guild and Penn Writers. She can be found online at www.marysangiovanni.com.